Rune Thief

Isabella Hush Series, Volume 1

Thea Atkinson

Published by Thea Atkinson, 2018.

RUNE THIEF

First edition. January 16, 2018.

Written by Thea Atkinson.

Acknowledgments

When I started this journey, I was on my way back to school for the academic year. Our organization sent us on a summit to pump us up for teaching the learners that would be coming our way.

While we were on that long bus ride, heading to the city 3 hours away that somehow turned into 7.5, I pulled out my notebook to jot down a few thoughts for the characters.

One of my peers who was sitting across from me (a woman who keeps her cool in the heat of the daily 'battle' of teaching and learning) asked if I was writing. When I said yes, she said, "Can you put me in your book?"

I told her only if I could do whatever I wanted with the character. She didn't hesitate. Unflappable as always. Grin.

Well, Kelly Setlakwe, you're in here, and likely to be in several books to come. I hope you like Kelliope.

<<<<>>>>

CHAPTER 1

Jewelry. For penis piercings of all things. That's how I got involved in this mess. I mean, who makes that sort of shit up about the kinds of things that are in a cache of legendary Incan gold?

Nobody. That's who.

So once I'd heard about it, I knew it was going to be my next gig. My next heist. Although, what I did wasn't petty theft. It was an art. It was how I knew Logan AKA The Lolli—short for lollipop—wasn't just talking out of his ass when he mentioned the gold. He didn't have the kind of experiential knowledge to pull that kind of detail out of his alcohol drenched brain cells.

No. He was the kind of guy who talked a good talk, but it was all from someone else's mouth.

The Lolli had a certain kind of kitch that made him useful to certain types. He took his nickname from his build. Tall and skinny and as red-faced as a cherry sucker from his years of addiction. He was loud and brash. And connected. Folks seemed to like him and so they put up with his mouthiness. Sometimes they even shot him some Intel by accident because he talked so damned much, it was easy to get caught up.

Which is how the remark about the Incan cache of jewelry started the rounds, and exactly why I bought into it.

No one else believed it, of course. Just me. The devil's in the details when it comes to a heist, isn't that what Scottie had al-

1

ways said, acting as though he'd thought up the adage and passed it down to me like a proud patriarch. Well, detail like those damned penis piercings was too specific to be anything but the real deal.

And I needed a haul. I would have settled for a ten dollar bill on the sidewalk by the time The Lolli had blustered that tidbit across the pool table at his beleaguered opponent.

Which was one small reason I was crouched right then in front of a painting hung far too low to be just a painting in the largest of the mansions on Valencia Boulevard. A mansion which just so happened to be in my own damn territory for Pete's sake. As though I wasn't already in a mess.

I shouldn't have been there. It was too damn close to home for any rational thief to consider. I'd call too much attention to myself when I'd spent a good three years covering my tracks and keeping my heists on the down low.

In came reason number two: the big reason I was crouched in front of that painting. I'd already been recognized. I knew it because a feeler had come my way via a sour faced patron at my favorite coffee shop. A stranger to me, really, and an innocuous thing until the man bought me a decaf latte no cinnamon and told the barista to write Sis on it when she asked for my name. Sis. Not Isabella. Not Izzy like most folks shortened it to. Not Ms. Hush.

Sis.

That my latte benefactor knew my name at all was a red flag, but to use that specific and unusual nickname? A gal like me knew what that meant. It stank of Scottie Lebans, and if she who hesitated was lost, then she who didn't tear off in a panic at that name was royally screwed.

I needed to fund an escape. And I needed to fund it fast.

My last heist had used up too many resources. Too many informants needed paid, too many cogs in the wheel needed greased. The things I did, I did on the sly and they never came cheap. Add to that the fact that info and opportunity had just sort of dried up, and I was in a mess. I got sloppy when normally over the last few years, I'd managed all my jobs cleanly and clandestinely.

I was proud of my network of Intel because in spite of Scottie's hot breath on my neck, I'd managed to build it into a spider's web. It had dozens of points of contact before you got to the hub, and even that seemed strung too thin, like a gossamer thread straining to reach wall to wall in an abandoned gymnasium. A breath could tear it down. That breath had come and I'd smelled its sulfurous belly for what it was.

Scottie had found me. And that meant I needed this gig.

I just had to get through the ridiculous pin pad security panel in front of me. Then, I might get out of here before the affluent Ken and Barbie of the Mcmansion got back from their soiree. It had already been a tight shimmy through a narrow skylight and a nasty climb down through the skylights in my black yoga pants with a four foot drop at the end because they had a sunken sort of floor you couldn't see from the top.

One of my rubber soles had come unglued from my shoe when I'd landed. It lolled like a tongue from the bottom as I'd scanned the recessed gallery of the couple's sprawling home.

Herringbone oak floors shone a pleasant nutty shade of stain intended, no doubt, to make the visitor feel like she stood inside the belly of an ancient tree. An equally burnished stairwell wound in a curve toward a second level of the gallery, one that was merely a walkway with blood rust stain that led the same visitor along a row of what I imagined were first edition books.

From where I stood, I could make out the worn look of leather bindings on books too thick to be made of mere paper. Vellum, no doubt.

Several dozen pieces of artwork peppered the olive colored walls, lit with perfectly bright, natural seeming iridescence. A statue of Napoleon stood guard at the far door, its own a sort of artistic piece of treasure. His hand clutched at something unseen beneath his breast lapel, probably pinching his nipple.

A Ming vase held its ground on a pinpoint plinth that looked weathered but sturdy and far too ivory-ish to be merely faux.

I could take any number of items and call it a day. But I'd come for the gold. And gold was what I was going to leave with. Seeing the collection made me all the more sure of the stash of Incan jewelry, and I told myself I could buy a dozen new pairs of rubber soled stealth shoes once I unloaded it to the right buyer.

I even had one in mind, several notches down the network and half a dozen Tarzan swings sideways. She would pay dearly for just one penis piercing because she had that kind of clientele.

But the job had to be quick to be effective, and I didn't need the added frustration of a panel made up of fractions.

I squatted on my haunches staring at the thing, feeling the hairs at the nape of my neck rise. A breeze somewhere, I told myself, cycling from the open skylight above me by the air exchanger and circling back toward me. Not someone watching me. Not a host of brawny men come to take me to what they might refer to as 'home' or to the person they would refer to as 'my fiancé' who would take up my goods as though my earnings were somehow his.

A bead of sweat slipped free of my hairline and trickled down my nape.

I was my own damn woman. I'd proven that these last three years. I was done proving it to anyone else.

I lifted the weight of hair off my neck, hoping to let the breeze mop the last of it up.

The matrix with its orange buttons gloated like a jack-o-lantern's grin.

"Damn," I muttered and clamped my lips closed at the sound of my voice.

It wasn't smart to speak in the midst of a heist. I'd learned that the hard way and had spent a night in jail because of it. It was just one more reminder of how desperate I felt. I could count on one hand the amount of times I'd broken my silence during a lift since then.

I planted my palm against the pad's face and inhaled slowly as though patience was an oily residue in the air. The room smelled of old dog and burnt hair. A terrible stink, really, for a Mcmansion. They needed a better cleaning lady.

I swallowed down the clump that had started to form in my throat when I imagined the men who would come for me if I tarried too long in the neighborhood and stared at the pad again, running my gaze from top to bottom and panning sideways. I had to stay calm. Focused.

I was so frazzled, I decided to hell with the silence. Since no one had come running at my curse and no voice-activated alarms sounded, I might as well go for a full finger bouquet. It might help me think. I was struggling to search for some secret sauce to the code before the couple swiped their key card or the video surveillance app picked me up and transmitted me to cell phones half a city away. Time was running down.

I rasped out the denominators audibly.

"Four, Sixteen, Thirty Two."

Easily reduced down to a half, but a half fraction was not on the pin pad. Just lots of easy to reduce fractions and a cluster of improper ones.

"Shit," I muttered. The sequence could be random, but experience taught me it never was. And it was always four numbers. And it meant something to the owner.

I shuffled on my feet, my thighs groaning from squatting so long. The muscles quivered more from suppressed anxiety than fatigue. I was here on prime time. My surveillance app hacker connection promised me thirteen minutes. I'd already spent four of them.

It was that thought that made me see it. Prime time. Prime numbers. Four of the fractioned buttons reduced and divided into prime numbers. And the resulting numbers indicated the order they needed to be pressed in. One. Three. Five. Seven.

My breath caught in my throat, making a sort of hiccupping sound. I touched each key reverently, steeling myself for an alarm.

Nothing. No bells.

No popping release sound from the safe door letting go either. It didn't open in a sleepy yawn to reveal its stained and yellowed teeth.

Nothing, in fact, but the irritated sound of my own sigh as I realized I'd been wrong. The Lolli was a blowhard.

Even now the police could be on their way, alerted by a silent alarm brought on by my error. I'd been foolish to come here and expose myself this way.

I counted my time in my head. Two minutes down the rope, four by now on my haunches, far longer than one minute trying to see through the puzzle of the buttons. Did I have enough left to get the hell out of there now and at least haul ass before the surveillance app turned back on and showed my face? I considered smiling for the couple and waving so that their cell phone app could show it was worth the price.

Just when I was about to scan the matrix again for a pattern I hadn't seen, something clicked loud enough to snag my attention. The lock in the safe had surrendered and the door that I expected to swing open slid upwards to reveal two drawers instead.

The slickness of it just begged acknowledgment.

"Wicked," I said to the polished brass drawer handles without meaning to say a word.

I whistled low in appreciation. Two drawers. Both the same size and depth. No doubt so much gold it needed to be stored in two separate boxes. I was giddy.

Then I realized the clicking sound from the safe hadn't stopped when it should have. In fact, it seemed to be coming from behind me.

It was getting louder, coming faster.

The hairs on my neck strained from the skin. I was being watched after all.

Just not by human eyes.

A low rumbling sound rolled across the room. The sharp intake of my own breath brought a shiver to my chest.

I should have turned around. I would no doubt get a full look at the attackers, give myself an idea of how much time I had before they sank their teeth into my skin, but I had come so far.

I reached for the first drawer with my right hand and hefted my satchel out toward the drawer with my left. I had seconds if any. That movement alone made the rumbling sound turn to growling. The clicking sounded faster. I knew if I looked over my shoulder what I'd see.

Pitbulls no doubt. Or Rottweilers. They were a favorite of security paranoiacs everywhere. Trained to attack without hesitation.

Whatever breed they were, they would not let me out without spilling more than a bit of my blood. I was sure of that.

I just didn't know how many rushed me until I yanked the top drawer open and started to upend its contents into the satchel. I did look then, because I needed to know how far away they were and precisely which direction they would come for me so I could roll out of the way.

I didn't have time for the second drawer. That was clear. I barely had time to scrabble to my feet and run for the rope I'd left dangling four feet above me.

The sheer size of the two pitbulls barrelling across the tiles at me made my bladder spasm.

"Fuck," I said, and I didn't care that it was audible.

I bottomed out as my knees gave way. The next sound that came from my mouth was a scream.

CHAPTER 2

The woman who could stay calm with two attack dogs hurtling at her simply wasn't human. I gawked at the beasts as they scrabbled in an almost comical flurry to get at me, slipping on the tiles and losing purchase in their haste.

But it was no laughing matter. They were coming for me. And I had no idea what to do.

I had seconds, if not a single heartbeat to get myself up and out of there before those teeth tore through my whisper soft yoga pants and plunged into my tender skin. And that was only if I was lucky. My throat would be a more tantalizing target and they'd go for that if they could.

I had to get up. I had to get out of there. One more heartbeat and I might not have another.

I know my fingers clenched into fists as they tried to push the rest of my body onto my feet and into a runner's lunge. The rubber lolling tongue on my left sole caught on the slickness of the varnished floor and I spilled onto my chest with my chin striking the corner of a gorgeous bit of herringbone.

I might have whimpered as I angled my face upward to catch sight of the beasts. My fingers still clutched the bag, my toes already dug into the floor as I tried to get up.

I half expected the whole thing to draw out in slow mo the way awful things do. I think some part of my brain even hesitated to send signals to my muscles because it couldn't grasp the danger fast enough.

But the time didn't stretch out at all. It rocketed toward me at the speed of stink.

I was completely blind to anything except the way those teeth loomed large as a 3D movie, the gums black and shining as the lips pulled back. Foam curled at the edges of their mouths.

I smelled rotten fish and old meat. My eardrum near burst with the shrill bark of fury that somehow sounded far closer than was possible.

They were on me faster than I could scrabble away.

I started kicking like a maniac, my legs working like they were arms flapping even as my forearm flew to elbow whatever bit of dog hide I could strike. One set of teeth clamped down around my calf while the other set dripped foaming saliva onto the floor as the beast tried to work itself past its partner to get a savory chunk of my arm.

I screamed into my shoulder cuff and ended up grabbing a bit of material between my teeth to bite down on as pain sliced through my calf and up behind my knee.

I lost track of the other dog in the haze of pain and terror. Everything narrowed down to the pain in my leg, the feel of the hot then cold wetness that soaked my pants and left them sticking to my skin as the dog shook me.

I was going to die here. I knew it as sure as I was being yanked sideways and backwards like a crocodile's supper being rolled over.

I knew the bite had broken skin and brought blood. That alone made my chest go tight. It felt like a lot of blood, and a lot of blood meant arteries and tendons. A wave of heat flooded my skin and then I went cold. Passing out. I was passing out.

I could not pass out.

This time, I heard my whimper. I sounded small and afraid and pitiful and it made me sick to my stomach I was such a coward. I'd faced a bully, for heaven's sake, one who delighted in watching his henchmen pull fractured finger bones out through the split skin of a traitor's hand. I hadn't snuck out one night under cover of darkness and ran like a frightened girl; I'd struck him with a baseball bat. I'd kicked him in the balls when he was down. I stood my ground and fought my way out in a gauzy nightgown and in my bare feet, by God.

I would not let a four-legged animal do me in.

Not now.

I'm not sure of the moment when things changed. I only knew in one instant I was kicking and flailing about in a panic, and the next, I had a flash of myself calmly packing my heist bag. That's when time pulled itself apart in cheese strings that were as gooey as they were elastic. I saw myself slip in gloves and a burner cell phone. A single blade that could snap open with a click of a button, better for jimmying than slicing and cutting. Rope. Carabiners.

I ran my hands again along the next item in my mind, feeling the cold metal against a hot palm.

An item I'd never had to use but packed each time almost like a religion or a superstition.

One, very slim, very long can of three shot pepper spray.

I just needed to get to it.

I rolled into a ball as best I could, trying to ignore the pulsing in my calf, the growling that was muffled in my pants. The second dog jammed his snout up against my heist bag. I punched down hard on its nose and made it yelp. I kicked out hard to dislodge the first beast.

I didn't think. I didn't have to. Instinct rammed my fingers into the bag and felt around till they found the telltale feel of cold metal. I was close. Too close maybe. I didn't dare pull my face out of the tucked posture and I didn't want to miss, so I had to let them come at me again. It took everything I had to look up and face them, to let them lunge for me again.

The spray sizzled out into the air and struck them in a focused shot of mist full in the face and mouth. It shot a stinking, hot load everywhere as I panned the can back and forth.

The dogs yelped and scrabbled to get away, knocking my hand and sending the hissing back at me.

I gasped for breath as my throat constricted. My eyes burned like hellfire.

But I couldn't balk now. I had to keep going. I dropped the can into my bag, heedless of the blood that nearly made me slip as I ran, weaving and stumbling, for the rope.

The dogs were both gagging and puking up slimy meat onto the floor and the smell of sick drove me harder to the knotted rope I'd left dangling.

Three minutes at best before they'd begin to recover. It wasn't a big can, the three shot spray. Just enough to give a gal a good run on a rapist.

Blind and coughing and groping for the knot I knew hung somewhere nearby, I kept a tight grip on my heist bag. I couldn't see a damned thing and I couldn't peel my eyelids open, but I kept telling myself the dogs would be in the same condition.

It was the only thing that kept me running.

It was a miracle if anything that my fingers touched the rope, but I knew when I felt the first clump of monkey's fist in the strand that I had hold of my tether. I pulled and leapt at the same time.

My right knee felt like it was one ball of flesh holding onto rags but I planted my feet onto the first knot and used the propulsion to push me up to the next. I hand by handed it up the two stories to the roof and lay on the slates on my back until the waves of dizziness receded.

I might have retched onto my shirt. It was all a blur.

It felt like an eternity before I was able to force myself to peer back down.

The dogs had recovered. They fought each other as they each tried to nom down on the puddle of blood I'd left. The loser had satisfied itself by tonguing the trail I'd left as I fled. Not just attack dogs, I realized, but trained like feral pigs to get rid of any invader they came across.

As sick as it made me to think I'd dodged a horrible demise, I felt stoked too. Whatever they'd been guarding for the owners, they'd felt it important enough to use man-eating attack dogs.

Incan gold indeed.

I'd been more than lucky to get out alive and I knew it.

I craned my neck to inspect the damage to my calf, groping in the dark over the bare skin with tentative fingers.

I'd need stitches. I'd need to wash my face and my eyes. I strained my hearing for sirens and heard none. No doubt there'd been no smart phone app or alarm. Just two really nasty doggies. Thank God.

I pushed everything back into the heist bag and climbed down the fire escape, mincing along gingerly as my eyes watered and my leg barked at me. It wasn't until I was several blocks away that I dared drop the bag to the sidewalk beneath a streetlight and crouch next to it so I could look inside.

Jewelry alright. Baubles upon baubles of costume junk. Nickel based chains painted gold. A few chunks of glass. My heart sunk. I felt as though I was going to be physically sick at the sight of useless junk I'd taken a bite over, and risked exposure for.

I couldn't even blame my bleary vision on the lack of true goods in the bag. I touched a few things to confirm with my skin what my burning eyes were already telling me.

A few tawdry bubbles that might have some value but not the take away I expected.

The second drawer. I should have pulled open the damned second drawer not the first. The first had been a decoy and I'd fallen for it. Rookies did that. What a stupid mistake.

My leg hurt even more just thinking about it.

I'd risked everything for this heist. My last dime.

The bites would no doubt fester, and the baubles would no doubt be worthless, but I hefted the bag to my shoulder anyway and hobbled on with my throat feeling like I'd taken a cheese grater to it.

I had to feel my way through the streets because my eyes refused to open all the way. My leg ached like a bitch and the cobblestone streets made for rough going. I was half mad at myself and half pissed at the Lolli. I should've known better. What had I been thinking to imagine that there had been a full cache of aging gold just waiting to be pilfered?

I was so busy grumbling to myself and limping along carefully on a leg that burned like the devil's kiss, I didn't see the guy who stepped in front of me until I smacked into him.

The heist bag slipped down my arm as I stumbled. It yanked on my shoulder enough that I dropped the bag to the cobblestones with the heavy thud. I froze as I heard the clunking of all that junk inside. Maybe I'd actually find a moment of luck tonight and he wouldn't take in my obvious stealth dress and booty bag and come to the conclusion that I was up to no good.

I excused myself politely. I didn't like the gravelly tone in my voice that indicated I'd been either yelling too much or screaming in pain. Maybe he wouldn't notice I smelled of puke and pepper spray.

I took a step to the left as he shuffled to the right. We did a short dance there together as I prayed I could get past him without incident. I made a quick dodge sideways again without thinking about the pain in my leg until it made me cry out. I winced instinctively.

"I'm so sorry," he said. "You okay?"

I peered up at him. Way, way up. Even with bleary eyes and nothing but dim light from the buildings and streetlamps, I could see he was a hulking sort of man, as wide as he was tall. I could just make out a set of long lashed eyes and a dimpled chin.

It was too late to just get by without incident. I'd have to engage. It would be a miracle if I'd get through the street and passed him now without every moment of this encounter burned in his memory. The best thing I could hope for now was just for him to think I was some unwashed derelict carting my entire livelihood on my back to somehow fall under the bridge somewhere.

"I'm good," I told him but he reached out anyway to grip the handle of the bag and help me ease it back onto my shoulder.

I had to cough up a good piece of my lung before my voice box would work, and then the sound was throaty and smoky. Like I'd swallowed a firebrand.

"Thanks," I muttered. "But I'm fine." I edged sideways, just out of reach.

I needed to get out from beneath that intense study. I felt like he was already adding up my obvious state of distress, the stink of pepper spray, the huge booty bag, and getting a whole slew of prime numbers from those fractions. I tried to shuffle past, as inconspicuously as I could, keeping my face out of his line of sight, trailing the edge of the building the way a mouse might.

He kept up pace with me no matter how quickly I moved. Kept trying to be so damn helpful.

"You need some help with that?" he said.

I was not happy about the way his voice made something inside me feel as though it was stuffed with warm cotton. I wanted to sink into it like the warmest of beds and sleep off the pain of a bad heist. That reaction was not the way I wanted to end this night. If I was smart, I'd recognize the smell of command about him and my terrified younger self would respond with the respect due that clear and present danger. Because that's what it should do. Respect the threat of danger. Run from it.

Instead, I twisted round out of long-ingrained habit and hated myself for it. Cell memory can be a bitch, and Scottie had ingrained the response in me with frequent, brutal reminders.

"It's not heavy," I told him. Maybe that would be enough for him to leave me be.

I didn't get far before his grip was on my elbow again.

I froze. Not sure what to do. By all accounts, he should have done what any city dweller would have done by now and leave me alone. Walk away with his nose in the air because I stank to high heaven.

What if he wasn't just trying to be helpful? What if he wanted to hurt me?

I'd used up the pepper spray. I had a knife in my bag if I could reach it. If he tried to accost me, I could try that, but it was a pen knife, no more.

"You better get that looked at," he murmured from next to me.

He smelled of vanilla and smoke. Like pipe smoke.

I, on the other hand, must have looked like I needed a medi-vac unit. Smelled like I'd gone to war. The pain and bleariness of my vision was affecting my reason. He'd asked me something, hadn't he?

"What's that?" I said.

"The leg," the man said. He jerked his chin toward my calf. "Nasty bite for a kitten."

I didn't look down. I didn't want to see it again. At least not until I was somewhere where I could do something about it. My stomach did somersaults just thinking about looking at it.

"It's nothing," I told him.

"You want me to look at it?"

"No," I said. "I'm good."

"That bag looks bigger than you are. Here. Let me give you a hand." He reached out for the bag and waggled his fingers.

He knew what I'd done. I knew he knew. It was all over his posture and it was a matter of time before he pulled out his cell phone and alerted the police.

I balked without meaning to, the way a teen might who had just shoved a pilfered chocolate bar beneath his armpit and caught sight of the mall police. And there was no taking back that reaction. It was a neon, flashing sign of guilt.

"Don't touch me." I backed away, trying to disguise the reaction by acting as though I was scared. It wasn't a complete lie. I was terribly afraid he would call the cops on me.

"It's alright, kitten," he said. "I don't bite unless asked."

He chuckled to himself as though I had just missed out on something wonderful and secretive. He tipped his fingers to his forehead the way a gentleman might if he were wearing a fedora as he walked backwards for several steps. He spun on his heel and disappeared around the corner, leaving me gaping after him.

I waited to be sure he was really gone before I picked my way towards the main street and then down several back ones.

I found a half-empty bottle of water lying on the sidewalk and after testing to make sure of its contents, poured the rest of the fluid over my eyes. It didn't completely fix my vision, but it eased up some of the extreme stinging.

The homeless old soddie I came upon leaning against a stinking trash can looked at me like I had three heads when I opened the bag under his nose.

"Wassat?" he said, sniffing the air and waving his hand like he thought I stunk.

No doubt I did. Blood was drying on my calf and the dog saliva that had run down my neck had an odor of old meat. The pepper spray made me smell like a ripe taco. Not the most delicate of perfumes.

I peered down at the man from swollen eyes, imagining he thought I was of the same sort of fortune. If he could catch sight of my eyes, he'd just assume they were rheumy from drink.

I squatted down painfully so I was at his level. My thighs still ached from the escape and the lingering scent of capsaicin made my nostrils burn.

"This," I said, jiggling the bag. "Is a cup of coffee for us both."

"What do I have to do for it?"

His look was wary, but beneath the grisly jowls there was an astute jaw and articulate eyes. A man down on his luck, not intelligence. But for my talents, I might be in the same stead. I let go a wheezing breath meant to sound encouraging not rheumy, but the running had made my lungs ache and it came out sickly.

"Well?" he demanded.

"Pawn it for me," I said. "That's all. And if it's a bit of booze you'd rather than a cuppa Joe, no judgment from me."

His gaze went narrow and he shifted up so he was leaning less on his side and more on his palm. He peered into the bag, snagging the edge with a grimy finger and hooking the material so he could twist it into the light of a nearby streetlamp. I shook it so the contents would jangle.

He pierced me with a sudden clear scrutiny.

"Sell it," he said, nodding with comprehension. "For you."

He stressed the word for instead of you, indicating he understood exactly what was going on.

I angled my bleeding leg away from him and shrugged my shoulders away from the clinging T-shirt. I tried my damndest not to give anything away in my expression. He might be homeless and in need of cash, food, and maybe a dram of whiskey, but if someone came behind me asking an old sot if he'd seen a young girl about yay high, he'd sell me out as quick as the coffee went through his cirrhotic liver. He had no reason to protect someone he didn't know.

It was up to me to change that.

"I'm a run away," I said, heeling my hand across my burning eyes. "I can't risk my parents finding me and I need cash."

It wasn't a lie, at least not all of it. It was true I was on the run, and it was true I needed cash.

He ran an assessing eye over my five feet three inches top to bottom, taking in what I knew was a mass of black curls and a nose that made me look like a teenager. I knew he'd assume the same thing everyone did when they saw me.

He grunted. "There's faster ways to make money for a young girl," he said and I wasn't offended. It was truth. I'd seen it hundreds of times. Considered it even back in my day.

"Indeed. But that's the sort of thing I ran away from."

His brow furrowed in anger. I had him. He was going to go for it. He felt pity and protection for a poor young girl down on her luck. I let my leg back into view of the streetlamp. Couldn't hurt for him to think someone had ill-used me.

"You can keep ten percent," I said. "Whatever you get for it, a tenth's yours."

"Twenty five."

"Twenty." I was feeling the kind of generosity borne of desperation.

He seesawed his jaw back and forth and dug a hand into the bag.

"Junk," he said as though he could see the tawdry dull color of the goldplate when we both knew the streetlight wasn't nearly strong enough for that.

"Not all of it," I said, hoping it was true. I'd seen a glint of yellow in the bag that was too clear to be anything but a yellow diamond. "There's a ring in there. Nice one."

"So you want me to pawn stolen goods for you, eh?" he said.

I nodded.

He lifted a thick chain from the bag and held it aloft as he quirked his head to the side and looked at me. I didn't dare relieve my trembling thighs to either sit or stand under that scrutiny. It all hung in the balance in that one moment. My safety, my carefully constructed anonymity. My future.

"You ain't no runaway kid," he said, breathing out a blast of stale booze. "You might look like one, but you ain't. You got too savvy a face on you for that. And it ain't just cops you're avoiding. That I can tell. Question is, who you running from, missy?"

CHAPTER 3

The man who had set me on a tear out into the night in my jammies might not be a name folks knew as a rule, but he had a way of knowing when his name was spoken, and he tracked the listener down with fanatical prejudice. Scottie. A man as possessive of the sound of his name as he was of his ten cars, his army of minions, and the woman – me – who had helped make him a shit ton of cash.

Best this old gent just think I was a little dirty and a little scared and a heck of lot in need of fast cash.

"Everyone's running from something," I hedged. "You, for example." I jerked the bag at him. "Homelessness wasn't a choice, was it? It never is. It's always the result of running from something big enough that you'd rather beg than earn."

I ran a keen gaze over his threadbare jeans and worn out doctor's loafers and watched him shift ever so slightly onto one hip. I'd hit the mark, sure enough. It was a bald and uncomfortable truth for many of the derelicts I met. But for my own love of comfort and warmth, I might be right there along with them. It was a truth that I tried to avoid as long as I could.

His jaw jutted out as he ran his tongue over his top teeth. Thinking. Not sure he wanted to get involved at all. But then he needed cash. He didn't have to say these things out loud. It was all written right there plain as the stamp on a whiskey bottle and I'd been reading labels like that for years.

It took at least a full minute before he pushed himself to a stand and swayed in front of me. I stood straighter with him so I could keep his eye. He reached out and plucked the bag from my hand.

"You don't have to be a bitch, little girl," he said. "Even an old drunk can see the nasty bit of blood running down your leg."

He spun on a dignified heel and lumbered down the shadowed alley way to what I knew was one of the local pawn shops. There were dozens of them in four blocks alone. Hundreds within the quarter. Who knew how many in the city.

It was why I chose this metro in the first place. For every open-doored, bar-slotted doorway that led to an honest pawn broker, there were four less reputable, gun-toting black markets ready to steal as quick as buy. Things got easier to move if you had a broad market to push things through, and when those items were questionable, you needed the swarthier type of buyer.

A stash of junk like I had was fine for a regular pawn shop. I'd be safe enough just letting the drunk pawn it off and take a cut. No one would bother to trace the loot. One diamond ring in a pile of crap wouldn't be worth the trouble.

I followed along behind him telling myself all those things and still not feeling easy about any of it. Probably had something to do with the blood still running down my leg or the stink of pepper spray and dog spit clinging to me, but I couldn't let go the feeling that something nasty was coming my way.

My mind fleeted over the memory of the man I'd run from years earlier, and the man who now seemed to have located me. I'd met him as an impressionable teen. I'd been sixteen and brash and pissed at having to live in half a dozen foster homes before I was ten. Scottie. I'd thought him handsome and dangerous and what girl at that age wasn't attracted to that? I'd wooed him for years with the ferocity and cunning of a back alley she-cat, not knowing that all along, he was a panther patiently stalking me until I caught him.

What a gal knows about a man when she's twenty four is far more savvy than even a run-away, dope-smoking alley cat teenager does no matter how edgy the living. The old drunk was right. I was running and for good reason.

If Scottie had found me after all this time, then he had never stopped looking. That meant nowhere was safe. It might as well have been him passing me that latte in the coffee shop and grinning crookedly at me as he murmured the nickname that oh so few knew. Sis.

I was so busy thinking about him that I almost missed the way the drunk in front of me lurched sideways through an open doorway. The sign that ran down along the outside wall read: 24 HOUR PAWN with the purple W fizzling in and out of phase and looking more sickly blue than royal purple. No glitz to the joint. Grubby windows. A cheap fan trying to hustle a bit of cool air from the hot August night and wrangle it into the even stuffier shop.

It was perfect.

I hung around the music section near the far wall, just out of sight of the man at the counter and well within earshot. I picked up a harmonica and tapped it in my palm, trying to look like I was a casual enough buyer that no one would bother me.

There was one other patron in the shop. He was tall enough that he could reach for the seamstress mannequin that hung from the wall above us that was studded with myriad gaudy brooches. He plucked a particularly ugly one from its shoulder and held it motionless in a broad palm. If he was interested in it, his head should have tilted down; he should have turned it over in his hand to inspect it. He did neither.

Instead, I watched him watching the drunk from the corner of his eye.

When he pulled an elastic band from his pocket and pulled his russet hair into a man bun, I knew he wasn't just a shopper interested in gaudy jewelry. He wanted clear view of the room and was opening up his peripherals all the while seeming to be nothing but a mere shopper whose hair was getting in the way. I knew better. I'd seen his type plenty.

But there was something more about him, something that set my memory alight with dark alleys. I felt a strong sense of deja vu, one that made my throat ache and made my heart race.

He was familiar somehow. My memory reacted the way your hands know the feel of slipping on well-worn heist gloves, the way your feet feel slipping into a pair of Himalayan fur slippers.

"You want that?" The proprietor called out to him, and he mumbled a no, he was just looking.

I knew that voice. I'd met up with it just an hour earlier in the alleyway. I ran a few quick measurements through my mind and came up with several, blinking red alerts. Was the man from the alley the guy from the latte shop? I hadn't been able to make out a face in the dark, just a shape and size. He certainly looked about the same build. Huge. Like all of Scottie's minions.

The question was: had I seen his type specifically with Scottie before? I tried to bring those days, all those burly enforcers he had clustered around him, to my mind. The image came clean of his profile. I scanned his jeans and perfectly pressed blue collared shirt. There was a telltale bulge just this side of his left shoulder.

A pistol or a knife, no doubt. I sidled my way around a display tree of shitty guitars so I could study him through the gaps in the pegs and trunk and still pay attention to my hustler.

He and the proprietor were arguing it seemed, in hushed voices, but enough to catch the man's attention. In my haste to get closer, I dropped the harmonica, forgotten in my hand.

"You break it you bought it," came a growl from the front without losing track of his argument with my drunk.

I squeaked out, "it's okay," and turned my back to the men, squatting quickly to retrieve the mouth organ and get myself out of sight.

There was a grunt from the counter and the old drunk pulled out his best act.

"I know most of it's junk," he said, "But my grandmother's ring is in there. That should pull a couple thousand at least. She came from the old country. Said she barely made it past the Bolsheviks with her life. Her charges weren't so lucky. Poor Alexei."

I had to stuff my fingers in my mouth to keep the snort from escaping. No one was going to believe he was descended from the Romanovs, but I found it interesting that he had elected to use that as a front. He had some education at least. He ratcheted up a notch or two in my esteem.

I peered around the guitar tree. In the full light of the shop, the drunk did look European. Hard edged jawline. But he had the look of Rasputin himself rather than of aristocracy.

Before I could so much as snicker, the other customer spoke up.

"That's ridiculous," he said and tossed the brooch onto the top of a glass case as he ambled toward the counter, unable, it seemed to mind his own business. "No one survived that execution."

The drunk turned his rheumy eyes on the intruder. His face from my viewpoint was indignant. I kept hoping the stranger would turn too, so I could nail it down.

"What would you know, young pup?" the drunk said. "It's true most died, even the old maid, but it was a botched affair. So much gun smoke." He puffed out his chest, looking ridiculously proud in his tattered clothes. "Are you calling my Oma, who was afraid of pillows till her dying day, a liar? My Oma? Who smuggled out a cushion full of gems and nearly lost her life for it."

The man eyed the old guy with something like mirth.

"Don't take it so hard, old man. My Oma once told me that the boogeyman would get me if I hung my hand over the bed at night. Omas lie. It's what they do."

"Not my Oma."

The henchman sucked the back of his teeth thoughtfully and pulled aside the edge of the bag to peer in.

"All Omas," he said pensively, digging a finger into the bag and rooting about with it.

"Nothing but costume baubles," he said of the contents. "Only thing worth a dime is the bag. Nice leather."

He straightened to what looked like a mountain sized height and looked the old guy in the eye before flicking his gaze my way. Our eyes met for several long seconds before I was able to drop mine to the floor. But even then I couldn't forget the way his had seemed to pierce straight through me. I felt exposed and uncomfortable, as though he'd stripped me down and dressed me back up after a negative assessment.

Not the guy from the latte shop, but still, he had the look of predator about him.

"I'll give you twenty bucks for the bag," I heard him say to the old drunk.

I couldn't help stealing another peek at him. Mistake. He was looking at me still, not at the drunk even if his hand was resting solidly on the old drunk's shoulder. I had to bite down on my tongue to stay focused. Something about him reeked of danger and charisma, and I'd been down that road before.

I fumbled over a Hummel figurine and nearly dropped it. I heard the man's soft chuckle again, the same smoky sound as from the alleyway. It was an effort not to look his way again and to study the proprietor instead, but I managed it by peeking up from beneath my bangs.

The proprietor's face went from bland interest over the bag of loot to outright disdain at what he obviously believed to be junk. I could feel the deal queering.

With a couple of sentences, the stranger had squirreled my con. I thought he did it on purpose. I knew right then that he most definitely remembered me from the alleyway. He was testing me. Waiting for my reaction the way a careful scientist might sit by a petri dish.

I had to stopper down my rage. Not only had one of Scottie's bullies found me somehow, but now this jerk was keeping me from salvaging my heist. My mouth opened before I could think any further about what the result might be.

"That's a grand story," I said, not quite coming out from the guitar tree, and keeping my face lowered but angled enough toward them that they could hear. "I'll take that ring, old gent. What do you want for it?"

I heard the old derelict shuffle his feet in confusion because this wasn't in the script anywhere and he obviously wasn't sure what to do. It had the desired effect on the broker, though. Those squinty eyes re-lit with greed. He thumped his fist on the counter.

"Nothing doing," he declared in an affected haughty tone as though the old and stinking drunk in front of him was the choicest of patrons. "This gentleman is here to do business with me." His use of the word gentleman sealed my suspicion that he smelled a profit in me and exploitation in the old drunk.

"You want the ring," he said. "Come back for it once it's in my inventory." He sent a nasty glare my way but it was all for show. He hoped I'd buy that ring and was already counting up his profits.

I would have leaned into the tree with relief, but my little show of spite had snagged the stranger's eye. He turned toward the cluster of guitars and I hurriedly averted my gaze, bending down to pluck a guitar string from the bottom of the tree.

At least I'd caught a good view of his face and his eyes before I'd ducked. Grey eyes, they were, set apart just perfectly in a boyish, but strong face. A face that could look innocent but had enough weather to indicate it had done a few hard things, seen even worse, in its day.

And he'd caught full gawk-eyed sight of me too. There was a tug of the corner of his mouth. A near smile on lips that were full and lined with the smokiest auburn stubble. A smile that could mean anything, but no doubt meant, "There. I got you."

He recognized me from the alley, and why wouldn't he, I realized. I stunk. I was still limping on my bad leg. Recognition by any stranger is never a good thing in my business.

I wished I hadn't opened my big mouth. It had got me a deal, sure, but at what cost?

I fled the shop, knocking over the mannequin on my way out. I waited around the corner, nervous and eager, to set onto the drunk's heels when he came out lest he abscond with the better part of my night's work.

I stepped in front of him as he rounded the corner, and bless his soul, he grinned widely as though he fully expected to see me there. He ratcheted up a notch in my esteem. Maybe I could use him again.

"I got $1000," he said so gleefully I knew he'd have settled for half that.

"The ring," I said, nodding, relieved at getting the cash. "Probably worth a heck of a lot more. But I'll take it."

He pulled his fist back. "Two hundred's mine."

"Of course." I waited patiently for him to extend his fist out again, clenched as it was around a fan of bills. My bills.

He looked wary. "You're sure?"

"I said so," I told him. "I keep my word."

I felt exhausted all of a sudden. He must have noticed me sagging against the building. He laid a cool hand on my forearm.

"You need patching up," he said.

I imagined going to the ER and trying to explain why I wouldn't leave a next of kin, what dog had bit me, and where should they send animal control, and that made me even more exhausted.

"What I need is a drink. A stiff one," I said.

He chuckled. "No reason you can't have both."

He pushed past me without explaining further and I had a moment of panic as I thought he was taking off with my cash. He was quick on his feet for an old guy.

I sighed audibly when I saw him disappear into a building just one block down. The sign overhead was for a pharmacy. I decided to wait and was rewarded when he exited again with a baggie.

"I can't stitch it up," he said of the wound on my leg. "But I can clean it and put some plastic skin on it."

I watched him keenly as he rinsed the wound with saline and prodded delicately with expert fingers around the swelling through the tear in my pant leg.

"The colloidal silver should help ward against germs. But keep it clean."

He angled his face up toward me and I knew in that instant he had spent years doing this sort of thing. He had some education and experience and if he was out here on the street, calling attention to that past would no doubt make him feel ashamed when he was so obviously happy to have helped me. I'd let him have his secrets. I had my own.

I left him heading toward the liquor counter right next door to the same pharmacy while I headed for my own respite several blocks away.

If I hadn't just unloaded the shit ton of cheap baubles for a less than impressive cache of loot, I wouldn't have decided to push myself behind the greasy bar in the seediest part of my borough. But I had, and only just barely, so ducking into the bar seemed the most appropriate response to the night.

Bloody but patched up, tired but needing to drown my fury and my sorrows, I didn't just want to get drunk. I wanted to get blitzed.

I should have been happy to unload the junk at all, but it was hard to feel grateful. As it was, I stared down at my shot of Canadian Thai chili moonshine and sighed.

"I thought this would do it, Fayed," I said. "But seems it's not."

I pushed the glass aside after I tossed it back and searched out the familiar face of the bartender.

"You made me open that cursed bottle," he said from where he stood at the far end of the bar. "You know what that means." He threw the words over his shoulder at me.

"Means I bought the whole damn thing because no one else wants this shit," I mumbled in a mimicked voice, his, and leaned back on the stool, hands playing against the sticky surface of the bar.

I tried to get a look at what or who had his attention so riveted that he wouldn't try to sell me that overpriced hit of ecstasy that I knew went along with the bottle if you paid enough.

"What about the Rot Gut?" I said.

Named for the tavern, the mixture was the house specialty of bottom-of-bottle cocktail. I secretly thought they emptied the glasses of leftovers into the fancy decanter they kept on the shelf, but no one had proven that – or seemed to care. What they were after—what I was after—was the snifter of crystallized absinthe at the bottom.

I tossed a crumpled fifty onto the counter to pay for the moonshine and pulled out one of the hundreds from the stash to lay as a companion to the first. I whistled sharply.

Fayed finally spun around, just enough that I could see the man he was talking to. Gorgeous enough to make me wish I'd gone home first to clean up. Creamy mocha skin and eyes the colour of money.

For an instant, I thought of the man from the alley, because this man eyes were very similar. Maybe not grey green like his, but where the back-alley man's gaze had an intensity that was almost frightening, this stranger's eyes seemed clouded with something different. Fear, maybe, or desperation.

He caught me looking and I tried to smile but came up with nothing more than a grimace born of my own sense of despair.

I grabbed the bottle Fayed passed me and upended it, pulling on the liquid to draw the crystal closer. The chunk was a hard, sharp weight that dropped onto the back of my tongue. I almost choked on it, and coughing and wheezing, I was too preoccupied to notice anyone had come close until I felt a hand drop on my shoulder.

I spun, my eyes tearing up as I tried to swallow down the clump in my throat. Eyes that were manic and veined with constricted crimson branches, met mine. I sucked in a breath. I wasn't sure why I'd thought they were the color of money. This close up, they were simply a terrifying shade of black.

"You watching me?" the stranger demanded.

I started to protest but he didn't give me a chance. He squeezed. Hard.

I wasn't sure what I'd done to draw his ire and tried to protest.

"You think you've made me?" he said. "Think again."

"Look," I said. "I don't know what you're talking about."

He ignored that, choosing instead to lean in and whisper close.

"I can hurt you," he rasped.

As though his words were a signal, a jolt of energy squirreled its way down into my collarbone.

I gasped, unable to do more than wince under his grip.

"One movement," he said. "Just one. And I can kill you."

CHAPTER 4

Kill me. Not like I hadn't heard that before. What was it about me that brought out such violent instincts in men? Whether or not it was an implied threat, it was still a threat. Unless I'd just pilfered this guy's stash, then I didn't deserve it. It wasn't my fault. It had never been my fault. I had to remind myself of that. A violent man was a violent man. It had nothing to do with me. It wasn't the result of me somehow massaging his baser side into an angry reflex. It was all about him. Dammit. Scottie had made that reaction far too normalized and it pissed me off that I went there first. It had been so long since my instincts didn't drive guilt to the front immediately that I found myself constantly talking myself down from moments like this. And that pissed me off too.

I shook him off. At least I tried to. He had a death grip on my shoulder with those daddy long leg fingers of his, and he kept scanning the room with that restless gaze then back at me. He had the look of a guy who thought I was about to whistle for the cavalry and figured he'd take 'em all on.

He doubtless thought he was scaring me, but after Scottie, I wasn't easily impressed that way. Not by mere words at least. He'd have to do a hell of a lot better.

His fingers dug into my skin through my jacket and I winced but refused to let anything show on my face. I wouldn't give him the satisfaction. Instead, I tried to twist sideways out of his grasp and when that didn't work I tried another tactic.

Sore as my leg was from the dog bite, I recoiled my foot and drove it hard and fast into the soft spot beneath his kneecap. Easy enough to do since sitting on the stool with short little legs like mine put me right about level to his knees.

He swore out loud in a language I didn't understand, but I didn't need to know the linguistics of it to know he was calling me something nasty.

I pulled my foot back again, thinking a second round might be in order, but he twisted just enough to the side to avoid the hit.

He loomed in close, pressing his body near enough that I could smell sandalwood and patchouli, both fairly exotic scents even for a man with his coloring. I was in the middle of telling myself that maybe he was of mixed descent and came from a culture where women were expected to act a certain way. Violence was easier to understand if it's justified. But then that hand on my shoulder slipped around the back of my neck as a means to control me.

While I couldn't help the way my chin lifted under the pressure of his fingers, I let go any kind rationalization I was doing for his benefit.

My response was very much like a cat being petted against the grain of its coat. I let fly a load of spit, but it missed its mark and fell to a splat on the floor between us.

I wondered where Fayed had gone and tried to look back over my shoulder to catch his eye. He wasn't behind the bar anymore. I looked over the stranger's shoulder for him. Not tending after any of the other patrons either. I'd been to the bar dozens of times while I'd lived in the city and I had gotten to know some of the regulars. They never so much as spoke to me, but they let me be, and that was about as much as I wanted.

This night, none of those regulars were here. In fact, the room itself was empty except for four dark and lean men clustered around a table.

They had the look of predator about them. A barely concealed perception of power controlled tightly within a container about to burst. While the man next to me was being a dick, he didn't have the same sort of presence, and I only truly realized it when I was able to compare him to the others.

He was scared, I realized. Something had him on edge.

Four sets of eyes lingered on me and the outcome of my skirmish. I caught one man scanning my face before letting his glance drop purposefully to my chest. One of his companions leaned into him and whispered something in his ear. They both laughed.

Something inside me burned.

I tried to pull my shoulders square, to gather some sort of dignity and command to my voice. I had let this get too far already. I was going to gather my things and I was going to get out of here and I was going to go home and sleep off my own frustration. I leveled the guy with a calm but cold stare. Give him a chance to defrost along with me and rethink the way this was going to go.

"I'm going to ask you nicely to let me go," I told him.

"What are you watching me for?" he said, refusing to give in.

He was obviously too far gone into whatever was making him edgy to even listen to reason. I yanked hard enough that I should have been able to dislodge his grip. It didn't and I ended up glaring up into his eyes.

I traced one bulging red vein to the tear duct and realized he hadn't blinked once since he'd stood over me.

"What do you know?" he said.

"Go pound sand," I said. "Whatever I know isn't any business of yours."

His hand moved to my wrist and he tugged at it, pulling me from the stool and onto my feet. My skin beneath his palm twisted and burned.

"Tell me now and I won't hurt you."

"You're already hurting me," I said.

I wanted desperately to rub the pain away, but I was still clinging to the half-empty bottle of Rot Gut and with it cold in my hand, I was struggling with the idea of hitting him over the head with it.

I was no delicate flower, but neither was I quite ready to take on a giant, and he was a giant. Now that he was standing, no, looming over me, I could see he was at least six eight, six nine to my five foot three. I'd have to do a jumping jack just to hit him in the crotch. I felt my head sway slightly and wondered if he really was that tall or if the absinthe was already hitting my synapses.

I thought I felt the slightest fluttering of absinthe's green fairy giving my insides butterfly kisses. Absolutely. The beginnings of a nice blitz well on its way. Except this wasn't a nice blitz.

I weaved on my feet. I leaned back so my head rolled backwards where I could get a better look at him.

I smiled at him, although I couldn't for the life of me figure out why. He certainly didn't give off any warm, fuzzy vibes.

"You're a big one," I said. "What's got you so spooked big boy? Those skinny boys over there chop down your beanstalk?"

I blamed the absinthe. I never knew how to shut my mouth while under its influence, never quite knew how to separate what I was seeing from what was real. Not that it mattered. The grip on my wrist was all too realistic and the way he looked at me, as though he was trying to work something out that couldn't be true, indicated that whether it was real or imagined, I was about to feel fifty shades of pain.

I brought the bottle in front of me at shoulder height, tilting the top toward him.

"You want some?" I said. "Maybe it'll take the edge off that paranoia."

"You're mouthy for such a little one," he said and leaned in closer. "And you stink."

I almost thought I saw a gleam of enjoyment in his eye. Shades of Scottie again. Well, I wasn't having it.

"Listen, buddy," I said, finding bravado from my frustration and intoxication. "Trolls belong in fairytales. Let me the fuck go."

The "boys" at the nearby table pushed back their chairs and stood as though I had somehow insulted them instead of the stranger still holding onto my wrist.

He cast a quick glance in their direction and then at me.

He smirked. "Toffee," he said. "That's all you are." He sounded relieved. "Nothing but a toffee. Soft and sweet. Maybe you better leave, toffee," he said to me and nodded in the boys' direction. "I happen to know they like them sweet."

One of them ran a long tongue across his lips. Despite the warmth of the absinthe crawling through my blood, my belly went cold. This was no place for me tonight. Even Fayed seemed to have vacated the premises. I was about to squeak out a confirmation when the man holding my wrist went positively rigid. I watched his eyes flick over my shoulder toward the doorway.

He let go my hand and was gone as though he were nothing more than a shadow by the time I turned back around to see why he'd released me.

Relieved and strangely confused, I thought I had suffered enough crazies for the night, and if I had got out of it all unscathed, best I beat a hasty retreat out the back door and find my way home before I could get into more trouble.

I was afraid I wouldn't make it past the herd of boys when Fayed came back into the bar from the back room, carrying a box of whiskey. When he plopped it down onto the counter, the boys eddied their way back to their table and sat staring at him as though he had interrupted something. No doubt he had. I couldn't fault his timing.

"Gonna call it a night, Fayed," I whispered across the bar. I didn't want those men to hear me, just in case, but I wanted a witness in case something happened. Someone to mark the time for me.

He sniffed loudly. "Good idea," he said.

I gave him a wave and staggered to the back door. No sense taking the time to backtrack all the way to the front again. The alleyway in the back of the building was faster route to my home anyway. And I was feeling as though I pushed my luck way too far already.

A blast of cold air struck my face as I opened the door and it sobered me up enough to remind me just how lucky I was. I was no further down the alley than five steps when someone pushed rudely past me, knocking me into the wall, cheek first. I skidded

along the bricks and fell on my hands and knees into a small puddle beside the dumpster.

"Hey," I demanded and craned my neck backwards to catch
sight of the jerk that had knocked me over, maybe give him a few
choice words.

The height of him gave him away. Stumbling and weaving
down the alleyway as though he was inebriated, the troll from
earlier clutched his shoulder as though it was about to fall off
and he was keeping it in place.

I started to call out to him to see if he was okay, when he collapsed right in front of me.

Half a dozen more feet and I would be able to stick my finger
straight up his nose. He hadn't even lurched sideways like I had
when he'd shoved me, finding the good fortune of rough brick
to graze against that could deflect some of the energy from the
fall. Nope. Just straight down. If he'd been a paper bag, he would
have been blown up and popped flat all within three seconds.

It took me all of two heartbeats to realize the jerk who had
accosted me in the bar, who had called me a Toffee, whatever
that was, was badly hurt. Maybe even dead.

It took me one more heartbeat to realize I was about to do
something stupid.

CHAPTER 5

Stupidity brought on by rash decisions and impulse wasn't something I cultivated if I could help it. Trouble was: I couldn't help it most times. It had got me in trouble all those years ago with Scottie, and I tried like the devil to avoid impulse like I avoided cheap red wine hangovers. But the guy—well, he just sort of collapsed like I've seen no one do before. It wasn't normal, not even for someone who'd been shot, and I'd seen that shit before too.

Just that one thing should have sent me in the other direction, but I imagined myself running from Scottie all those years ago in nothing but my jammie jams and no one to help me for miles. I'd hidden in a ditch for hours, waiting for daylight so I could make sure that the color and make of the cars going by weren't Scottie's. I still remembered the feel of the nylon hem of my nightdress sticking to my thighs from the wet and the way the dead leaves gummed up between my bare toes. It would've been nice if someone had come by to help me then.

I imagined the man, prick though he might have been in the bar, might need help the way I had back then and I felt an irresistible urge to do something. The young Isabella cried out for me to help. She egged me forward, carefully at first, crawling forward on my hands and knees for several seconds before I was able to push myself to my feet. My steps were slow and wary, the physical me of the present warring with the younger, barefooted Isabella who cowered in a ditch with muddy water up to her ankles.

The ache in my calf from the dog bite was a reminder of how ridiculous it was for me to get involved, and the feel of cobblestones grinding into my knees as I dragged myself to my feet reminded me that I wasn't exactly in the better part of town.

The alleyway stank of old garbage and vomit. Old booze and cigarette smoke, maybe a bit of pot clung to the underbelly of the air currents that wafted by from the main street. Another reminder of its locale. A person could get hurt getting involved down here.

And he was obviously drunk, probably pissed off someone else in the bar that wasn't as inclined as I was to take his verbal abuse. I'd seen the look of those guys. They didn't look the least bit tolerant.

If I knew what was good for me, I'd just keep heading home like I planned. I couldn't risk exposure anyway, and if he needed an ambulance and I called 911, they'd want a name. I could offer a fake one, but the best thing to do for my own survival was just to walk away.

But what kind of person would I be if I did that? Those burly gents in the bar no doubt had a devil of a time at his expense, and although he'd been a bit of a prick, he was in need of help.

He didn't look so tall now, all curled around himself. In fact, he seemed much shorter than me and that was small indeed.

He was sucking in air by the time I reached him and the sound of it raised the hair on the back of my neck. My own lungs ached just listening to him strain to breathe. His thin, wax-coated duster had bunched itself up around his torso like a shroud.

The street lamp overhead washed him in a sort of sickly yellow glow and showed me his face far too clearly for my comfort. I'd seen men die before and I knew that gray pallor that crept up along the throat like the swell of a bloated tide. He wasn't going to make it, not unless he got help fast. I'd never seen anyone swat away Death's cloak when it was lying close enough to smell the mothballs.

"It's okay, buddy," I murmured. "You're going to be okay." I didn't believe it for one second, but the words came of their own accord.

I could feel the flood of urgency starting to shrink my veins away from my skin. My mouth went dry. I recognized all the signs of shock and told myself to breathe slowly. I couldn't let the stress reaction make me stupid. Foolish mistakes happened when the blood washed out of the brain like a tsunami as it flooded its way to the core. I'd seen it time and time again. Too many times.

I wouldn't be that person. I would be rational. I would make rational decisions that would make a difference for this poor guy.

That determination lasted until I knelt next to him and saw the way his face had begun to contort. There was no humanness in the way his features screwed themselves into tiny constricted knots. Whatever was causing him pain was dancing an Irish jig across his skin in stilettos. Blood streamed from his eyes and his nostrils.

Blood. From his eyes for heaven's sake. I heard my own sharp intake of breath and that was the thing that scared me the most. I was afraid, I realized.

"You're going to be okay, buddy," I murmured, a touch of tightness in my voice that made me wish I hadn't spoken at all. "Help is on the way."

His eyes rolled back in his head, showing me nothing but the white and his chest arched upward I ran a quick scan over his body head to heel but couldn't find so obvious that I could use any of the long-dormant first-aid training I received back in my lifeguard days.

"Do you have a phone?" I asked him. "Where are you hurt?"

I peppered him with questions as I reached out to lay my hands on his chest. Name, where was he from, did he have any family? Ridiculous questions, really, but I was really interested in getting him to respond. Trying to calm him down so that the frenzied heartbeat in my own chest would settle into a more normal rhythm. Let me breathe. Let me think.

There was still a pulse, though. So he was alive. But he wasn't doing so great. I tried to pull to mind the first-aid training Scottie had made me take years earlier.

Priorities first. He was breathing. That much I could tell as I leaned my ear down to his mouth. Muttering something I didn't understand. Maybe Latin. He thought he was dying. Giving himself the last rites or begging for forgiveness. The hairs on my body seemed to stand up with each syllable he muttered. Was the air around me getting hotter? Or was it just his breath washing over my skin?

I ran my hands down along his neck, checking for a pulse. Feeble and timid, the triggering against my fingertips told me he wasn't long for the world. Something sticky and warm met my fingers.

More Blood. Coming from his ears. I moaned out loud and let go a series of curses I'd heard from some of Scottie's ex-marines.

His thready pulse quivered beneath the heel of my hand.

I'd have to call an ambulance. But there was no way I was doing it from my cell phone even if it was my monthly replacement burner. It still had five days left of minutes.

I chewed my lip, thinking. I'd felt something in his pockets, hadn't I? Maybe one of those things was a cell phone. I needed my gloves. I had to scrabble backward several steps before I found it where I'd dropped it when he'd bumped into me.

Everything always went into my heist bag in specific compartments. I always tucked my gloves into an outside pocket that was flush against the bag. I yanked them from the pocket and rammed them onto my hands as I ran back and knelt alongside the injured man.

I ran my hands down along the outside of his jacket, my fingers moving instinctively, searching through the items by touch and processing exactly what they were from years of experience. A wallet. Pack of gum. A pocket knife.

As if my hands had a mind of their own, each of those got dumped automatically into my bag.

I checked the other side. Digging in, I felt as though something burned through the gloves. I yanked my hand back instinctively and then sighed at my foolishness because I knew it wasn't possible. Nerves. That was all. I dug back in and wrapped my fingers around something square. I extracted it and threw it into my bag along with the other items.

I didn't find the cell phone until I reached the fourth pocket.

There it was. A big bulky thing that was either far too old to be of use or so new, it might have that infuriating optic unlocking recognition.

"Kelliope," he muttered as he tried to roll onto his side. "Infacto fae mortem."

Delirious. I hoped he was far enough out of it to feel no pain but I doubted it. He still writhed beneath my hand.

"Hold on, buddy," I murmured. "We're going to get you help."

"Infacto," he said again, stressing the middle syllable. His eyes rolled sideways and up again. "Mortem."

"Yeah, yeah," I said.

I couldn't watch it anymore. I felt for his hand and found his index finger. It was cold and clammy. Time was running down. I pressed the pad of his finger onto the phone. As it lit up, I could see it was indeed one of those newfangled phones, the ones that allow for optic security and that measured your alcohol blood level. But the poor sod hadn't thought enough to lock it down.

"You are one lucky fuck," I said, noting quietly that I imagined he didn't think so at the moment.

Holding onto the tip of his index finger, I pressed the three numbers: 911.

Relief washed over me as I pressed the last button and dropped his cell phone onto his chest. I did my best to hold him still, to keep him from thrashing around enough to knock the cell phone off his chest while I listened for the operator. She'd hear his breathing. She'd hear his gagging. The cell phone GPS locater would do the rest.

I'd done what I could. I just hoped the ambulance would arrive fast enough. The high-pitched voice came through from the speaker and I let go a breath. A woman. Despite the high pitch of her voice, she was calm, far calmer than I had been. Two heartbeats after asking what the emergency was, she was already telling him help was on the way.

I sagged in relief at those words. I fell back onto my backside from the crouch I'd been in. The muscles in my thighs were screaming and I accidentally put my hand out to catch myself on his arm.

It was that moment when his eyes rolled back to land on my face. Bright green. Impossibly so in the dim light. Just like the color of money.

I thought I heard a crack of thunder and a blast of light spilled into the alley as though someone had thrown open a door.

The man at my feet drew in a sharp breath and grabbed hold of my forearm. His fingers dug into my skin.

"Buddy," I said and tried to yank away again. "What's with you and your death grip?"

Before I could tell if he was going to answer, a jolt of hot pain went up all the way to my elbow as though someone had Tasered me where his hand met my skin.

I winced and tried to break free but those eyes pinned me with a hard, panicked gaze.

"Behind you," he said.

Everything in my stomach seemed to fight for the exit all at once at those words. Behind me.

Scottie.

My heart thudded in terror.

He'd murdered this man just to teach me a lesson. He controlled me. He would always control me. I thought I heard myself whimper and then I sucked that back in.

My eyes squeezed shut, sending explosions of colored lights into the blackness beneath my eyelids. I inhaled a bracing breath through my nose. Then I spun, almost so fast that I felt a moment of disquieting vertigo.

Nothing there.

A scuttling sound echoed in the far part of the alley next to the dumpster. I waited, breath held, but still nothing. It didn't do anything to soothe my fear or offer relief from it; rather the sense of dread magnified the heavy claustrophobia that still clung to the air.

But something had shifted. Something was different. I only realized what it was when I looked back over my shoulder toward the fallen stranger that it was because the grip on my arm had disappeared.

And so had the dying stranger.

CHAPTER 6

A bad trip. That's what this all was. Had to be. There couldn't be any other explanation for a flesh and blood man to disappear into thin air. I had touched his clothes with my own hands, felt his blood on my fingers. If he was a figment of my imagination, then it had to be because I had choked back far too much alcohol and chased it with that huge crystallized chunk of absinthe.

It didn't comfort me to think that particular combination of substances—one that I had enjoyed on occasion over the last three years to pleasant distraction--could have caused a hallucination so realistic, it was wrapping my insides up into knots. But there it was. The most logical explanation.

To quote a famous fictional detective, once the impossible was ruled out, what remained had to be the truth of it.

I swung around in the alleyway, almost staggering off my feet as I scanned the cobblestones for the stranger one last time. A rat scuttled out from behind the dumpster with a rag of wet paper in its mouth. It froze when it saw me then waddled forward brazenly.

I stomped my foot in its direction and wavered drunkenly on my feet as I did so. When the vile thing refused to scoot off afraid, I yelled at it. Its steadfast refusal to halt had me hightailing in the opposite direction.

That wasn't like me to just flee like that, but it was obviously time for me to haul ass home.

I woke the next morning to a hot pain raking across my belly and feebly scratched at what I knew was causing it in an attempt to brush away the discomfort. A hissing ball of fur met my fingers. My cat, obviously. Enjoying the warmth of my skin.

She'd been a snooty thing from the day I'd found her as a kitten six months earlier, swiping her double-pawed foot at a rat who seemed to think she was dinner. Something about the way she stood her ground despite the scrawny, wet and tiny thing she was prompted me to pluck her from battle and pop her into my pocket. She hissed in there in a roiling ball of fury the entire way home. I'd yet to find a suitable name for her that could encompass all the aspects of her personality.

I gave her a weak swat now, to rob her of the chance to scratch me again. Just that one movement sent goosebumps rising all over my body. It was a strange enough sensation, it chased the drowsiness away.

That was when I realized I was naked.

And sprawled across my armchair in my living room with what felt like a fist of bony knuckles digging into the muscles of my neck.

And with flakes of dried drool coating the corners of my mouth.

And with a throat that felt like someone had put a burning match head to it.

The ache in my right ear told me I had slept with my earlobe folded over on itself sometime during the last several hours. I had a headache that made me wonder if it was possible for a skull to squeeze into a single clenched ball of bone somewhere behind a gal's eyes.

All in all, pretty much par for the course the morning after a binge like I'd indulged in. But it was the way my calf felt like it was on fire that made me squeeze my eyes closed again, focusing on the thread of some half remembered bit of information.

It took several seconds for the evening to come flashing back. Every bit of visceral reaction I'd suffered the night before at the hallucination the absinthe had given me tripped its way through my consciousness again. This time wearing combat boots.

As bad as I felt physically, the memory that I'd had a shitty heist quickly shoved out the nasty hallucination because while that had been nothing but imagination, I couldn't escape the fact that a bust heist meant I didn't have the cash I needed to get the hell away from Scottie's bandits.

And that was of paramount importance.

I moved my hands in front of my face to make sure I wasn't actually having a seizure. I stuck my tongue out. Everything seemed to be working. Painful and sluggish, but physically capable of proper movement. At least there was that. Absinthe. Never again. Chasing the green fairy simply wasn't worth this agony.

I groaned and rolled onto my side, testing the weight of my head as I tried to lift it up from the cushions. I spied my clothes littered all the way from the door to the foot of the chair. My favorite heist gloves were in a ball next to the door.

My heist bag lay on its side next to the coffee table.

Given my nudity and hangover, I wondered if I still had any money left in the bag or if I'd wasted it all. I spilled onto the floor on my hands and knees and crawled over to it, wincing as my calf fetched up on the cat's indignant swipe.

I crouched there with the bag in both hands and heaved it onto the coffee table. It upended and all those bits of things slid out and across the glass surface.

None of it was mine. A quick gaze over the contents, mundane as they were, told me most of it would have had to be the castoffs from the pawnshop.

A pack of gum. Something long and crooked and distinctly woody looking. A straight razor—I winced at that one, the shiver of memory reminding me of the stranger at the bar's words to me. That he could hurt me. Kill me, even. Good thing that was all fanciful green fairytale.

I flicked my finger around the contents on the table, following up with my gaze until both fell upon an inch square tile of some sort. I cocked my head, thinking. That incredibly realistic hallucination had included something square.

I reached out for the little tile and as my fingers wrapped around the edges, my palm burned. I dropped it without thinking to the floor. It sat on the carpet upside down looking ridiculously ordinary.

I laughed out loud.

"I've got to get a grip," I said to the cat who had taken to batting at her food dish and squalling in my general direction.

"Okay, okay," I told her. "I get it. You're starving."

I scooped up the tile with my nails and tossed it onto the table again. It had an interesting heft and it even more interesting face now that I looked at it. Definitely old looking. Maybe a couple of centuries. It reminded me of ancient Greek mosaic piece. It wasn't complete by any stretch as a picture, but looked like it could certainly fit into something bigger.

Pretty in its way, but useless. I sighed and groaned my way to my feet.

I strode to the kitchen and pulled open the bottom cupboard to pull out the box of cat food.

"Might be able to sell it to that creepy old antiquities dealer on 11th," I said out loud. More to convince myself than anything else.

I hated going there and only did so when I had something I couldn't unload anywhere else. I'd have to put on the wig and fancy boots again. The old creep had a fetish for dominatrix and I always sold better to him when I was dressed up. I hated that, using sexuality to score like an old cliché. But he paid better that way and who was I to complain about a few extra dollars in my pocket.

"What do you think, cat?" I said and in response, she jumped onto the counter to take a swipe at the box.

Absently, I moved to scoop her off the sideboard and toss her next to her bowl.

I didn't get the chance to touch her. Before I came within half a foot, she lifted her back in a sharp arch and hissed at me. Fully arched back, sharp canines showing.

"You little bitch," I said, hardly able to believe her nerve while at the same time admiring the moxy.

"On your own terms, I guess," I said. "I get it. But just remember which side of your bread is buttered."

Tuna it was then. She had never truly got used to the box food. Couldn't say I blamed her. It looked dry and unappetizing.

I rattled the drawer and pulled out a can opener, snapping it over a can of cheap fish. Just the sound of the soft hiss it made as the seal was broken sent the cat into a frenzy. She wound in a circle like a dog chasing her tail.

I opened the can into her bowl with a smacking sound and stood back with my arms crossed, waiting for her to dig in. She literally leapt for the bowl but as she got her nose to it, she started snarling and backed away from it as though I put poison in it.

"Seriously?" I said. "It's not that cheap."

I lied and I knew it.

"Okay," I said, conceding. "Milk it is." I yanked open the fridge door and pulled out a jug. It splashed over the edges of the bowl as I poured without so much as kneeling over.

"Well?" I said.

The hissing continued. I toed the bowl toward her.

When she refused to come closer, I leaned over to scoop her up. This time she scratched me on the wrist. Quick, so quick I didn't see it coming until the pain shot up my wrist and blood welled on the surface of my skin.

I glared at her.

"If you don't want to eat, then fine. You can starve. I have things to do. "

I lifted my wrist to my mouth automatically, thinking to ease the pain.

Except there wasn't just a bloody scratch on my wrist. There was also a small red mark next to it. I stared at it for a long moment, trying to figure out how I had got it.

I searched through my memory banks of the night before, filtering through the hallucination with tiptoeing feet because those few moments were too vivid for my queasy stomach, but came up dry. It didn't look anything like a tattoo. Instead of being inked into the skin, it seemed to sit on top like a henna mark. I scratched at it with my thumbnail. Nothing. I wet my index finger and rubbed at it. It stayed crisp.

No doubt there were some parts of the night that I had blacked out, but if I was honest with myself, I knew that during that hallucination, that stranger had grabbed my arm. Hallucinations just didn't leave a mark.

So he'd been real. No doubt the tat had been something I'd paid for in the alley and my absinthe-hazed mind had made the rest of it up.

"Nice nightmare," I muttered to myself. "Couldn't have given yourself a nice, spa day as a vision, could you, Sis?"

Obviously my mind wasn't wired that way, at least, not under all the stress of the Scottie threat. Even so, I resolved to visit the bar again later on to check in with Fayed. He might have a different take to clear a gal's muddy memories.

I reached for the cat again and this time she snarled at me and took off like a shot toward the bathroom, her favorite hiding place whatever she flipped the kitty litter all over the floor and I yelled at her. I sighed, frustrated.

After a quick shower, I pushed everything to the side of my closet as I dug deep for the more costume aspects of my wardrobe. Meant for the times when I needed to meet with parts of my networking and didn't want them to see the real me. The antiquities dealer on 11th Ave was just one of them.

It involved a long blonde wig with a shock of red running through it and lots of leather and thigh-high black boots.

I topped it off with a long trench coat because that kind of garb drew attention.

I grabbed a cab for several blocks and hoofed the half dozen remaining ones with the feeling that I had somebody following me the entire time. I was confident that even Scottie wouldn't recognize me in the garb I had on, but it didn't ease the sense of vulnerability.

By the time I made it to the shop, I was a bag of nerves and I couldn't throw myself through the door fast enough. I leaned against the door after it closed, scanning the shop with a nervous eye.

The proprietor, who always had a keen eye for folks entering his shop, was out from behind the counter in record time.

"Ms. Foster," he said managing to make it sound like the name was sliding around on a greasy plate. "I'm desperately delightful to see you again."

Everything was desperately delightful when it came to him. He reminded me of so much of Ron Jeremy, I shivered every time I saw him. There was a bloated look to his face, as though rivers of water ran through his tissues and couldn't find a way out. His eyes were less piercing green and more a girlish fingernail polish neon. He had a long black ponytail that he let lay over his shoulder and that left grease stains on his gabardine shirt. He wore cowboy boots with silver toe tips that peeked out from beneath 70s style trousers.

He constantly held onto a vaporizer although I never saw a plume of smoke come out the end. I always wondered if perhaps it was an affectation, something to keep his hands in motion so that his customers wouldn't notice that he was stealing them blind with the other one.

I pulled in a bracing breath. I could do this. Just get it over with.

"I have something I think you'll be interested in," I said.

"You always have something I'm interested in," he said and in case I didn't get the inference, he licked his thin lips.

I groaned inwardly and tried not to shudder visibly beneath the coat. He was the sort of man who bargained better when he thought he had the controls. Before I could change my mind, I slipped off my jacket and let it hang over my elbow.

I knew that the black vinyl hot pants outfit was a bit over the top. The bottoms barely skirted the crest of my backside and the mesh cut-out left my navel and everything all the way to the shoulder bare except for two narrow strips that barely covered my nipples.

The whole gaudy thing was held together by a collar with decorative spikes that lay against the black mesh at the collar bone. Even the boots were too much, and although my feet were killing me, I couldn't have worn anything else. One thing I had learned from Scottie was that men would do anything for a woman in thigh-high black leather boots.

It was Scottie's face that allowed me to stand there, as good as naked and vulnerable, letting that disgusting gaze of the shop-keeper's linger over my skin. A gal can do anything for a man if she wants to, and she can do anything to avoid him. I told myself that a lascivious stare was nothing to the things Scottie would do to me if he caught me.

I sauntered my way across the shop with my trench coat flung over my elbow as though it was a casual thing when the whole time my arm was shaking beneath it.

I passed the candy counter at the front, ignoring the smell of sugar floss and licorice and ginger that clung to the air as I breezed in. I'd never seen any kids at the counter, and I suspected its existence was more to cover up the stink of must and old paper that coated the underbelly of the shop's air.

I resisted the urge to grab a chocolate bar on the way by and held the proprietor's greedy eye with my own until I got close enough to lean over the counter.

I tapped the glass counter with my fingernail. I wished I had the forethought to polish the nails, but he didn't seem to notice if they were grubby and slightly chipped. He was too busy trying to see around the narrow strips that covered my breasts.

"I've got just the thing to put in your showcase," I said giving the counter another tap.

"And what's that?" he said without lifting his gaze from my chest.

I dug into the pocket of the trench coat where I'd dropped the tile. It made a clattering sound as it dropped onto the counter.

"Not sure what it is," I admitted. "Thought you might know."

I watched his face carefully and although he dragged his eyes from my cleavage, the way he took in the tile as it sat on the counter... there was hunger in his eyes that had nothing to do with my dress. The piece was valuable alright.

"You think maybe you have enough money to put that in your showcase?" I asked him.

He shook his head. "Worthless. Never seen anything like it. Waste of my money."

"We both know that's not true." It was a risky move but I had to bluster. It was the only way to project value onto the thing when I had no idea what it was.

He picked up the tile. "Warm," he said, looking me over. "Very warm. Where exactly have you been storing this little thing?"

I ignored the inference in his tone. "Do you want it or not?"

"Might fetch a price," he said with his gaze lighting on the tile. "Might not. I ain't interested in spending the money to find out."

He was lying. I could tell by the way he fidgeted behind the counter. He had seen something like it before, and he did know what it was worth. A hell of a lot was my guess.

"Okay, then," I said, pulling the trench coat over one arm. "I'll go elsewhere."

"Maybe we can strike a deal," he said.

I narrowed my gaze, suspicious. "What kind of deal?"

"For a thousand," he said. "I'll take the tile off your hands for you, but you have to do something else for me."

"You ask me that every time I come here," I said, lifting the tile from the counter and tapping the edge of it against the glass. "I'm not going to do that for you."

He cocked his head at me, the effeminate green eyes narrowing pensively.

"Two thousand," he said. "Just ten minutes out back. That's all I need." He sidled out from behind the counter, running his palm along the surface of the glass in a way that made me feel nauseous.

I took a step back, a shiver running down my spine that had nothing to do with the air conditioning. A nest of spiders might have just scuttled across my skin.

"Do you know how cute you look?" His tone had all the charm of a slithering eel. "Like a little girl all dressed up in nasty clothes. Desperately delightful."

"Fuck you," I said.

"Oh darlin', if only." He ran his hand over his crotch and I watched in horror as those trousers bulged out obscenely.

I backed away, shaking my head. Sure it was a goodly amount of money and part of me knew that all he wanted was for me to beat him up a little. Heck, I might enjoy knocking that smarmy look off his face, but no. I didn't need cash that bad.

I spun around on my high heels to leave and went all off kilter, lurching sideways, as he yanked on my elbow. I landed against his chest and lost my footing. His greasy mouth up against my ear.

My knees went out from beneath me as the panic hit.

"I've been a good boy," he said and ran his hand down along my ribcage till it met my buttocks. He squeezed hard.

"You've made me wait long enough."

CHAPTER 7

The heat of the owner's palm through the vinyl hot pants made me think of dark nights when I was a kid. Despite the openness of the shop we stood in, the smell of tobacco and old paper, I was back in the twin bed of my childhood covered with too many blankets for a spring night. Those swaths of flannel and wool were a force field of sorts. One last bastion of protection against hands and fingers that would burrow down beneath the sheets, seeking my skinny, goose fleshed legs. He was close, so close. I could feel his erection against my thigh. His ragged breathing deepened, and I knew he was inhaling the scent of me.

I had one horrible thought: that his tongue would dart out to slip into the corner of my mouth. I retched as I stood there, paralyzed by memory in his grasp, and sick with guilt and shame for playing the part I'd had in my own demise.

I stared at his mouth from the corner of my eye. That girlish, bloated gaze ran the column of my throat as though he were imagining running his tongue down my skin.

A thought, bright with hope squirreled its way through my mind: submissives obeyed.

"Get your disgusting hands off me," I growled.

I could've sworn his eyes rolled back in his head at my words. I knew then I had him. He'd never dare disobey the mistress he hoped I'd play. Hope buoyed my next words.

"You are a pig," I said, meaning every word and enunciating clearly, each syllable spat out with venom and authenticity.

"You are repulsive and disgusting and if you don't drop your hands, I will cut them off."

"That's it," he rasped out. "Be nasty to me."

I expected him to let go. By all counts, he should have.

He didn't.

Instead, he started pulling me toward that back room of his. I found it difficult to fight him off in my high-heeled boots, and since he was so much taller than me, I couldn't even buck my way backward to get loose.

"You're disgusting," I said in a much smaller voice, and he made another sound that reminded me I wasn't going to get anywhere with that tactic.

I was suddenly terrified. I remembered watching Pulp Fiction and all that went on behind closed doors for the poor up-to-that-point villain. I'd started out the villain in this story, hadn't I? Coming here dressed like this? Knowing it would increase my odds?

With the beaded door looming in front of me and it's strangely reddish glow coming from within, a swirl of possibilities started dancing around like a kaleidoscope in the back of my mind. What if he wasn't just a strange old geezer who liked to be dominated? What if he liked to play other games as well?

I gave one last yell, but this time it was nowhere near commanding. I sounded like a mouse squeaking out its fury at a cat.

If he said anything in protest, I didn't hear it. All I could focus on was the way the back of his neck bulged beneath his hairline and the smell of him that reminded me of sour grapefruit flesh and boiled ham.

"Let go of me, prick," I said. I gave one long, hard yank and wrapped as much composure around myself as I could.

We were halfway across the floor toward his back room before I remembered the tile. I craned my head to see the counter and noticed it wasn't there. I hadn't put it in my coat. A quick survey of the floor revealed it hadn't fallen down either.

That meant he had it.

We had reached the beaded door by then. I thought I could see a dungeon of sorts through the gaps in the strings. The back wall was lined with whips and other paraphernalia. A freestanding closet hunkered in the middle of the wall with a door that hung half a jar because it was warped in the middle. Who knew what sort of things lurked inside.

My stomach twisted. My knees went weak.

I wasn't a southpaw by any stretch, but I clenched my non dominant fist anyway and swung around in his arms with as much thrust as I could manage. I let the punch fly with the movement, hoping it would clock him right in the chin. Instead, it glanced off his jaw.

He gathered me close, pulling my arms back around my midriff and crossing them over my waist.

"I never used to have such a hard time with women," he complained and laid his lips down on the top of my head. It was a gentle kiss, almost like something an older man would give to a young child, creeping me out even more.

"I've been around a long time," he said into the wig. "And in my day women begged me for pleasure."

I didn't want to think of the kind of woman who would ask for this man's touch. My mouth went dry with terror.

"You are delusional."

He pushed me toward the curtain. "I'm old, yes," he said. "But not delusional. I have far too many of my faculties left and not enough of others. More's the pity."

With a gentle shove, he let me go enough that I could lift one of those high-heeled boots I wore and bring it down hard on his instep.

I lurched free the next second and made to bolt.

But he had my tile. And I wasn't about to leave it here with him. That would just add insult to injury.

I swung to face him. The look on his face had changed from lust to anger, not the pain I expected. In fact, he looked like I hadn't hurt him at all.

I stretched my palm out, demanding my tile. I cleared my throat to gain courage.

"You have something of mine," I said.

He smirked at me. "It's not yours and we both know it."

He lunged for me, and I ducked sideways. But for an old guy, he was fast. He seemed to anticipate my moves and grabbed my wrist, yanking it up behind my back and leaving me hanging over my stomach in pain. I was breathless with it.

"This isn't part of the deal," I said. "You need to take your hands off me."

His breath was almost too hot the back of my neck. And it was very wet. As though a line of hot oil had beaded on the vertebra at the base of my skull and was running down along my spine. I couldn't help but shudder.

My wig fell askew. I tried to blow it back into place and away from the corner of my eye. I squirmed in his grasp.

"Did you hear me?" I demanded, trying to squirrel up some bravado in the hopes that some of that submissiveness still lingered in the basest parts of his intentions. "I said let me go."

Any reply he might have offered got lost in the sound of the door chimes as we both realized someone had come into the shop.

We both swung to the sound. I remembered the full lips and the thick cascade of russet hair of the man who filled the door frame. The man who'd been in the alley and the pawn shop. He still wore a suit—a Desmond Merrion no less. He was taller than I remembered, hitting the top of the six foot eight end of the robber's scale beside the door.

"I hope you're paying her handsomely for that exquisite bit of violence, Errol," he said.

Humiliation burned in my throat. Even though I knew he couldn't recognize me as the girl from the pawn shop, not with the blonde wig, I lowered my gaze to the floor. Shuffled a few steps away from the proprietor as he relinquished his grip on me.

A step or two more and I'd be free. I prayed for those few steps, that I'd be able to make them.

"What I pay her is none of your business, Maddox," the shopkeeper said.

This man Maddox shrugged. "That may be true," he said. "But I've never known you to have to fight so hard to pay a girl so much, Errol."

Errol. I might have laughed at the absurdity of this creep having the same name as one of history's most romantic heroes if I wasn't inwardly hyperventilating.

And I might have been grateful for the intrusion if I wasn't so doggone antsy to get out of there. I pulled my overcoat back on, not bothering to make sure it was straight or if it gaped open at the front, and I swung around to face Errol. I laid my palm out in front of him flat.

"Bastard," I said with a shaking voice. "Give me back my goods."

A long line slinked over his lips into a smile. Then he shrugged.

"I thought I was buying it from you," he said.

"You thought you were buying a lot of things," I said and grabbed it from his hand.

It was difficult to keep my face averted from Maddox, but the wig was sufficiently long enough to cover the side of my face.

Maddox sent a long gaze in my direction. He was careful not to let his glance slip below my throat, but it was too controlled for me not to know he worked at keeping it discreet.

Something fidgeted inside my chest at that look. Most men, no matter how hard they wanted to, wouldn't be able to avoid stealing a glance at a bare thigh or swelling cleavage. Not this man, apparently.

He was too controlled, I realized. A man who could keep his baser self in check under unusual circumstances. It should make a gal feel safer. It didn't. All it made me think of was Scottie and his nearly antiseptic calculation of cause and effect. My heart hammered. I skirted them both as I headed for the door, pulling my trench coat tight across my chest as I ran the line of aisles like a mouse might, tight along the edges. My hand shook when I reached for the door handle.

"Maybe try a red wig next time," Maddox called out to me. "Men dig redheads." He chuckled.

It stung, and the words drove me from the shop. I collapsed against the outside wall, beyond thankful to get out of there.

I couldn't wait to get back home. First thing I would do would peel off this disgusting garb and throw it in the trash can. I didn't think I would ever be going back to that shop again. Costumes were a very necessary part of my job, but this one would never be pulled into rotation again.

Instead of walking the rest of the way, I hailed a cab and caught the driver peeking at me in his rear-view mirror.

"Yeah, yeah. I'm a prostitute," I said, angry for a whole host of reasons, not the least of which was humiliation. I'd felt it plenty enough times with Scottie that I knew what it was. But I was a different girl now and if I could acknowledge the shame, I could recognize the anger that came with it.

And that was the other thing. The thing that bothered me the most because I wasn't sure if my sense of humiliation was from the tightly controlled and willful way Maddox had managed not to look at the rest of me. Or if it was because he was actually able to do so in light of the blatantly sexual attire.

"You have a problem taking a working girl's money?" I said to the cabbie.

He muttered a few choice words beneath his breath and I pretended not to hear them. He dropped me off in front of the brownstone and I shut the door to his cab a little harder than I wanted to. I gave him a feeble smile because I had already started to feel shitty about treating him poorly. I held out a dollar bill as an extra tip.

Maybe he was having as hard a day as I was, and I was just coloring everything with my own frustration.

He tipped his cap with a motion no one could have called grateful.

"Money like this," he spat out. "You can call me anytime."

On a good day, I might have engaged. But I was weary. Down to the marrow weary.

I sighed heavily and headed toward the broad steps that led inside.

My landlord, Mr. Smith, was at the front door. Although I imagined his name was an alias. It looked like he was fiddling with the lock. A strange enough occurrence that it made me stop a few feet away so I could watch without him noticing me.

He was an old curmudgeon who had been a bug in the zoning committee's comfortable bedding for as long as I had lived in his apartment. I suspected he kept me in the brownstone just to piss them off because as long as he had a tenant, he couldn't be rezoned. It was no secret the brownstone sprawled over an area that most of the more elite residents wanted to turn into a green space so they could up their optics and garner more tax cash.

It wasn't like him to fix things. In light of his feud with the neighbors, he was more inclined to 'distress' his property occasionally. Besides, my lock did not need fixing.

I knew he would recognize me regardless of the wig and glasses because the only person coming out of or going into his purposefully shittily-kept old brownstone would be me.

I halted at the bottom of the staircase. "Whatcha doing, Mr. Smith?"

He swung around like a kid caught trying to stick a fork in an outlet. That's when I noticed the lock did indeed need fixing. It was hanging outside the door as though it had been yanked through.

"Changing the locks?" I asked, wary. First the henchman in the coffee shop and now this.

"One of those damn bums decided to take a rock to the door," he said. "Probably wanted a good place to sleep."

We both knew there weren't any bums in the neighborhood. They got run off. His complaint was for the neighbors, one of whom was hovering about her garden, trying to pretend she wasn't listening.

I chewed the side of my cheek, trying to think of some way to explain it away without making him worry about me. He was a blustery old man, but I knew he kept me on for more reasons than just trying to annoy the neighbors. I imagined I reminded him of the daughter who lived a country away.

"It was probably one of your neighbors," I said loudly and jerking my chin toward the labor clutching a set of gardening shears. "Didn't you say the zoning committee would be meeting next week?"

He started muttering at that, cursing the committee up down, left right, and seven ways to Sunday, to quote all of the clichés at once. I slipped my hand into the gap between the door jamb the door and was pulling it open when he halted his tirade midstream and put his hands on his hips. The screwdriver in his fingers fell to the platform with a thunk.

"Is that why you've got some seedy looking john hanging around outside the building," he said. "Helping me fight the fight?"

"What's that?" I said over my shoulder.

"That guy you have hanging around." He stooped to pick the screwdriver up and tossed it end over end before catching it by the handle. He gave me a broad smile and pointed the tip at me.

"Nice touch. He looked pretty haggard. Ought to piss them off royally."

"Sure," I said, trying to smile back and feeling as though my lips were catching my teeth instead. Everything had gone suddenly dry in my mouth. My tongue felt like sand paper.

Another woman might have written off the broken lock or the strange man hanging around. I knew what it meant: Scottie had found me and sent his henchmen to collect me.

I'd waited too long.

"Thanks, Mr. Smith," I said and wasn't surprised to hear the tightness in my voice. "I'm glad you like it. Say," I said, as though something had only just occurred to me. "Do you think my hired derelict decided to raid my kitchen?"

I wanted to know if there was a chance someone—likely, Scottie's minion—was still inside waiting for me.

He winked at me, buying into the conspiracy. "No way," he waved the screwdriver the way a fencer might. "I ran him off toot sweet." He gave a meaningful look toward the neighbor holding the burning shears. "He probably found some other place to hole up."

Relieved, I thanked him and went inside. I couldn't wait to peel the hot pants and dom boots off. Scottie's minion might be gone for spell, but he'd be back. He might even still be lurking around somewhere unseen, but as long as Mr. Smith was out there he wouldn't risk being noticed again. The next time came, he'd be sure to do so under the cloak of night.

That left plenty of time to for my mind to skip track into a groove more useful than fretting. Fretting got a gal nowhere. I needed to unload the tile like yesterday if I wanted to get clear of

Scottie post haste. And I was sure it needed unloading...and that it would collect a fair amount of cash.

If I'd doubted it, Errol's reaction to it, sealed my thought.

I did have one other lead I might be able to use to unload the goods. Kassie. She was a young runaway. Maybe no more than twelve at best, and I tried to give her as much business as I could to help sustain her on the streets. It was my way of keeping her safe in the face of the awful conditions that the street could force a girl to endure.

I wasn't foolish enough to report her so she could find her family again. She didn't want her family to find her. Whatever she'd run from, she thought it best to be an anonymous tooth in in a very large gear. Much like I had.

Besides, she always gave me good Intel. I wasn't sure where she got it from, who or what she had to endure to get it, but it was always useful.

I had already decided to give her a call when I opened the door to my apartment and was struck by the undeniable stink of rotten eggs. I gasped and held my breath. It wasn't like me to forget something like a pilot light or to leave the gas blazing.

One more bit of evidence that I wasn't myself lately.

I ran to the windows to lift them open. Curtains billowed in and sucked back out as the breeze wafted in. A horn blared from somewhere outside. I ran to the stove. The pilot light was fine. In fact, everything was fine. Nothing was out of place.

Then I saw my cat.

She perched atop the fridge in a tight ball of hissing fury. She looked odd, and not just because she looked terrified of me. Something was wrong with her coat.

I edged closer.

"It's okay, cat," I whispered. "It's alright." I held my hands out for her to see, slowing inching up to her.

I didn't have to get close enough to pick her up to see parts of her fur were burned down to the mottled brown skin.

Or that the shapes of those scorch marks looked exactly like human hand prints.

CHAPTER 8

My hackles rose on the back of my neck. What if the person was still here, quietly assessing me, ready to launch with deadly intent or bolt out the door? What if Mr. Smith had been wrong?

I froze in my spot, straining my hearing to pick up any noise of the apartment. Nothing met my ears but my own breath. I inhaled deeply and silently. No aftershave. No perfume. No smell of soap or cigarettes.

I glanced at the cat from the corner of my eye. She watched me back, blinking balefully. No agitation except when I reached for her.

If the cat had decided the coast was clear enough to glare at me rather than cower from an intruder, then I'd take the evidence of her senses over mine. I relaxed.

She did too, and I figured it was me who was agitating her. I took another step backward to give her space. She folded her feet beneath her chest and settled into a ball where she could watch me from those slitted yellow eyes.

I was in the clear, it seemed. For now. No one else was in the apartment, I was sure. And now that I could relax and let my other senses kick in, the ones that made me good at what I did, I could assess the circumstances.

I would've expected things to be upended, drawers open, things broken the way unskilled thieves did things. This invasion was nothing like that. Everything was as neat and tidy as when I'd left it. Granted, there was the trail of clothes I'd left the night before, the usual pair of socks hanging from the side of my sofa, and the occasional toast crust sitting cold in the middle of the plate, but those were things I'd left. Those were things I was used to seeing. Whoever had come into my apartment, had left no scent, no mark of having been in there at all.

Nothing was out of place except the cat. She hissed at me from the top of the fridge when I tried to pluck her down from her perch and assess the damage. One swipe at me with claws extended, and I backed off, hands held aloft so she could see them. She could be a handful when she wanted to be.

"Okay, Miss Hiss," I said. "I get it. Leave you the Hell alone."

I tried to eyeball her skin from where I stood to see if there were burn marks beneath that scorched fur. Was that a blister I saw bubbling up on her back or just a dollop of olive oil from the decanter she'd knocked over? I used the distraction of righting the bottle with one hand to touch down on her back with my opposite one. She squalled at me and leapt straight from the fridge to the counter top like I'd cattle-prodded her.

Not injured then. Just incredibly pissed off.

I crept around the apartment, looking for clues that something had gone missing. Checked my usual hiding spaces. Everything was intact and in its usual spots—even the bug out bag hidden in the ceiling tiles.

I couldn't exactly call the cops to report a break-in. I couldn't really complain to Mr. Smith either. What would he do? Change a lock? I knew enough not to put stake in that kind of 'protection'.

Besides: I knew the signs. Whoever did this was looking for something specific. I got the feeling they had not rifled through my things at all. And whoever had left the marks on my cat had done so intentionally. They wanted me to know they had been there. They wanted me to know and be afraid.

That sounded a lot like Scottie. Part of Scottie's modus operandi was fear, and it worked well for him. I knew the way he worked. I knew how his workhorses did their deeds. It was never in secret. What they did, they wanted the intended to know about it.

But Scottie's workhorses weren't exactly the subtle type. I doubt it was them. But the problem with that was if it wasn't them, who was it? And how they had managed to burn such a perfect pattern into my cat's fur.

And following up on all of that awfulness, exactly what kind of message were they trying to send?

They wanted me to know they had been here, that was clear. If they wanted something, they hadn't searched my apartment for it. That meant they must have thought it was in my possession. Not squirreled away somewhere in a drawer.

"The tile," I said more to myself than the cat. Only a couple of people knew I had it and only a couple of people saw it at all, but only one of them wanted it bad enough to try to sidetrack me in his back room while he stole the thing right from under my nose.

So it was valuable. Very valuable. I stuck my hand in my pocket to wrap my fingers around the tile, still strangely warm in my palm. Rather than feeling angry or afraid at being left unguarded, I felt giddy.

The question was, just how valuable? Was it valuable enough to reach out for Intel? And who would be the best person to do that? Who had the best network available without me having to come out in the open?

"Kassie," I said, pulling out my burner cell phone and shooting off a text. For whatever spider's web I had been able to create in my three years here, she had managed to make several of them. No doubt she had cobwebs of connections lingering in the dustiest, dirtiest of places.

I supplied a burner phone to several of my contacts each month and I knew there were still three days left before the time on hers ran out. I snapped a pic of the tile and sent that along for good measure.

She answered me back in moments. I wrote that I would meet her in the usual place and then I went straight to my closet and pulled off the offensive dom costume and pulled on jeans and a T-shirt. I pulled a cap down over my hair, tucking up the curliest bits at the temples and the longest bits into a ponytail that I pulled through the opening of the back. Sunglasses. Sneakers.

Next, I grabbed my bug-out bag full of wigs, cash, and a bunch of granola bars and fake IDs. I wouldn't be coming back to the apartment for a long time, not until I figured the rest of this out. The apartment was to be considered compromised until then.

I endured several scratches from the cat, but I eventually shoved her down into the bug-out bag as well and zippered her in, leaving a small enough hole in the top that she could poke her head out for air when she needed to. She growled at me from inside but didn't poke her head out. I imagined her all balled up in there, waiting to dig into any finger that reached in.

I met Kassie behind the upscale sushi joint three blocks away. I always hoped she'd go in after I paid her and ask for a round of fresh California rolls. I worried she didn't eat enough. She was so damn skinny.

"Your purse is meowing," she said, but there was no look of interest in her expression. Mostly, she just stood very still, as though the act of moving was painful.

It had taken me all of three years to get the girl to give me more than two extra words at a stretch so I was surprised enough to answer her.

"My cat's in there."

She stared mutely at me, and I had the sense she was thinking I was an animal torturer or something.

"She needed the air," I said. "It's not good to coop things up too long in a stuffy apartment."

Kassie ran fingers through her crop of orphan Annie curls as she considered that information. She blinked at me but didn't move until I pulled at the zipper to see if the cat would poke her head out to prove she was just fine. True to form a double-paw shot out and scratched me. I yelped and pulled my hand back, sticking the wound in my mouth.

"Damn thing," I said.

Kassie snuck closer, leaning down to peer into the gap in the zipper. I thought I saw a hint of a smile.

"It needs a name," she said.

"She'll get one when she learns to behave," I said. "So. Did you get my text?"

She blinked several times at the question and then rolled her shoulders the way a fighter might before facing an opponent. She looked over her shoulder. I knew she hated coming out in public at all, even if it was the back of the sushi place. The location was very close to a busy street and she was antsy, skipping from one foot to the other as she watched me. I thought I heard her counting beneath her breath.

I placed the bugout bag on the cobblestones between us. She nudged it with her toe, straightening it out so it was parallel to the building.

For a punk kid, she had her fingers in a lot of pies. A lot of connections. I might have pitied her if she was pitiful at all. She was a tough little thing and was always discrete. My entire enterprise depended on discretion when I couldn't do things for myself. And I trusted Kassie. Enough to go out on a limb and push her further than seemed normal, even for her.

"You got the picture, then?" I said.

She made a sound that might have indicated she agreed, but I never knew what those noises meant. She rarely said much that wasn't a straight answer to a probing question or to detail her Intel. I waited to see if she would name a price for the Intel. I hated to start off the bargaining.

I knew she didn't have the same aversion. She'd give me a price that was way too high and I'd give her a hundred bucks. She never refused it. Sometimes I suspected if I tried to give her anything other than the hundred, she'd run shrieking down the alley way in panic.

"What do you think of the tile?"

She shrugged, again nudging the bag with her toe.

"Throw it in the trash," she said.

"You mean it's worthless?"

I didn't think so, and I didn't think Kassie did either. I waited patiently but it took a long time before she spoke again.

"You don't want it," she said.

I jammed my hands into the pockets of my jeans to keep from giving anything away in my body language.

"I sure as hell don't want it," I said. "But if it's valuable, then I need it, or at least I need the money you can bring me if it's worth it. I've got people on my tail. I need to know if it will pay my way out."

It wasn't fair to press so, to even bring up the question of my own safety in light of her own tenuous lifestyle. And especially when she seemed so reticent, but I couldn't afford to think about her sensibilities. Not with Scottie breathing down my neck.

"My life might even depend on it," I said.

She met my eye for a long moment before she dropped it again to the bug-out bag.

"I won't help you," she said.

I listened carefully with my eyes as well as my ears. It was often the things Kassie didn't say that were the most valuable. For example, I noted she said wouldn't help me not couldn't. She wouldn't look me in the eye, either. Not particularly strange for her, except she wouldn't look at the tile in my hand.

"What's wrong?"

"Just get rid of it."

I stepped closer, fully expecting her to bolt. When she didn't, I pressed on.

"You can come with me," I said. "If you're scared. If it can pay for the both of us, I'll take you with me."

She gave me a strange look, one of disbelief and surprise, but not one of hope like I expected. Instead of taking me up on the offer, she sighed and kicked the bag. The cat inside yowled.

"I know a guy."

"Someone who will buy it," I said, pushing aside my discomfort at her ignoring my offer and grounding myself in the reason I was there in the first place. "It has to be someone who will buy it, or someone who has a connection who will buy it."

I hoped it was the first one. I didn't want to add too many links to the chain.

"He's got no scruples," she said. "Dangerous. But he'll probably buy it. Probably the only one who will."

It was more words added up in one moment than in a full year of dealing with her. I had to fight the urge to hug her.

"Thanks," I said simply. I pulled out a one hundred dollar bill from the bug out bag and passed it over. She took it without touching my fingers and shoved it in her shoe.

"So where is this guy?" I said. "I'll give you ten percent of the cut and take all of the risks. You don't have to worry about getting caught in the middle."

"Show me," she said.

"Show you?" I crinkled my forehead in confusion. "You mean the tile?"

She nodded. "If I send you to him, I need to see it."

"What does it matter?"

She shrugged. "Is it real?"

"Real compared to..." I let my thought trail off because, as usual, she was confusing me. "I showed you the picture," I said. "It's real enough."

She pursed her lips as though she thought I was being dense. Maybe I was.

"Authentic," she said. "He'll know. He knows stuff."

"What kind of stuff?" I wasn't sure why she stressed the word so strangely. "Is he mafia? Yakuza?" I would have to stay clear of this contact if that was the case. No sense getting my little panties wadded up again with that pile of dirty laundry.

She gave me a peculiar cant to her head that made me think she was trying to decide something about me.

"I can take care of myself," I said, not wanting her to feel responsible for the information.

She grunted with one of those inscrutable noises again.

I reached for the tile from my pocket and she edged expertly sideways the way a practiced germophobe might.

I held my hand up, tile facing out at her from my palm. She was particularly skittish for a kid that rarely reacted.

"I just need to know if he can move this for me and if I can trust him," I said. "That's all."

"He can," she said. A certainty to her tone.

"So. A name. Description? A way to contact him."

"Someone like you doesn't contact him."

"Someone like me?" I said.

"Yes," she said. Very formal.

I told myself she no doubt needed to keep some things to herself if she was going to keep on eating.

"Okay," I agreed. "No problem. So you set it up."

She gave me a curt nod. "Fayed's bar. Night fall. His sort hangs out there."

His sort. I tried not to feel anxious about that. Not just for myself but for the girl who might know that 'sort'.

"A name?" There. I did a good job of not letting the concern show in my voice.

She sighed. "Maddox."

The tile fell free of my hand with a clatter to the sidewalk at the name. I remembered the way Errol had quailed at sight of the

Maddox I'd already met. It was an unusual name, certainly not one a gal ran into often.

I told myself it might not be the same guy even as the dread clogged up my throat. With the way my luck was running, there was no doubt about who it would be.

I leaned to pick up the tile because it gave me a moment to recover and to phrase a question just the right way to the girl. Like, what the heck was she doing connecting herself to a man like that. My fingers closed around the tile and I yanked my hand back when it burned my fingers.

"This damn thing keeps burning me," I said to her.

I craned upwards but she had already melted away into the buildings or alleyways. One moment she was giving me that baleful, non-affected stare, and the next she just disappeared. I hoped she went into the sushi joint, but I imagined she wouldn't stick around any longer than she needed to. I was never sure where the girl came from or went to.

I yanked my sleeves down over my hand and leaned down to work the tile off the sidewalk and into my pocket. I gave it a pat from the outside of my jacket. Still warm. In fact, my entire waist grew warm beneath its heat.

Stranger still, my wrist, where that strange little henna mark sat, burned. I eyed the sidewalk where the tile had landed, bewildered and sure I could figure out what the root cause was of the heat.

Pushing the improbable into the realm of impossible, there on the pavement was an exact stamp of the marking from the tile.

I hunched over, trying to get a better look, and flung the bag over my shoulder. The cat squalled and moved around inside, making my grip tenuous.

"Patience, cat," I said and leaned further.

Yes. A stamp. Scorched in like the hand print on the cat's fur.

That did it. I was not high on absinthe this time. This time, I couldn't explain it away.

When met with the terrifying impossible, a girl should feel afraid.

But I wasn't a girl any more, and all I felt was giddy. At least until I caught sight of Scottie's henchman heading my way.

Then the terror flooded in just the way it should have in the first place.

CHAPTER 9

I recognized the man from the coffee shop who had bought my latte, and I was pretty sure he recognized me too. If he was indeed in Scottie's employ, then he was hired long after I'd taken flight because I didn't remember him from my tenure. That didn't mean he wasn't a threat to me, though. Scottie might be many things, but he wasn't a stupid man. He would send someone to fetch me that wouldn't give away his intent by showing me a familiar face. All the better to take me unawares.

Except the man had tipped his hand when he'd bought my latte. He had lost that element of surprise. Probably didn't even know how important it was. Some men were just like that.

Lucky for me, he was one of them.

I gave him a quick grin, letting him know I knew him for what he was. He smiled in return. That perverse delight in knowing he'd threatened someone was written all over his face. Well, I wouldn't show him my fear. I wouldn't give him that satisfaction. Back in the coffee shop had been different. I'd thought I was safe. I had become complacent in all of the little safeguards I had thrown up around myself to remain invisible from the likes of law enforcement and my past.

He was a mere three feet away by now, shouldering his way past a group of teens shoving greasy pizza slices into their gobs. A particularly surly looking youth swore at his back and gave him the finger when he pushed past. It would take no less than two heartbeats for the man to grab hold of me.

I stood my ground stubbornly. We both knew he wouldn't do anything to me in the middle of a busy street in broad daylight, but he wouldn't let me out of his sight of either.

That meant I couldn't go home. It also meant I couldn't just wait it out and explain myself away in the hopes he'd take pity on me. Some guys were like that too. They took one look at my diminutive stature and girlish looks and felt all fatherly and protective.

This one was not one of those sorts.

But there was one more good thing about being small. I could give just about anyone the slip. I just had to wait for my moment.

He had his eyes pinned to me as he trolled forward, coming at me down the sidewalk. I stood stock still, letting him think he had me. I scanned my environment from the corners of my eyes, careful not to look like I was going to bolt. A tall man in a suit stepped outside the door of the pizza parlour with a sixteen inch box cradled in his arms. He was about to heft it above his head to avoid a kid on a bike.

It was my chance. I stepped sideways, thinking to melt behind the even taller man who was blabbering into his cell phone beside him.

One moment of self-satisfaction was all I got, then the feeling of victory popped like a balloon.

Someone bumped me from behind as I sidestepped and I ended up stumbling forward, right into the arms of the brute I was trying to avoid. I almost dropped my bug-out bag and my cat hissed from its confines.

At the same moment, his arms went round me as though he was a man meeting a long-awaited lover. His chest felt very much like a brick wall. The muscles beneath my palm had no give.

And yes, there was a pistol beneath his jacket.

"I can see why the boss wants you so bad," he said over my head, laying his chin down over top my ball cap. "You're small enough to fit in a man's pocket."

I adjusted myself in his arms, taking my time to run my fingers over his chest and slipping over his ribs, letting the back of my hand linger over the pocket with the pistol. It was small, an afterthought weapon. The other one was no doubt tucked into his hip band.

"You got a thing for little girls?" I said. "Cause that pocket feels pretty hard for something so small."

He didn't laugh.

"I got a low tolerance for smart-ass bitches."

He withdrew his arms to squeeze my hand with meaty fingers. He pulled the arm of the hand not gripping my bag around his waist beneath his coat. Ah. There was the bigger gun. Holstered to his side. I should have known.

"Like them submissive and compliant, huh?" I said. "I wouldn't have figured it for a genteel knight such as yourself. Then again: Such is the dichotomy of attraction."

"What the fuck are you on about?" he demanded.

"Can't stand smart women, either, I guess," I said.

In response, he pushed me hard enough in the direction of the alley that I started to panic. What if Scottie was there waiting for me? I might be all bluster and vinegar in front of a minion, but the real thing was terrifying.

"You've been tormenting my land lord," I said to distract him. "Scottie won't like it if he knows you've left a trail." I stumbled beside him as he walked me along to the mouth of the alley. I slipped my free hand casually in my pocket, then swung the bug-out bag wide.

"You might be cute," he said. "But you're bat shit." He aimed me to the left of a crowd of women inspecting each other's shopping bags. "Who am I to question if the boss likes 'em crazy."

"My landlord," I said, keeping the conversation on track because it was the only kind of reason I could find that he would care about. "You've been hanging outside my building. He's in a delicate spot with his neighbors. He might decide to report a suspicious-looking hang-about."

He gave me a shove toward the alley, not so inclined to look like a fawning lover now that we were close to being out of sight of the street. I lost my grip on my bug out bag's handle and the cat inside mewled in fear. I might have grabbed for it with my other hand, but it was already full of pistol.

I didn't bother to peer into the gloomy and damp spaces. I didn't want to peer in there and find whether or not a shadowy figure about five feet six inches tall and seven feet wide lurked within waiting for me.

The brute had released me in his macho move of aggression and I spun around, his tiny pistol in my hand, right at groin level. I wasn't above grinning at his surprise that I'd liberated it.

"What Scottie wants of me is something you wouldn't understand." I braced my feet and leaned sideways to pick up the bag. When I came back vertical, I jammed the nose of the pistol upward.

"My guess is your sack is fleshy enough to muzzle the shot," I said. "But I'm also guessing you don't care about the noise."

He went rigid.

"You wouldn't," he hissed.

"I'm crazy," I said. "Right?" I was terrified he'd find a way to strong arm me but I kept my expression carefully placid. Confident. That's how a dangerous threat looked, right? Arrogant. Cocky. Determined.

His mouth twitched. "I never went near your apartment. I have no idea where you live."

He was telling the truth. I could tell by the slightly desperate tone in his voice. He thought it was about me telling on him to Scottie.

"Doesn't matter," I said.

"What do you want then?"

"Take out your gun."

"What?"

"Your gun. Take it out." I wiggled the nose into the folds of his trousers. "Take it out and lift it high over your head."

"You really are crazy."

I flicked aside the safety and I knew he heard the latch engage.

"Okay. Okay." He took pains to move slowly so I wouldn't get nervous or retaliatory. He pulled it in front of his jacket. "Now what?"

"Raise it over your head and fire."

"But—"

"Fire," I hissed, "or I will."

"You won't get away with this."

"I've got nothing to lose," I said. "I fire, the cops come. They arrest me. I'm safe." I shuffled my feet sideways, giving myself the space to spin and run. "You fire," I said." The cops come. They arrest you. I'm safe."

"You'll never be safe from the boss's reach."

"I've got a snub-nosed pistol breathing in the stink of ball sack that begs to differ."

He sighed heavily but I knew he would give in. Didn't matter if Scottie was just a breath away in the alley. My guess was it was just the two of them.

Far too many seconds had already gone by that I was losing my sense of surprise and the upper hand that went with it. Just in case my abductor was thinking he could turn the tables, I pressed the mouth of the pistol a little harder into his junk.

I heard someone scream before I heard the shot he fired. By the time chaos erupted around me, with a dozen cell phones moving in a blur to ears and photobomb position, I was at least a yard away, sprinting down the block and dodging down the alley on the other side of the street.

I didn't bother to look back and see if the guy got away, but I was willing to bet his face would be plastered all over the news come suppertime.

Cat meowed from inside the bag, furious at being jostled about.

"Suck it up," I told her.

I ran without stopping to look back or sideways. I knew exactly where I was in the city and exactly how many alleyways and streets I needed to bolt through to get clear. With any luck I'd left the man behind me to face dozens of irate citizens and maybe even a policeman or two. But just in case I hadn't, I planned to abscond to the one place I knew most people refused to frequent.

Rot Gut Alley. Straight to the bar where Fayed would be coming on for his shift in a few hours.

It had taken me a lot of patient finagling to get accepted there. While I wasn't exactly safe, Fayed had given me the cursory going over. Until the last time, when the stranger accosted me and the bar patrons had made a move on him, I'd been safe there. No one touched me when I was there. I wasn't foolish enough to think it had anything to do with anything except Fayed. It was his acceptance of me that lent me that safety, and I'd never felt that any more keenly than that night.

I was never really sure why Fayed preferred the night shift. He'd once told me that he refused to work days and who was I to argue that? Besides, it suited me fine. The man with his obvious pull working during a time frame when I was most likely to frequent the place worked in my favour. More than that, I always had a feeling that he had his own secrets and that suited me too.

In fact, as threatening as the bar could be to a stranger, and had been to me at one time, once I had been accepted by Fayed, there was an almost code of silence that hung in the air. If you knew what it felt like, you could take it like a pulse.

I fell into a dark corner of the bar and put my bug out bag, cat and all, down onto the chair next to me. Breathing hard and with lungs burning, I left my back to the wall and pulled out the chairs from around the table, pushing them aside so that if I needed to make a quick run, I could do it unimpeded.

I didn't expect Scottie's henchman to follow me in here, and I certainly didn't expect Scottie to have taken up the pursuit.

Even so, a girl didn't get this far away from dangerous men by being sloppy.

I did a quick check of my cell phone and pulled my cap down over my face. At least two hours before Fayed's shift. From the smoke hazy windows, I could see the sun going down outside over the shorter buildings. The mere hint of darkness made me feel just a little safer.

I hailed a waitress for a glass of water and lemon and crossed my arms over the table, waiting quietly to catch sight of either Fayed arriving for his shift or for the man named Maddox.

I'd already decided it couldn't be the same man. If his sort hung out here like Kassie had said, surely I would have seen him before. And I would've remembered him had I lain eyes on him. He was far too large a man, far too handsome a man, for anyone to forget.

It was Fayed who arrived first. I watched as he stooped to clear the lintel of the doorframe on his way in from the back, and realized for the first time how tall he was as well. I was short enough that everybody looked like Giants, and so I rarely took notice of exactly how much taller than me people were. A gal doesn't want to be reminded that she looks like a kid.

But I rarely got an opportunity to study Fayed from a quiet corner where he was unaware I was watching him.

It almost seemed that the moment he arrived, was some sort of signal. Like cockroaches scuttling from dark corners when the lights go out, the room seemed to fill with all sorts of people. Fayed took his place behind the bar, with his hands displayed shoulder width apart, fingertips touching down on the surface. From there, he surveyed the room, nodding to patrons he obviously knew, which looked like everyone. A couple of them made a concerted effort to approach him. To both of them he gave a silent nod and the shoulders relaxed visibly before they found a place at a table close to the door.

He looked ethnic, with a hint of Whistler's Grandmother. His blue eyes made the ethnic skin all the more creamy looking.

He crooked his finger in my direction and I realized he'd known I was there all along. I grabbed my bug out bag, fully prepared to pull a few bills from the interior to pay him to keep my presence here tonight a secret.

I slid into place on the stool in front of him. He scanned me top to bottom quietly before he spoke.

"You've been running," he said.

I wasn't sure how he would know that, since it had been at least an hour since my panicked sprint. I probably looked like a mess, all sweaty and adrenaline soaked.

"Nothing keeps a girl in better shape," I said.

One black eyebrow quirked almost humorously.

"You don't look like the tracksuit type," he said.

I held my hands up in surrender. "You got me. Truth is, I'm looking for someone."

His face closed up. "No one ever comes here," he said pointedly.

"I understand," I said. "But I'm not looking to get anyone in trouble. I'm actually supposed to be waiting for someone."

While his expression didn't change, I noticed his shoulders relaxed.

"Well then if you're waiting for someone, they should be along shortly." He made a move to slip away but I wasn't done with him.

"Actually," I said, reaching out and touching him on the forearm. "I was hoping you could give me some background on the guy."

He swung that lamplight gaze on to me again. "Scary sort?"

"Blind date," I said carefully.

"We don't get many blind date hookups here," he said.

I shrugged. "I'm here so much it's like a second home," I said. "I feel safe."

He smiled for me, revealing perfect white teeth with rather longish canines that I'd always thought looked rather predatory.

"You are safe here," he said. "I wouldn't let anyone hurt you. Not while I'm here."

The way he said it made me think there were plenty of people that frequented the joint who would hurt me after all. All those men I'd assumed had accepted me and let me be out of respect or some hard earned moxy. For a second, I was taken aback and felt uncomfortable. I couldn't help looking over my shoulder. Sure enough, two men averted their gazes as I scanned the room.

The back of my neck crawled.

"I guess I've been lucky, then," I murmured, turning back around to face Fayed. He too had caught the eyes of those men and his expression had been a hard, ugly one until he noticed me watching him. Then it softened, not enough to look fawning. Just that bland, careful expression he always wore.

"The sort of folks that come here aren't always the friendliest," he said by way of explanation. He leaned down to pull out a bottle of Rot Gut and I shook my head. I had to keep my wits.

He pursed his lips and flicked his gaze to the men again before putting the bottle back under the counter.

"Well then," he said. "Tell me who this blind date is that you're meeting and I'll let you know if you can trust him."

I told him I didn't know much about the man, just his name. That he was connected. That his "sort" hung out there.

His eyebrows cocked at the words sort, but he said nothing until I dropped the name.

"Maddox?" he said. "You're meeting a man named Maddox. Tall guy. Man bun?"

I nodded. The bugout bag stretched and undulated. My cat poked her head up through the hole in the zipper. One look at Fayed and she hissed, the prissy thing.

"Get back in there if you can't be civil," I told her. She withdrew back inside and I shrugged at Fayed.

"Rescue," I said of her. "She doesn't trust anyone."

"A sound policy," he said.

"So," I said. "Do you know more about him? Maddox, I mean."

"I know a Maddox," he said. "Fits the bill. And his sort does hang out here."

"And?"

"You trust me?" he said.

I nodded.

"Then trust me when I tell you to leave. Don't stick around to meet this guy. Whatever "date" you think you have with him, it's not what you think it is."

A scuffle sounded from the side of the room where the men had taken up spots near the door. I turned to look but Fayed grabbed my arm.

"Trust me," he said. "Stay away from him."

"Too late for that," said a drawling, dusty voice from behind me.

CHAPTER 10

The voice reminded me of roasted dates and smoky bacon. I knew it was Maddox behind me without turning around to confirm his russet hair, probably pulled up in a man-bun exactly like he had in the pawn shop. His grey eyes would look like they'd been chinked out of an ice block.

Fayed's fingers lingered on my hand in a warning touch, and his gaze flickered over my shoulder. I knew it landed on Maddox behind me, but there was no welcome in his gaze. Rather, it was confrontational as he leaned back against the bar and crossed his arms over his chest. Pectoral muscles flexed beneath his charcoal T-shirt and his full mouth twitched.

No harm would come to me while I was here. That's what Fayed had said. I repeated it to myself in my mind. Even before I turned around, I could see in my periphery more stocky men filtering in and finding seats throughout the room. The buzz of conversation was laden with curses and threats one man to another, and yet it was the man behind me that made me nervous.

No harm would come to me. I inhaled slowly. It was ridiculous to believe Fayed's words could give me the courage to swing around on the stool and face the man I knew waited behind me, but it did. Fayed didn't seem the type to deliver warnings like that.

I spun so fast I was surprised to see him as close as he was, and was dizzy for a second as I tried to let the blur of him come back into focus.

There Maddox stood, all six foot eight of him. Closer than I expected. I should have felt him long before this if he was that close. Smelled him even, but I hadn't. Chalk one up to my fear factor, losing track of the basest things.

He wasn't wearing the manbun he'd wound into his hair the first time I'd seen him. Electing instead to wear his russet hair down around his ears. In this light, admittedly neon-sign lit with a taste of shadow from the darkness of the room, his hair reminded me of a fox's. It spiraled in loose waves that some men might call effeminate but most women would die to twirl their fingers in.

I swallowed down an unexpected clump of lust. It was just nerves and the giddiness of dodging Scottie and his henchman, best I remember that.

I noticed that the men at the door had vacated their spots beside the exit and retreated to the shadows, leaving Maddox with nothing behind him but a gaping door and several upturned chairs.

I didn't want to think about the kind of man who could make hardened criminals like the ones I knew frequented the bar turn their chairs over in their haste to make a wide berth of him.

Fayed's warning echoed in the back of my mind as I extended my hand for an introductory handshake.

"Ms. Foster," I said, deciding to use my alias rather than my real name.

I didn't use multiple personas like some thieves and cons. Far too easy for a girl to forget herself. I relied on my careful networking to keep me invisible. My real name was one most people didn't know, and I'd used my alias so often it came easily enough from my lips to sound genuine. It was a recent thing that it didn't also bring to mind the foster homes I'd languished in, so I used it often in place of my true surname.

"Isabella," I tacked on.

He looked at my hand held out in the air, a slight quiver making it shake, and when he didn't take it, I pulled it back against my side and shoved it into my pocket. I wanted to call him an arrogant prick, but I remembered how badly I needed that money.

"You have something for me?" he said.

"Maybe," I said, trying not to sound surly in the face of his rudeness. I couldn't help thinking that he had seemed a lot more interested back at Errol's shop. But then I had been dressed as a dominatrix with a blonde wig. Now I was just me. The ball cap I imagined interested him far less than the blonde tresses. No doubt he had no idea I was the same woman and had already decided I wasn't worth his trouble.

"I don't have a lot of time for coyness," he said and laid a hand along the surface of the bar. He tapped it twice, obviously trying to get Fayed's attention. He needn't have bothered. I could tell Fayed was watching the exchange keenly. "I have things to do."

"So don't we all," I said and met his gaze with more courage than I felt. "You think you're the only one who is busy?"

His gaze took in the ball cap, and the way my hair had escaped its confines along the temples and lay plastered against my face by sweat. I would have given anything in that moment to yank out my blonde wig and shove it on my head and remind him that he had once tried very hard not to look at me.

I felt exposed. I wished I had just said that homeless guy here for me to do this part. He would have been easy to find, and I might even have been able to give Scottie the slip without feeling as though my lungs were on fire from running. It was ridiculous of me to take this sort of risk. Even wearing a cap and jeans, I was too easily be recognized. But then Scottie did that sort of thing to me. He took my last nerve and ran a cheese grater over it.

No doubt I was off my game, and it would be foolish to try to make a deal when I wasn't in my right mind set. Desperation almost always ended up in stupidity.

"Well," he said when I didn't answer. "What do you have?"

I hesitated. Was I being desperate? I didn't even know what I had, how did I know how valuable it was?

He rolled his eyes in the direction of the ceiling, heaving a sigh at the same time.

"If Ms. Foster here feels like she needs to be wined and dined then maybe you should get us a couple of glasses," he said to Fayed.

Fayed turned around and headed for the more expensive bottles toward the left of the bar. I secretly smiled to myself thinking he obviously didn't like this Maddox one bit and planned to make him pay handsomely.

I was inclined to agree.

"I'll take the Dom," I said over Maddox's shoulder. I didn't pretend not to see the sly smile Fayed slipped in my direction.

To his credit, Maddox asked for the same without complaint. Then he turned to me with a smile that looked pasted on. I wondered how gorgeous he would look if he truly smiled with full-blown authenticity. Even his pasted on smile made a girl's heart race.

"What? Are you going to make me wait all day?" he said. "Are you going to try to pawn off another bag of crap?"

"What makes you think I have junk?"

He shrugged. "You didn't have much more than junk for sale at the pawnshop."

"To be clear," I said. "I was in the pawnshop, but you've got it all wrong. That old guy was selling his own junk. I wanted the ring. That's all."

"That's how I remember it happening," he said. "But that doesn't mean that's the way it went down."

"If you thought I was going to pawn off crap, then why are you here?"

"I am here," he said, "because a mutual acquaintance thought I should meet you. You obviously managed to con her."

He threw a wad of cash at Fayed and pulled at the two champagne stems, pushing one toward me. He settled onto the stool next to me and it was only then that I caught a fragrance that might have been aftershave. It smelled strongly sexual but I couldn't name it. I edged a little further over on my stool so I could catch a better whiff.

"So," he said and slid the glass closer to me. "Assuming she wasn't conned, you must have something worthy of my interest."

I lifted the glass to my lips, peering over the rim at him and pretending to drink. It might have been a mistake, ordering the booze. For some reason, I was already feeling dizzy. I toyed with the stem. He was deliberately trying to sway me, trick me into divulging my goods.

"Look, I know you've got something," he said over his glass. "Kassie doesn't ever reach out to me, and she certainly doesn't set me up. So whatever you've got, she thinks it's worth my time. I only want the rarest, most unusual of things."

He took a long drink of his champagne before setting it down purposefully on the bar.

"Think of me as the godfather of pawn," he said with not one trace of humility. "No one calls me to sell their grandmother's necklace."

I felt decidedly queasy at the use of the word godfather. Two people had warned me about this guy. I needed to be careful. If he was the godfather of pawn, he'd not stop till I showed him something and I most definitely wasn't going to show him the tile. Not till I sussed him out.

I kept a rose colored diamond in my bug out bag along with some cash for emergencies. He wouldn't want it, I knew, but it would get more in the way of Intel than just blindly passing off the tile. If the tile turned out to be something connected to a nefarious group like the mafia, then I definitely didn't need that.

I peered sideways to see Fayed busily scrubbing the bar nearby. Just out of earshot but close enough to intervene if I needed it.

I shot him an encouraging smile that I didn't feel.

I pulled my bag from the stool next to mine and slipped my hand in through the hole I'd left in the zipper for the cat. I felt around what I knew were several pairs of panties and a wad of cash. The cat's belly, soft and hot, met my fingers then shrank away. It was right about when I got my fingers deep into the corner of the bag that I noticed that all those burly, nasty looking men previously huddled about pitchers of beer had slowly but decidedly begun herding toward the back exit.

Strange thing, that. And not at all a good thing.

Not when a gal was in a bar of derelicts.

I froze, my fingers touching the diamond finally, and I glanced at Fayed. He was clenching the cloth as it lay on the bar surface. His eyes darted to the space beneath the bar where I knew he kept a gun. The cat hissed from inside the bag and dug into my hand as she tried to scramble out past my wrist.

I was still jamming her back inside and trying to duck down at the same time when Fayed leapt toward me.

No harm, he'd said. The words flashed through my mind as I spun stupidly, like a dazed drunk to meet whatever danger he figured was threatening me. I assumed that danger to be Maddox. He wanted what was mine and would take it by force if he had to, just like Scottie had and leave me with nothing.

But that wasn't it. Not at all. Maddox was turned back to the door, and his expression was shifting from curious interest at what I planned to pull from the bag and realization that something—everything—had changed behind him without him noticing.

The lag pulled out like taffy, sweet in the way it gave you time to react, but laced with the dread that what it allowed you to see was definitely not good for you.

That one second that pulled out time into threads of sticky goo revealed a petite woman dressed all in fatigues. She didn't look frightening enough to send a bunch of hardened men running for the exit.

Yet they ran none the less.

There was something different looking about her. Something peculiar, as though she didn't belong.

I was still trying to work out what was wrong with her when Fayed slammed into me over the bar and carried me, stumbling to the floor. It was then that I realized she had lifted her hand, palm facing toward me, and that a ball of purple light had gathered there in her palm.

It sizzled that light, and in the moment Fayed struck me and knocked me into Maddox, that glow flashed forward and struck the bar where I'd been standing.

It splintered like a tree trunk and sound rent the air even as my scream died in my ears.

CHAPTER 11

Another blast of light came hurtling across the bar at me, narrowly missing my temple but only because Fayed pushed me down onto the floor hard enough my teeth rattled when I struck it. The light skidded past me, hopscotching along the floor till it met a patron's foot on the other side of the room. Evidently, he wasn't as fast as Fayed, and he howled in pain.

He went down hard, grasping for his foot, which by then was nothing but a mangled mess of blood and flesh.

I caught a whiff of burning hair and skin as the man raked at his pant leg in an effort to cradle his foot. The light was dim enough in the bar that I couldn't make out how much of his foot was ruined in the strike, but I could clearly see his leg was covered in a pelt of hair.

I thought of dogs and bears as I gawked at it. My mind reeled as it tried to piece together animals and legs and human men, and then it bucked back, resentful and furious when I tried to add a bolt of lightning to the equation that could do that to a man's foot. A bolt of light that had apparently been marshalled from a woman's palm.

Exactly why that man's foot was so hairy at all, I didn't want to stuff into the complexity of it.

Fayed grabbed for my hand. His fingers dug into the skin as he yanked me behind an upended table and we fell onto the floor behind it, both panting.

I felt the hot well of blood, and he sucked in a breath at the same moment I did. I imagined he must have hurt himself, the inhale was so sharp.

"You need to get out of here," he rasped.

"What the hell was that?"

I stole a look sideways at him, hoping he'd have an answer that made sense. His face looked strange, all feral brow and pointy teeth.

I gaped at him, still trying to process all the discordant images and make sense of them. Fayed didn't look like Fayed anymore. A streak of light had cracked a hole in the bar, and some woman as small as I was had sent an entire room full of hard-core criminal types for the exit.

I was obviously fear-drunk. Too glutted on my terror to get away from Scottie, the anxiety of meeting someone no one seemed to think was a good idea, and the knowledge that where I'd felt safe really only tolerated me, to really be capable of making judgment calls on what was happening around me.

No absinthe or booze this time. My senses were simply on hyper overload. Whatever part of my mind delivered reality and sorted out peripheral thoughts had shut down. My brain had started serving me up living nightmares instead.

I absolutely would not, and could not accept that Fayed now looked like a creature from a cheesy vampire movie.

I felt stupid and slow with it all. Shock, some still working part of my mind whispered. My body felt icy with it. Even Fayed was cold. He wasn't even breathing.

The woman bellowed that she wasn't after a drink. That Fayed had better serve up what she wanted or else.

"Fayed," I tried. I wanted him to help me make sense of all this.

"Isabella," he barked. "Get the hell out of here. Now."

The sound of combat boots tapping across the floor echoed against my cheek as I lay there. They paused. Tapped twice in thought.

Fayed buried his face in my shoulder.

I tried to move. The silk of Fayed's hair brushed against my cheek.

"I can't," I whispered into the mass of it. "You're lying on top of me."

He grunted but he didn't move. I felt him trembling against my body but I didn't think it was from fear. It was something else. Like restraint.

"Fucking idiots," hissed Maddox. Because I was squashed down beneath Fayed, I had no idea he was with us behind the table, and the sound of his voice startled me.

"You're going to get yourselves killed," he grumbled.

The pressure of Fayed's weight eased up a bit, and I realized it was because Maddox had begun to haul on his arm. He gave two rough yanks but Fayed was stuck to me like a bug.

"Let go of her," Maddox ground out. "You need to relinquish her."

Relinquish. It was such an archaic, prissy word. I almost laughed. Almost. Except for the combat boots clunking about, coming our way, and the smooth, whiskeyish voice that accompanied them, I might have.

"Fie fi fo fum," a feminine voice said and then she chuckled, a horrid, light and tinkling sound that was more frightening than seeing Fayed's suddenly feral features.

"Fuck," Maddox said.

The combat boots scuffing along the floor paused. Maddox growled at Fayed to let go and then I was stumbling to my feet, clawing my way out of both their grasps as I grabbed for my bug out bag.

"Run," I heard Fayed shout.

It was a crisp sound that shot out amidst the din like a bullet and I wasted no time to see why his voice went dead flat in the next instant.

A thud sounded like a heavy bag being struck by a boxer. I knew without having to look that he had fallen to the floor. Injured or dead. If he had taken a hit to give me the chance of escape, I wouldn't waste it. I didn't think about why I needed to. I just ran.

Next I knew, I was sprinting headlong across the bar and thanking my lucky stars that I was small enough to dodge in and out of tables and chairs as wood splintered around me and balls of light sailed past. I had one thought: get the heck out of there.

The glowing Exit sign over the back door was nothing but a blur as I panned the wall for another assailant. My life with Scottie had taught me a good many things I never wanted to know, but they came in handy now and then. Like where there was one killer, there was another. Backup in case the first one fails.

The exit was only a short sprint away. Sizzling and cracking sounds much like thunder and lightning splintered around me. I was vaguely aware of someone chasing me, of my cat yowling in her bag. I pretty much agreed with her. I was terrified too.

I didn't have the time or inclination to check and see what happened to Fayed or Maddox. For all I knew, they had been struck by whatever weapon the female soldier struck them with.

It was even completely possible that she was in cahoots with Maddox and was the bad cop backup to his good.

I was pretty sure I could get away, but I needed a contingency plan in case I had to drop the bag. The tile wasn't safe in there, and I already decided it was more than just valuable. It was priceless. Deadly priceless.

I dropped the tile into my pocket as I hit the back door. Whoever or whatever was behind me was breathing hard. Anxiety or nerves, or just plain out of shape. Didn't matter to me. I just wanted out of there.

Something caught my foot and made me stumble as I burst through the door into the same alleyway I'd met up with the stranger the night before. It smelled the same. The same rat huddled next to the dumpster. I spilled over the threshold onto my face, and as I struggled to find my feet again, strong hands grappled for me beneath the armpits and hauled me along with him.

I staggered and fought to keep up, juggling the bug out bag with the cat inside, unbalancing it in my grasp with every step.

"Drop that stupid thing," Maddox said. "If you can't keep hold of it."

My lungs were already burning enough to make answering him nearly impossible, but it didn't stop me trying.

"Fuck no," I wheezed out.

My legs from the earlier full out run hadn't yet recovered enough to power me through another terrified sprint. I stopped dead in my tracks, hanging over my knees. The bug out bag hung between my legs on the cobblestones. The heaving of my lungs as they tried to pull in oxygen was making me nauseous. Sweat had broken out all the way down my back. I knew I was going to be sick.

I was making horrible wheezing sounds.

"It's mine." I rasped out.

He shoved me ahead of him, ignoring the fact that water had begun to run out my mouth. I was going to be sick. I couldn't help it. I stumbled and fell to one knee.

"Now is not the time to be clumsy, little girl," Maddox said. "We have to keep going. She won't stop."

Won't stop. My stomach lurched and I buckled. It was damn tough to keep my grip on the bugout bag, but by God I wouldn't let it go. I heaved up nothing and heard his disgusted groan. Then when I couldn't stop heaving, his palm lay against my back, snicking in between the shoulder blades.

He patted me there. As though that would help.

"Don't," I managed to get out between heaves. I held one hand out as I shuddered through the last of it.

"Are you through?" he said. "Because we need—"

"To get going, yeah I know." I bit the words out and pushed myself to my feet with the aid of the brick wall. "What in the hell does she want anyway?"

I inhaled and forged ahead, my legs feeling like lead.

I peered sideways at him. He was still walking sideways toward the mouth of the alley with all the appearance of a man frustrated at my pace. Was this some con? Was he trying to get me off guard and steal the tile?

I wasn't on absinthe now. I was terrified, but not stupid. Occam's razor and all. He had agreed to meet me to discuss an item of value. He had seen that tile in the antiquities shop. He was setting me up somehow. It wasn't Errol who had broken into my apartment for the tile; it was Maddox.

I backed away from him, pulling the handle of my bug out bag. The cat inside meowed shrilly enough to echo off the walls on either side.

His brow furrowed as he halted and glanced at it.

"You have a cat in there?" he said.

I shrugged. "Some girls carry ratty dogs in their purses."

That was it. Casual conversation. We were too far in for me to pull out the diamond and try to pass him that off. *He knew.* He knew I had that tile and we both knew now just how valuable it was. Valuable enough for him to hire a female soldier to lay siege to a back alley dive of a bar.

But he didn't know I'd made him. And that gave me an advantage.

I'd have to dazzle him with banality until I could slip away. I edged along the brick wall. If I knew anything about human nature, he'd look over my shoulder any time now, act like he was afraid of what was coming at us. Try to make me think this was all a strange, but genuine attack.

As if on cue, he jerked his head toward the back of the alley behind me. I bolted, using his distracted attention as my chance.

Another crack of lightning froze my feet. I couldn't help looking back, like Lot's wife, to see what was behind me.

A ball of light exploded against the wall, then broke into several slithering trails that skittered along the bricks.

I gasped. I couldn't help that either. And when it struck my bug out bag, it made a sizzling sound.

There was a snap and the stink of burning leather.

I dropped my hold on the bag in the same instant as the snapping sound. More out of reflex than anything, but good thing I did.

Because the bag disappeared.
Cat and all.

CHAPTER 12

A sound escaped me like I'd never heard before. Up until that point I felt stunned, yes, afraid. But this had gone way beyond anything rational. For a gal so good at puzzles, I was having a hard time adding any of these pieces up. Several gears in my brain were struggling to shift and turn to unlock something unlockable. I was frozen with it. So many strange little pieces: a seedy bar. A woman in combat fatigues. A weapon made of light.

These bits of puzzle weren't fractions and prime numbers or even someone's password made up of children's names and birth dates. None of these pieces fit together. They didn't even look like they came from the same picture.

I couldn't move for the complexity of the riddle, even when the woman stood in the open door frame, drenched in the hazy light that spilled over her from inside the bar. I got a good look at her then. Cropped black hair, pixyish almost, that framed a face with gracile, angelic features.

Her fatigues shifted color as she moved, as if the camouflage pattern woven through the material was a living texture. She couldn't have been a hair taller than me, and she reminded me why so many people told me that I looked like a kid in grown up clothes. It always pissed me off, but looking at her, I could see how apt a description it could be. Her diminutive stature made her look harmless even if the entire room had lit with fear at sight of her.

If she looked harmless, she certainly didn't give off an air of it. She straddled the threshold with both boots set wide apart. Her hands flexed at her sides the way a boxer's did before shoving hands into balls of gloving heavy enough to incapacitate a healthy opponent.

She gave one last shake of those hands, and then raised one of them again, straight at me, palm facing forward. I watched, dazed, as swirls of blue and purple light abandoned the street lights and neon signs and gathered there on her skin to light the alleyway around me.

She watched me with her head cocked to the side, maybe trying to assess whether I'd run or fight. I could make out every bit of her expression as she grinned with the slow realization I'd do neither.

She had me. She knew it. And it was the cold and calculated expression in her eyes that terrified me the most.

My limbs wanted to explode into motion, they even twitched, but my brain couldn't send the signals out. The synapses were stuck on trying to solve the puzzle like a gummed up ON switch to an old fashioned VCR.

The light fled her palm and streaked toward me. I heard it sizzle as it gobbled up the air. It was going to hit me. I was dead.

Rough hands grab hold of me and jerked me sideways.

Just in time.

The blast struck the wall behind me and broke off into thousands of splintered stars. I stared at the place it struck in the abandoned warehouse. Rubble rained down the side of the building and fell to the cobblestones. Nothing but a gaping hole remained behind it.

"Move," Maddox ground out. I swung my stunned gaze sideways to see him hovering over me. So we were both still standing. I hadn't collapsed after all. Strange. I couldn't feel my legs.

I started to say so, to tell him that I could not move unless a bulldozer scooped me up, but he took one look at me and cursed. His arm went around my waist as though I was a 20 pound bag of flour and that he was dragging me with him as he ran, hoisting me against his hip now and then when my feet bit into cobblestones.

We fled together, zigzagging up and down back alleys. It was full dark but the city had come alive with light. Crisscrossing iron bars covered the doors of the more reputable shops and floodlights in the eaves of the buildings lit up their façades as well as the sidewalk in front. Blurs of faces moved past me.

And I recognized the path he was taking. The docks. We were headed toward the docks. A far seedier part of town than even Fayed's bar. A place where no one would be be safe let alone a woman of my stature. Just knowing what he might have in store for me was enough to put some steel back into my spine.

I struggled out of his grip and managed to get free. But the effort dropped me to the sidewalk.

My legs were shot. My breath raged in my ears, my heartbeat hammered in my temples. My chest shuddered when I realized that I'd only gotten this far because of his grip on my waist. I was fooling myself if I thought I was participating in the escape. He'd been the one doing the running. I was just being dragged along for the ride.

I could move faster unburdened by the bug out bag, but the back of my mind kept chanting over and over again that this couldn't be happening and I refused to let go the one last thread that tied me to reality. I pumped my arms, kept flexing my fingers, expecting to feel that handle in my grip. I sobbed each time my fist closed on empty air.

"You need to get up," he said, reaching down.

I flipped over onto my side, holding my hand up.

"Don't," I said. It was one word but it held everything burgeoning in my psyche. My fear. Threat. The plea for this to all be over.

He loomed over me. His russet hair clung to his face. He brushed it back and re-wrapped it into the elastic. I fancied I heard him breathing hard until he spoke and proved he wasn't winded in the least.

"I can wait," he said but the words had the feel of a man who wanted to check his watch.

"What in the hell was that?" I gasped out.

"You must have pissed someone off, that's what that was," he said.

"What kind of answer is that?" I refused the offer of his hand and instead pushed back against the step, hugging my knees as I pulled them up to my chin.

He shrugged at my refusal and crossed his arms over his chest as he regarded me.

"What kind of question was it?" he said.

"What do you mean what kind of question? That was some crazy shit back there."

He crossed one ankle over the other and leaned against the building. I wondered how such a lazy stance could look so coiled with tension but it did. I expected him to pull out a cigarette. Instead he sighed and crouched so he could be eye level—sort of—with me.

"A crazy question is something one asks when the answer is obvious," he said.

"And the obvious answer is?"

He sighed. "You crossed one person too many."

"Me?" I said. "What makes you think all that was about me?"

I crossed a lot of people in my time. It was part and parcel of job. But I'd never seen things I'd seen tonight.

"Because it wasn't about me," he said.

"That's no answer." I lifted my chin. I'd done a hell of a lot of things in my time, and I knew people. He was hedging. He knew exactly what was going on. His body language was all over the knowledge.

I'd already ruled out the possibility of him being behind the attack. He'd run too frantically with me at my side him to be anything but afraid. And whatever it was he was afraid of, he was being careful now.

Not for the first time I wished I'd sent a lackey and sussed out this entire heist. Things had gone from bad to worse ever since I put the sole of my foot down that skylight to steal the Incan gold. Maybe even before that. Maybe even when I'd let that stranger buy me a cup of coffee.

"Heist?" he said, looking down at me with his head cocked just enough that the streetlight lit up half his face. The half I could see looked wary. I realized then that I was muttering to myself. I slapped my hand over my mouth to keep from saying more.

"What did you steal?" he demanded.

"Nothing," I said between my fingers.

"You just used the word heist." He pulled my hands away from my face and held them. "You must have stolen something pretty valuable to have Kelliope after you."

"Kelliope?" I said. I'd heard the name before somewhere, hadn't I? And he'd thrown the name out as though I should recognize it and be afraid. In fact, there was a distinct note of awe in his voice that made me uncomfortable. "Is that her name? That soldier from the alleyway?"

"Soldier?" he said. "Kelly is a soldier the way a Hot Wheels Porsche is a car. I'm surprised you don't know that."

I didn't like the way he said that name again. It had heft to it. A dread that made me try to inch away from him instead of answering because I had the feeling no matter what I said it would be wrong.

"Why is she after us?" I said. "Who is she?"

His gaze traveled my face to my throat, down to my knees and up again.

"You took something," he said, and his thumb went to my chin. He tilted my face so that he could look in my eyes. The glare from the streetlight made me squint and I felt like I was under interrogation. His face was still in shadow. "Something Kelly wants. So what is it?"

I squirmed beneath his touch, feeling like a kid and a doomed woman all at the same time.

"Nothing."

"Kelly doesn't chase anyone for nothing."

"Nothing anyone would kill for," I said, and hated the way my voice went all shrill. I was out of my depth, let alone the sheer panic that still coursed through my thigh muscles in memory. I leapt for the only rational thing I could.

"The diamond," I said. I'd stolen it so long ago, I couldn't remember if the mark had been a woman or a man. How rich they were. If they hired mercenaries. But it was the most likely explanation.

"So you did steal something." He eyed me with an I knew it look and I shrugged.

He shifted his hand so that the webbing between his thumb and index finger slipped up beneath my chin, and his fingers lay against my throat. He had very large hands. The palms were calloused. A man who did labor. Hard labor. I wondered if that labor included hurting people. My breath caught. I wondered if he could hear my heart slamming against my ribs. I could feel his palm against my throat as I swallowed the fear down.

"The diamond. It was in my bag," I said.

"Not a diamond," he said, shaking his head. "Not something so worthless."

I didn't dare move beneath his hand, a rabbit beneath a Wolf's paw. Instinct told me to lower my eyes, but I couldn't. My gaze was pinned to his like Icarus's gaze to the sun.

I made a sound somewhere between a grunt and a sigh. While the hand on my throat didn't move, the other one started running down my shoulders and arms, playing across my waist and into my pocket. I held my breath. I could feel the weight of the tile in the other pocket. If he decided to check there...

Which of course he did. His hand crossed over my waist and fumbled into the other pocket. I expected him to pull his hand back as soon as his skin touched the heat of the tile. Instead, he withdrew it and held it outstretched on his palm in front of my face.

He tilted it toward the light. The sound of his intake of breath told me he knew exactly what it was. Despite the fear, a sense of victory took flight in my chest. Yes. Valuable all right.

"An Odin rune," he murmured.

"It's mine," I said. Whatever an Odin rune was, I'd earned it with blood and sweat and not a small amount of terror.

"Where did you get it?" He sounded almost righteously angry.

"None of your business," I said.

He let me go at that and closed his fist over the tile. He squeezed. It seemed like he was testing the heat of it, the weight.

"It's real," he said. "I can feel it." The wonder in his voice was almost painful.

I wanted terribly to reach out and pluck the tile from his hand but I was afraid to move as he held it to his heart. Some sort of rumination was going on behind his gaze even as it held mine.

"Where did you get it?" He leveled me with that gaze and when I refused to answer he shook his head. "Never mind." He sounded exhausted. "Doesn't matter where you got it. You're screwed."

"Screwed?" I said. "She got the damn diamond." I thought of my bug out bag and the way it had just fizzled into nothing. "Or I guess she got it."

He canted his head to the left. "It's not the diamond she's after, I told you," he said. "It's this."

He pinched the tile between his finger and thumb and held it in front of me. I stuck my hand out for it but he tossed it lightly and caught it again in his fist.

"This is what you came to sell me," he said.

He pushed himself to his feet and I bolted to mine, thinking he planned to abscond with my future. He held his hand up in a halting gesture.

"No worries, Kitten," he said. "I'm not interested in the kind of future that's in store for you."

He said future like he'd heard me say it, and I most definitely did not. Even so, I didn't like the inference in the statement, as though whatever was coming was a thing to dread. Well, maybe it was, but what choice did I have? Run from an insane soldier woman or Scottie. It was all still running.

I squared my shoulders and held my hand out until he laid the tile onto my palm. I slipped it back into my pocket and patted it from the outside. His eyes followed the path of my hand and rested on my pocket.

"I've only ever seen one before. A forgery, that one. Nothing like what you have there."

"So it's valuable?" I said.

He chuckled darkly. "Oh yes. You've got the real deal there if Kelliope is after you."

He jammed his hand in his pocket. "At least the Fae believe it's real or they wouldn't have sent their most notorious assassin after you."

He dropped the words the way a skilled negotiator did. Letting them sit there quietly awaiting comprehension. I heard Scottie do it a thousand times. It was very much akin to 'you can tell me which Fed to talk to or I can break your fourth rib. You can tell me how much of my money you skimmed away or I can make you swallow your teeth.'

A person needed time to work through both of those things and a good negotiator gave the poor sap all the time he needed to realize that there really wasn't a choice anyway.

"Assassin," I said, my mind landing on the word that made the most sense.

I thought of the man in the alley who had disappeared. There'd been a blast of light then too. He'd been afraid. He'd told me a 'she' was behind me. My throat hurt almost too much to speak as the full weight of the realization descended.

I'd been fooling myself before, setting myself into a tunnel visioned spiral because all I could think of was Scottie and the dread of him was bad enough. I didn't want to think there was something worse. How stupid had I been, anyway? Blinded by bias despite the vivid picture right in front of me.

"The guy in the back alley," I murmured to myself. "She killed him. She wanted the rune and she killed him for it."

"I don't know what guy you're talking about, but yes, she will kill for it."

I shook my head to clear it of the ridiculous thought that a woman could blast a man out of existence with a beam of light. The army was getting pretty advanced.

"You expect me to believe the army has an assassin unit? And that they want to kill me for a stupid piece of stone." I started to pace, working my way through the information as though it was a trench of muck.

"Bone," he said and when I gaped at him, he cut off whatever else he was going to say in favor of a new train of thought.

He peered at me even closer.

"What are you?" he said.

I shrugged. I didn't know what he wanted for an answer and I was already too sunk into the forest that I couldn't see the wood.

"Oh my God," he said. "You're not anything, are you? You've got Kelliope after you and you have an Odin rune and you're not anything."

He raked his hand through his hair and sent me a look of outright pity.

"You shouldn't have it," he said with a note of urgency. "Give it to me." He held his hand out.

"The hell I will. You'll pay like anyone else."

"How much?" He said. "Tell me now. I have $10,000 cash on me."

My gaze flicked to his pocket. $10,000 was a lot of money. For a piece of stone. No, bone.

But it was also a hasty figure. One offered in desperation. If he was ready to give over $10,000 right away, it had to be worth more.

"Now," he said." Right now. I can give you the money and you can be gone and be rid of all of this."

Now I was beginning to understand. It really was all just a ruse. He almost got me. I'd been afraid there for a moment. Really afraid.

"There is no assassin is there," I said. "Because if there was, no amount of money would make a risk worth that."

"You're wrong," he said. "You have no idea what you're mixed up into. If you don't want to tell me where you got it, then just sell it to me. I can help you. You came to me, remember? Why hold it back now?"

"How do I know $10,000 is a fair price?"

"Honey, you're not in Kansas anymore," he said. "There's things you don't understand."

"I understand that someone who wants this thing enough to kill for might want it enough to pay for it."

He laughed at that, implying I was a complete idiot and I glared at him.

"Well, darlin', it's your funeral." He slapped me on the shoulder. "Suit yourself."

His hand ran down the length of my arm until it met my fingers. He lifted them to his mouth and kissed the tips then slipped my hands back into my pockets. My chest went all tight at the touch and I wanted to throttle my stupid libido as it panted beneath his gaze.

"It's your death," he said. "Take your chances with the fae's best assassin. See if she'll give you a fair price *and* let you live."

He turned heel and strolled off into the shadows. I sank back down onto the first stair, running the events through my mind. Things hadn't been right ever since that heist. A strange new mark on my arm. Fayed's peculiar transformation. The tile having heat that came from within when stone—no bone—didn't produce heat.

Nothing added up. Too many weird and unexplainable things. Starting with that guy disappearing just like my bugout bag. I had a pang of grief as I thought of my poor cat, but I pushed the concern aside. Something interesting hovered on the fringes of my awareness, something that buzzed because Maddox had used two words to describe that woman in fatigues.

Fae and assassin.

Fae was not a word a man like Maddox would use. It was too ludicrous, too Goth teen or nerdy gamer.

Unless he believed it.

Occam's Razor be damned. There was no easy explanation that could cover all this weirdness and still be grounded firmly in the normal order of things. Not unless it meant those who played were entrenched in the belief of something out of the ordinary, playing with weapons that shot light and destroyed walls. I felt the burble of manic laughter clawing at my throat. Would that it was some sort of Dean and Sam Winchester Cosplay.

I wasn't the kind of gal to believe in fairies and unicorns and magic. I believed in a roll in the hay with the Winchester boys, but not their creed. Give me good hard cash, a bed with a dozen pillows. A life without fear. Those were the things I believed in.

I didn't need to understand what these actors were playing at or why. I didn't need to care what *it* was.

I just needed to understand the things I'd always counted on, the things that made me and people like me such an integral part of society's seamy underbelly. Things that were as constant as the stars: that knowing human nature was a selfish, greedy thing.

And a selfish, greedy nature was very good at getting me what I wanted. All I needed was a good deal of cash to buy me a new life in a new city. And I needed a buyer. The best buyer. If the people I dealt with believed in all that Dungeons and Dragons hooey, then I'd meet them where they played.

I was going to get my life back. Come Hell or high murky water.

And I wanted my damn cat back too.

CHAPTER 13

The first step in solving a puzzle—any puzzle—is simple. You need to be clear about what the end result should be, what the riddle really is. Puzzles have a way of looking like something else. Like the Half Lady Old Man picture, perspectives can change the outcome.

The way I saw it, only a few people knew I even had the—what had Maddox called it?—Odin rune? The stranger from Fayed's bar had died for it in that back alley. I knew that now. He hadn't just been a figment of my imagination. I gave him a brief thought as I hobbled along on legs that had ran far too much for one day and were still trembling from exhaustion.

He'd had the rune in his pocket. I had stolen it. The antiquities dealer had wanted it bad enough to try to tie me up in his back room. Maddox had wanted to buy it from me, he said, to keep me out of the trouble it would cause.

The so-called Fae assassin wanted it bad enough to try to kill me.

Whatever it was, it was deadly valuable.

I limped my way across town, following well-lit streets and staying on the busiest of the thoroughfares. No more back alleys for me until I was ready to confront whoever leapt from the shadows to challenge me, kill me or steal from me. And yes, I was worried about those things in that order.

The city at night was much like the city during the day except it was filled with people who thrive in the shadows or have no choice but to venture out in the dark. I'd always thought it was regular folks down on their luck who would want to remain in the shadows but after today, I realized it was far worse.

What are you, Maddox had asked me. As though I could be something other than human. As though something other than human was entirely possible.

The city looked like it had wound ribbons of light around its streets. Faces were a blur as they moved past me. The exhaust of cars idling as they waited for traffic lights reached out to my nostrils like a heavy musk.

I was walking like a zombie, following the trail of lights when I caught scent of oregano and roasted tomatoes.

I was famished. The fact that I didn't even know I was hungry was testament to how deep into the thinking process I was. It explained why the lights looked blurry, why the faces distorted as though they were behind panes of watered down glass.

It wasn't until I had to stop and lean against a building that I realized it was because I was spent and I wasn't seeing clearly. My eyelids kept trying to close but I stubbornly pressed on until I couldn't anymore.

I'd run through my adrenaline. That last pit stop a body makes before it's about to crash into a burning wall was already clearly on the horizon. I needed fuel.

"That you?" Said a familiar voice.

I swung my gaze sideways. Through the thicket of meanderings, I recognized the pizza parlour where I had met the old drunk. I recognized the old drunk too. He leaned against the building with a paper bag in his hand, held outstretched toward me.

"Yeah," I said slowly. I recognized my reluctance to pull out of the deep hole of thought I was in. My voice sounded thick with thought.

"Hell," he said, pushing himself off the wall with his foot and leaning in close to peer into my eyes. "You okay?" He nudged me with the bottle.

I shook my head. I couldn't risk even one drink to dull the panic. I needed my wits.

"Not okay or don't want to drink," he said of my response. "Never mind. Both the same things to me."

When he took a pull from the mouth of the bag, I had the feeling he was glad I didn't want any. He eyed me over the paper bloom.

The bag came away from his mouth just enough to speak again. "How's that leg of yours?"

I leaned sideways to peer at my calf. I'd forgotten all about his patch job of the dog bite. It seemed so long ago.

"Fine I guess."

"Don't look fine," he said. "Looks like it's giving you some sort of fever."

"That good, huh?"

"Let's just say I feel like I should do the chivalrous thing and give you my bedroll for the night."

I found myself chuckling at that. He smelled faintly of urine and something akin to vinegar but I didn't want to offend him.

He looked down at himself and grinned. "I don't look like I have a bedroll, do I?" he said.

I shook my head. "You don't look like you have much besides a wet cardboard box, no offense."

"You got me there," he said and lifted the bottle again. "But if I had one, I'd give it to you."

I collapsed against the wall next to him, pressing my shoulders into the bricks and using the way they dug into my shoulder blades to keep me standing. Then thought better of it and skidded down onto my haunches. I was exhausted. I hadn't realized exactly how exhausted until I finally let my legs rest.

I stretched my legs out, and worried a discarded cigarette butt with the tip of my sneaker. A bus pulled up to the curb in front of us with a squeal of breaks and stink of diesel. I rested my head against the wall and before I realized my eyes had closed, I felt him nudge me with his knee.

"What?" I said.

"I asked you if you wanted a slice of pizza."

"You buying?" I expected him to say no and laugh at the joke, but when he confessed to having enough money for two slices, I decided to accept his chivalry. Especially since he looked so hopeful.

I nodded and he disappeared into the yawning door of the pizza parlour. My stomach gurgled in anticipation. I put my hand across my belly to calm it. That was when I felt my cell phone in the pocket of my hoodie. My cell phone. I could've sworn I put the tile in my pocket. I pulled it out of my bag before Kelly had blasted my cat and bug out bag into nonexistence. I knew I hadn't dropped it.

That left only one thing. Maddox. He must have stolen it.

The bastard.

I pulled out my cell phone and tapped the screen, typing in Kassie's number. If she had gotten in contact with him before, she could do so again. But this time she'd tell me where to find him, not just to meet him. I wasn't about to let him get away with stealing. Not from me. Not after everything I'd gone through.

Instead of texting, I let the phone ring. She picked up after a single ring.

"Your friend Maddox stole my goods," I said without preamble. It wasn't quite midnight, but I didn't care whether the girl was sleeping or roaming the streets.

"Let it go," the girl said. "It's not worth it."

"I'm not going to let it go." I pushed myself onto my feet and held the cell phone closer to my ear. "I want to know where I can find him."

"You won't like it," she said.

"I don't like any of it anyway," I said. "But he has it and it's valuable and I need it."

"It's good as gone," she said.

Despite how tired my legs were, how many people were pushing past me, making me bob and weave on the sidewalk, I started to pace.

"You don't understand," I said into the phone. "I have to have it." I couldn't tell her I planned to bug out. She might not give me the information I wanted. I needed her to believe things were status quo, even if they were a bit desperate.

I took a long pause to calm myself. No doubt I was sending off jittery vibes through the phone. Kassie wasn't a girl to trust jittery.

"I'm just pissed," I said, which was true.

She said something that I barely caught through the cell phone because in the next moment my wrist burned like someone had branded it. I dropped my cellphone with a clatter to the sidewalk.

I clapped down on the painful wrist instinctively with my other hand. It stung like a son of a bitch, and I worried there'd be a wasp beneath my hand, ready to dig its little ass back into my skin. I peeked beneath the palm with a fearful eye and caught sight of the forgotten mark. The little henna tattoo I'd obviously paid to have painted on myself in a fit of absinthe induced euphoria. I'd forgotten it was there in all the hubbub. Except it didn't look normal.

Now it was bubbling on my skin like water on a hard boil. It took a second for me to realize the hissing sound was coming from my own lips and not my skin.

Kassie's voice came up at me with a note of unusual urgency in her tone.

"Isabella?"

"I'm alight," I said toward the phone and through gritted teeth. I fell back against the wall. I didn't feel aright. In fact, I most definitely felt all wrong. Marks didn't just bubble and boil on bare skin. Not of their own accord. And I most definitely was not high.

I was losing my mind. That was what. I tried to count backwards to the last time I'd slept. How many hours did it take for a mind to begin hallucinating? Seventy two? Forty eight? My chest shuddered with my hitching breaths as I tried and failed to breathe without hyperventilating.

And through it all, I couldn't take my eyes off the damn mark. All I could do was brace myself against the stinging that remained and hope it wouldn't get worse.

Then, as suddenly as it had begun, it stopped.

So why didn't I feel relieved? Why did I feel as though something worse was about to happen?

I twisted my wrist in front of my face, twisting it this way and that. Normal. No sign of boils or bubbles. Just a reddish trail of ink. I scraped at it with my nail.

"Kassie, you ever get a henna tattoo?" I said to the phone on the pavement. Someone bumped into me, kicked the phone out of reach. Kassie's voice got lost in the sea of trousers and skirts.

In the next moment, someone clamped their hand down around the mark the same as I had. Male fingers with a soft but broad palm.

I expected to see Maddox when I lifted my gaze to the face of the man who held me.

It wasn't.

I'd only seen the face in the soft light of Fayed's bar and then again in the dark shadows of the back alley behind it. But I knew the features, the eyes. The face. I would never forget it.

The guy who was supposed to have disappeared into thin air.

"Where's my Odin rune?" he said.

CHAPTER 14

I started to protest, but in the next instant, his hand left my wrist to shoot up to my neck. Those long fingers of his dug into my jaw while the heel of his hand rammed hard into my voice box.

I gagged as I tried to swallow and my eyes shed water. I didn't expect him to hoist me by my chin up above his head, and as my feet lifted off from the ground, it became harder to breathe. I gurgled beneath his grip as I fought to suck in air.

I had lived in the city for three long years, and I'd lived with hoodlums before that. I knew a city's underbelly. I knew people wouldn't want to get involved. They'd try to hide their gazes in their purses or their feet as they shuffled past things that made them uncomfortable, but I thought surely someone would be aghast enough at a woman my size being hoisted several feet into the air by her neck that they'd try to intervene. Shoot off a phone call to the police. Point. Stare. Something.

No one did anything. It was as though they couldn't even see me.

My eyes rolled in their sockets toward the door of the pizza parlour, hoping to see my drunk.

I rolled my eyes back toward the street, hoping for an outraged expression in the crowd and finding nothing but disinterested strangers.

I tried to call out to someone and coughed instead. The stranger's grip tightened.

"You haven't answered me," he growled.

As if I could with his hand cutting off my wind. I tried to kick him in the shins and found I didn't even have the strength for that.

My eyes flicked sideways over my assailant's shoulder again, hoping to see my old drunk strolling out from the pizza parlour with two slices of pizza in his hands. I wished so hard I almost expected to smell the oregano, and then I realized I couldn't in fact smell anything.

I couldn't feel a waft of breeze whisper along my cheek. Everything seemed to be filtered through a wash of UV light or night vision goggles. Nothing was clear anymore. Colours that should be vibrant echoes of yellow streetlights and neon signs shifted into a greenish glow, and what wasn't tainted by an ab-sinthe-esque hue was blurred and mottled as though the scene was a drawing on a chalkboard that something had run their sleeve over.

I had passed out before. Once when Scottie decided that his new favourite kind of sex play involved choking the breath out of me. This wasn't like that. This was just sort of... Dead feeling.

"Where is the rune?" the man said.

I struggled to meet his eye, to try to tell him without words that I didn't have it. To tell him that if he didn't stop soon I would never be able to get it or find out where it was.

His face was as placid as a lake at dusk. He felt nothing for my welfare, that was obvious. Choking the life out of me didn't affect him one bit. This close up, I could see every bit of stubble on his jaw, the scar that scored one of his eyebrows in half. I could see the look of determination in his eye.

I coughed beneath his palm as I tried to form a protest. I expected him to drop me back down onto the ground as he heard me struggling to speak, but he didn't. He tightened his grip.

Something flickered in his gaze and in that heartbeat between thinking I was going to pass out and deciding to kick to life with that one last bit of oxygen, there was a relaxing of the bubble of perception.

I could hear the traffic. I could make out a flush of color in my surroundings. He smelled of smoke and something that made me think of witches stirring bubbling cauldrons. Sulfur. That was it.

"No sense struggling," he said and leaned in closer. "No one can see us."

His lips touched down on mine and he drew in a long, yogic breath. I sagged against him, unable to even lift my hands to grip his forearms or scrabble with desperate fingers up to claw his face.

The edges of several bricks where they met mortar joints were digging into my back. I took a strange solace in the fact that they felt very real. The parts of my vision that had gone greenish started to turn black as I lost the last of my air to him.

He must've known he was stealing the rest of my air and that very soon he wouldn't have a puppet to question because he retreated. An angry look crossed his expression and he shook me like a man might shake a rag.

At least he eased me back down so that my feet met the ground again. His grip loosened just enough to let air seep down my throat and into my lungs. But he still held me pinned against the wall. His whole body leaned into me again, trapping me there.

"One more time, human," he said. "Where is my rune?"

"What?" Human, he'd called me.

He shook me again.

"You know exactly what I'm talking about. You stole it from me."

While his fingers didn't leave my throat, I could breathe easily again. I sucked in air greedily. The freefall sense of being untethered, of the tingling in my skin and floating sensation in the back of my head, started to recede. The pulse in my temple hammered as my heart tried to push air into my blood. I could feel it racing through my veins. I would live.

I tested out my voice and was happy to hear a note of brashness in it that I didn't feel.

"I don't have anything," I told him without lying.

He canted his head just enough sideways to tell me he knew I was using truth as camouflage. Not a stupid man. Even so, I didn't expect his next words.

"Do you know what I am?" he said.

The way he phrased the question—with what instead of who—made my skin go cold.

"A bastard?" I blinked at him innocently, trying all the while to reign in my imagination and its insistence on playing me a video of Lord of the Rings.

It didn't anger him like I expected. Instead, he smiled.

"Indeed," he said. "I wear it like a good suit, I know. But beyond my parentage, do you know who you're dealing with?"

"A violent prick?"

This time I didn't say it quite so congenially. I wasn't sure why I was tempting fate. I knew he could easily squeeze the very last bit of air from my body. I just knew that I wasn't going to give in to violent persuasion. I was done with that shit.

He put both of his hands flat on bricks on either side of my head and then he laid his forehead against mine. He closed his eyes, let his nose run along the bridge of mine. If he'd been a dog, I would've thought he was scenting me. Laying his own smell on me. I considered bringing my knee up between his legs, but found I was strangely compliant, like I was in the throes of a nice high.

"I'm a sorcerer," he said as though he were telling the greatest secrets to a new lover he wanted to impress. As though it meant something. "A tracker."

I tried to dance my mind around the things he was telling me: sorcerer. Tracker. All I could think was I needed to escape. Which meant I compounded my stupidity.

"Some tracker," I said, thinking of the tile I'd taken. "Your shit is gone."

He gripped my wrist and twisted it hard enough I cringed. The pad of his thumb ran along the henna mark.

"Mine," he said of the mark. And then it felt as though he had branded me with a hot iron. I tried to pull my hand back, but he tightened his grip.

"You're my 'shit,'" he said. "And because you're my shit, and because I have a very healthy relationship with the blackest of magics, I could pull your skin from your body with a whisper."

My skin went cold at his words. Sorcerer. Black Magic. I started piecing together all of those discordant chunks of puzzle that until now wouldn't slip one groove into the other.

My perspective had clouded my vision. My bias had kept me from seeing possibility. And that was the cardinal rule of puzzle solving. You had to step outside of the things that you knew in order to see other possibilities. If you couldn't, you had no chance in hell of solving a puzzle.

Fayed had not looked anything like himself in those moments when Kelly had attacked the bar. Kelly's purple blast of light. Maddox asking me what I was.

I had entered the looking glass. There was almost a giddy sense of relief in admitting it to myself. Once I allowed the impossible, everything shifted. It wasn't prettier by any stretch, but at least it made sense.

I recalled the way he'd been lying injured in the back alley.

"Kelly hurt you," I guessed. "Back at the bar. She got to you."

He gave me a queer sort of look that said he didn't expect me to say that, but it said more. It told me he was telling the truth.

"It was fortunate you were there," he said. "You have impeccable timing for a human."

I grit my teeth as I realized one more thing. The burn marks on my cat. The burning in my wrist. They were connected.

"You're the one who broke into my apartment."

The pain in my wrist receded, and he nodded. "I didn't have the strength yet after the fae's attack to physically collect the tile but I needed to know you still had it."

"She's good," he said. "Kelly is. And she's ruthless. And she is determined. She won't stop until she gets it."

There was a strange note in his voice as though he was mourning something already gone.

"I thought you were one of hers at first," he said leaning in close again and sniffing my neck. I looked at him out of the corner of my eye. "You have a peculiar fragrance to your skin."

I rankled at that. I thought of Scottie and all of the times he told me I belonged to him and that everything I had, everything I was, was his.

"I'm no one's," I said.

He made a noncommittal sound deep in his throat. But he seemed to relax. Not enough to let me go, but enough that I could see I was no longer a threat to him. He just wanted something from me. He would bully me until he got it.

"So you're tracking me because you have no idea where your goods are?"

"Tracking flesh has its benefits," he said. "And its disadvantages I will admit. But one does what he can with the skills he was born with."

I had to agree there.

"So where is it?" he said.

"I told you I don't have it." I held his gaze. "But I know who does."

"Then you will retrieve it."

I thought of the blast of light Kelly had thrown at both Maddox and I. I recalled his warnings. I thought of my poor cat, gone now along with my bug out bag.

"If you think I'm going to die over some ridiculous a piece of stone –" I said.

"Not stone," he said. "Bone."

"If you think I'm going to die over some piece of bone—"

He lay his palm over my mouth and I gasped beneath it, trying to suck in air. Even my sinuses were clogged with what felt like muck. I could imagine myself beneath the sea, silt washing into every orifice, seeping into the small, open spaces.

He was going to kill me. Right here. Right in the middle of the street and I couldn't do a damn thing about it.

"There are only two factions that know this thing exists," he said, laying his mouth against my cheek so he could funnel the words into my ear. "One of them will just kill you. The other will kill everyone you know. Care to guess which one I am?"

I shook my head.

He let go my mouth and I hauled in air like a greedy vacuum. My chest lurched with the blast of intake. I couldn't do more than nod. My cap fell off my head and rolled into the gutter.

"Good," he said. "Good."

I couldn't let this maniac find me at any given moment, take his leisure with my life. If I was going to do this, I wanted at least one thing.

"The mark," I said. "Can you at least take this damn mark off."

"That stays until after delivery."

Until after. That was better than nothing.

"Fine," I said.

The wash of absinthe-hue receded from the street. People's faces came into focus again.

"You have 24 hours," he said. "Find the rune and press your tracking mark. The clock is already ticking."

I nodded because I couldn't seem to speak around the thickness of my tongue.

"If you don't, I'll not only burn your brownstone down, I'll find you and wear your skin like a damn poncho."

CHAPTER 15

He disappeared as quickly as he'd come, and everything that had been washed in green went back to normal. The sounds of street life, of vendors calling out to hock their wares, hookers taunting johns, brakes blaring: It all came rushing back like a floodgate had opened.

I sagged against the wall on legs that felt like they were about to buckle. I clutched my hand to my chest and worried the collar of my shirt. What he'd asked of me put me square in the middle of danger no matter which option I chose. It was a hell of predicament.

I would have to find Maddox.

I kicked along the street, searching for my phone. I found it next to a trash can, dirty and scuffed but still functioning.

I was punching the numbers onto my cell phone screen when my drunkard finally exited the pizza place. I could smell him and the oregano long before I saw him. In the aftermath of being assaulted in the middle of the street by stranger, I would've thought I'd lost my appetite, but the smell of burning cheese and yeasty bread made my stomach grumble.

"You look like you've seen a ghost," he said as he handed over a slice that hung from his fingers like an over sized tongue.

I pulled the thing toward my mouth with a bit of hesitation, knowing the man who offered it probably hadn't washed in days. Maybe weeks. But hunger has a way of winning out over niceties like that. It was as though, having faced my death, I was ravenous to taste, smell, breathe again. The pizza tasted glorious.

I just caught a bit of hanging cheese with my tongue before it dripped to the ground. I chewed thoughtfully for a long time, watching him as he savored his piece. So he wasn't too far gone if he could spend a little bit of money on food instead of alcohol. Maybe he wasn't as derelict as I believed. Maybe he could be more useful than I thought.

"How would you like to make a little more money?" I said to him.

"Depends on what it is I have to do for it," he said.

"Nothing criminal," I said.

He shrugged. "I have no problem with criminal, it's how much time it will take."

Translation: he was running a little low on blood alcohol content.

"You can multitask," I said. "All you have to do is hang out on a specific street and watch a specific apartment."

I stationed him outside my brownstone. He could do double duty; Mr. Smith would think I'd sent him to help with the optics and if I needed to return home, I could check with him before I went in. It wasn't fool proof, but it was something.

He shrugged good-naturedly and I gave him the address, giving specific details about where he should stay so that it is out of sight of the more affluent neighbors who might run him off. It was comforting to think I had a lookout and I felt a twinge of guilt for my poor cat who could have used a warning before that sorcerer decided to burn her fur down to the skin.

Sorcerer. I seemed to be taking that information pretty much in stride. And here I was making those contingency plans for something I didn't understand. Was I so ready to accept that a supernatural world bubbled beneath my feet? Maybe three days ago I'd have laughed in someone's face who suggested such a thing.

After feeling the very real struggle to breathe beneath a very real hand, feeling the burn deep down into my bone from that mark, acceptance of it was a moot point. Whether I wanted to believe or not, there was no other explanation.

Just thinking about it all made me tired. But there was something else prickling along my skin as I watched my drunkard weave his way down the street through pedestrians and the occasional hooker. And that was the sense of an entire new world opening up to me. One that might provide escape, one that Scottie couldn't find me in. One that might have an entirely new treasure trove of goods to plunder.

One of the other special gifts Scottie wanted me for was my adaptability. He would've called me pliable. Had called me pliable, actually. Submissive even.

I reached for my cell phone. I tapped the numbers for Kassie's burner into the keypad. She'd connected me to Maddox before. And she was my only lead back to him.

I had 24 hours, and that meant I couldn't waste any time. I walked while the phone rang on the other end, keeping my head down.

When she answered it was with the customary clipped sentences.

"Here," she said through the other end of the line.

"The milk has gone bad," I said. She'd know what that meant.

The phone went dead on her end and I slipped mine back into my pocket. If I knew Kassie, she would have dumped the burner phone as soon as she hung up. She was a smart girl. She knew things had gone wrong. She wouldn't risk anyone contacting her again. Not even me.

I booked an uber to get to the meeting location. My legs were spent and tired and I was in dire need of sleep. I leaned back into the leather seats of the Volkswagen GTI and closed my eyes.

I hoped to catch five minutes over the ten minute drive, but the wash of green haunted the inside of my eyelids and I snapped my eyelids back up and again, choosing instead to stare at the city as we drove. I knew I wouldn't be able to sleep again until I shook off the dreaded sense of threat that was even now tightening my muscles.

I hopped out of the uber three blocks away from the meeting place. It was a habit I had begun years earlier upon fleeing to the city. If you always assumed someone was following you, you never went directly to the destination. So I had that driver drop me off at Chinese restaurant three blocks away. I went in the front door, and then begged a server to let me out the back. I inched along the back alleys until I found the library. Kassie would be waiting inside. Thriller and mystery section.

She was sitting cross-legged on the floor holding open an aged Agatha Christie on her lap.

She looked up when she heard me approach and closed the book so quietly I doubted even the dust mites inside were disturbed.

"Trouble," she said.

I nodded. "Trouble you can't even imagine."

I sat down next to her and let my legs stretch out across the aisle. It felt good to rest them and let the muscles go flaccid. My hands found a place on my lap as I leaned back against the column of hardcover book spines. I examined the mark on my wrist with renewed interest.

I wondered if the sorcerer was a bit voyeuristic and was lurking somewhere about in that haze of median world. It gave me the shivers. The faster I was rid of this thing, the better. It was bad enough worrying about Scottie finding me, but now knowing some other dangerous man could call himself to me in a heartbeat through this thing made every hair on the back of my neck stand and flail about wildly for rescue. My chest felt tight with panic.

"I have to ask a favor of you," I said still looking at my hands. "You need to tell me how to find Maddox."

Something in me wanted to reach out and use physical contact to create that connection that might encourage her to give me what I wanted. But it would have the opposite effect on her. I knew that. I respected her need for space. We were sitting next to each other, but several feet apart. I was careful not to get too close.

I let her think that over. It might take a moment or it might take ten. I couldn't rush it. I felt bone weary with the waiting, but there was nothing for it to be done. Waiting is hard work.

"No," came the short answer.

Then she was on her feet and pushing the book back into its place on the shelf. It was so abrupt, I reached out and touched her leg without thinking. She recoiled as though I had burnt her. Her face crinkled up like a wolverine sensing a threat. I scrambled to my feet, holding out my hands in a placating gesture.

"I'm sorry," I said. "I didn't mean to do that. I'm just exhausted. I've had a hell of a day."

I pinched the bridge of my nose, and when that pain wasn't quite enough to rattle my brain into the here and now, those fingers crawled up to my scalp and tugged on my hair. Both hands ended up on top of my head, fingers interlaced as I regarded her. She hadn't moved. But she looked like she was ready to spin on her heel and tear off down the aisle like a terrified rabbit.

I was desperate. I realized how desperate when I stared at the way my hand snaked out and clutched her sleeve and the way she yanked away from me because I couldn't let go.

"I need to know, Kassie," I said, inching closer, instinct trying to close the gap so I wouldn't feel so exposed. "I can't tell you why because I don't want you to be in danger, but I need to know. Every minute I stand here doing nothing, is one I can't afford to lose."

She canted her head to the side. The mass of soft looking curls lay across her cheek in an endearing way. She reminded me of a cherub for all of three seconds until she spoke again and the note of dread in her voice ruined the warm and fuzzy feeling.

"You won't like it," she said.

I swallowed down the instinctive fear and searched for something courageous to say, something that wouldn't make me sound like a frightened little girl that had gone one step too far into oncoming traffic.

"There are lots of things I don't like," I said.

She blinked several times as she watched me, and I knew that what was going on behind that gaze was considerable examination. She looked older in that moment, ages older. It was the eyes, I realized. The maturity in the depths was staggering. Whatever she searched for, I knew she was weighing what she saw against a heavy control and that if I had any hope of getting what I needed, I had to let that assessment find me as light as a feather.

I felt like a deer about to pluck an apple from the bottom of a baited tree. I could hear my own breathing.

But I waited.

I didn't know the outcome until her hand snaked out from mine, closing the distance between us. Before I realized she had moved, I saw a little penknife in her hand. Too late, I tried to back away but she sliced into my forearm just above the hennaed mark.

The girl who spoke the rare few words suddenly started rattling off dozens of them. They sounded ancient, those words, as though they came from a time before language had stretched into the sophisticated pattern of syllables it was.

The room spun as she spoke. Spines of books made a kaleidoscope of color and shapes in the racks. The back of my head felt as though it was on a carnival ride all by itself

My knees buckled. I had to reach out to grab the book stacks to keep from falling.

The last thing I heard before everything went black was the English words she whispered in warning.

"Don't stay too long."

CHAPTER 16

I found myself at the bottom of a long set of granite steps with an iron railing that, even in the dim lighting, looked like it had seen better days. The individual treads had been scuffed so much, they were worn in the middle from the erosion of a thousand feet over hundreds of years. I knew the city was old, but not that old. Even the door in front of me looked as ancient as the steps. With a breadth of several feet and a height that belied that of a normal cellar, its iron hoop door handle was set in the European style—smack dab in the middle—and big enough that you needed both hands to yank on it.

Functional and undoubtedly solid. Maybe a foot thick. But in its way, through the haze of the light from a streetlamp, I could tell how lovingly it had been carved by its maker. Gothic faces glared at me from the wood. My fingers roamed the surface of the two of them closest to the door handle as I imagined some artisan in the distant past labouring over it by candlelight or oil lamp. The teeth were sharp still, too sharp to believe they were made of just wood. I imagined there were other materials worked into the woodwork and leaned in close to see if I could make it out in the darkness.

To my night vision, admittedly not the best, it looked like wood alone but how they'd managed to survive the centuries without getting chipped or knocked off, I couldn't imagine. Nor could I imagine how fine the artisan had to file the grain to get the teeth sharp enough that they were still at point all these years later. And the tongue was there too, realistic enough that it felt like it moved against the pad of my thumb.

I yanked both hands back against my chest and peered even closer, my eyes crossing in the darkness.

"Get a grip, Sis," I said to myself. "It's just a door."

I chewed my nail in thought. I needed to get in. Did a gal knock, rap, or just yank it open? I was strangely loathe to do any of them.

I didn't need to see the other side to know there would be a thick iron bar with a lever that would stick into the wall and create a stiff, unassailable brace. If a gal thought she wanted to trip down the halls of imagination, she could imagine it being barred against an invading horde.

But I'd had enough of fancy these last few days. Even these last hours to know that I would quite happily settle for nice, normal criminal types to what might be beyond that door.

I thought I knew almost every dive in the city, every back alleyway, every place a person could hide or retreat. It smelled of both sulfur and candy floss. Two warring fragrances that made me think of scorched sugar left on a burner too long. The grate beneath my feet ran with old water that rose murky to my nose. The gurgling noises it made as it fled down the pipes and sewer system gave off a faint odor of fish.

So I was near the docks, then. That was good to know. I could imagine the streets then in my mind, puzzle my way mentally through the maze toward home or a place of safety. The city had a long convoluted history with the sea. Another reason why I had fled here when I'd left Scottie. While the shipping lanes might belong to the more nefarious gangs, and network of people that Scottie might well have to hand, there were also plenty of independent fishermen. Any one of them would secret a fare across the ocean for the right amount of money.

That was the first thing I'd checked out on my arrival, and I made a habit of reassuring myself of that every quarter. A gal could never be too careful.

But it took more than transportation cash to escape a man like Scottie. And now with the tracking mark on my wrist that could bring to my splintered heel a self-proclaimed sorcerer, one who would fry me down to my toes if I didn't retrieve his goods, no amount of money would be enough to find sanctuary.

I needed Maddox. And I needed to find a way to make sure he handed over what he had stolen from me so that I could get rid of the mark that tied me to a man more dangerous than the one I'd fled.

And that meant I had to get in.

I didn't wear a watch, but a quick check of my cell phone told me I was down to 23 hours. I licked my lips, testing for fear and finding it. I told myself that was a good thing. Fear meant I hadn't quite lost my grip. Fear had its place and could be very useful in unusual circumstances. I told myself that fear would keep me vigilant.

Then I inhaled a long bracing breath, slipped both hands into the iron hook and lifted it. I dropped it three times against the wood beneath.

And I waited.

I expected the door to remain closed, and to see some strange sort of wary eyes peering back at me through an impatiently snapped aside grate. Much the way it happened so often in thriller or mystery movies. Just knowing I thought that might happen indicated I was still securely anchored in the reality, and it was a damn good thing because with a fourth and final rap, the door simply melted away with a shuddering movement.

I stood there, paralyzed as I watched it shake loose any sense of form or function as I knew it. When it was done transforming, I stood in front of a transparent wall that writhed with light and colour as though those two elements from my world were a living, breathing, snakelike entity in another.

Unnatural, natural, or supernatural, inanimate things just did not look like that. Even special effects on film couldn't create that roiling mess of light and ... was it skin? I shuddered.

Like the terrifying moment I spent with the self-proclaimed tracker between worlds as he'd hung me above his head by my throat in the middle of a busy city street, my vision went awash in green-tainted colour. The sky above me and the looming skyscrapers that jutted into the shadowed clouds all turned hazy and green. The stone stairs behind me blurred.

And yet the world over the threshold was just that much more in focus.

I knew that if I took a step over that threshold, I would be entering a world where I didn't understand the rules—if there even were rules. I could be stepping over that threshold to my death. My world was real. I understood my world. I understood the threat of dangerous men. I could handle what I knew. I wasn't so sure I could handle things I didn't even know existed.

But what choice did I have? I couldn't outrun the tracker. I waffled as I stood there, trying to decide whether or not it would be preferable to just jump on a ship and get the hell out of Dodge. For all I knew, that tracking mark on my wrist was only good for a few miles. I could test it out what it would do over a whole country. A continent, even.

While my mind was trying to push me to step over the threshold, my feet were dragging me away from it. Everything in my viscera told me going forward was not a good idea. The very hair on the back of my neck leaned away from it and strained toward the stone steps. This was not a good idea. I knew it. Choice or not, I had taken on too much this time.

I butted up against the bottom tread with my heel before I even knew I had taken several steps backwards.

I clutched the iron railing that led back upstairs to the street. I needed to go forward into that mess, but I couldn't force myself to move toward it. Was that groaning sounds I heard coming from within? Screams?

My ribcage hurt for all the hammering my heart was doing. I could barely hear my own breathing through the pounding in my ears that was all but drowning out the horrible sounds coming from the threshold.

"Sweet Jesus," I said out loud. That wasn't groaning. I knew groaning. That was a sound unlike any other I'd ever heard. It was if a thousand voices had blended together in an eerie chant and then simultaneously reversed. Add a few fingernail rakings down an old fashioned chalkboard and you might come close to the effect of the sound.

All in all, creepy enough to make my skin try to crawl off my bones and slither up the stairs behind me.

Which was exactly what I decided to do.

I took a step, backward up the stairs. No way was I doing this. I'd just have to find a way to con the tracker. Maybe I could pay someone to make one of those tiles. I could picture it pretty well by memory.

I took another step. Yes. That's what I'd do. And if that didn't work, I'd pull a Scottie and pay someone to kill him.

I wasn't aware I'd spoken that last until I heard someone repeat the name from above me. Whoever had spoken had heard me say Scottie's name and, surprised, had echoed it.

I met the eyes of Scottie's henchmen for several heartbeats before either one of us reacted.

His response was a slow, slithering smile. One that said, "I've got you now," and mine was to merely blink in sheer terror.

Then he moved so abruptly it made me startle. His hand went beneath his jacket and I knew that in one more moment he would extract his gun. I knew too that he would shoot me somewhere incapacitating and then he would carry me off, still breathing and living just in hell of a lot of pain to where Scottie waited.

Without thinking, I spun on my heel and took the three remaining lunging steps toward the portal that still seethed with energy.

One step over it, and everything after that changed.

CHAPTER 17

I felt a cold rush of terror. It wasn't a natural thing to be between worlds. Everything hurt. I felt as though two sharp teeth had sunk into my neck and that blood, hot and thick, was dribbling down my neck. Something cold and slippery brushed against me. What parts of my skin that didn't feel like they were on fire were trying to crawl off my frame. Whatever had brushed against me slithered around my hand where Kassie had cut me. I could swear a long, rasping tongue ran over the wound. I convulsed in revulsion, my teeth chattering like wooden chimes in a breeze. A sudden flash of myself as an eight-year-old lit up the synapses of my memory and showed me lying on my side in bed curled into a shivering, weeping ball. Everything started closing in on me, choking off my air.

And then it was gone.

Everything cleared with a vacuous sound that made me gasp out of sheer release. Behind me, the wooden door reappeared, taking again its original form, except from this side, the smooth panel of oak was covered with fist sized creatures who appeared to be lodged up to their shoulders in the wood's belly. I knew without a doubt their heads poked through to the other side. I shuddered, knowing in that moment when I had lain my hand against the door, what I had perceived to be artistic carvings actually had been the faces of those creatures.

That meant the tongue that had licked my thumb had been real.

I thought I might faint just thinking about it.

I stepped away just in time to avoid the sharp barb of one of their tails as it flicked up and down and side to side. It stuck into the back end of the creature lodged next to it, and in retaliation that creature sent its own tail, this one with a stinger, into the first one's thigh.

The same movements echoed along the surface of the wood and back again like a tide returning to shore and retreating again. I wavered on my feet, wondering if I'd done the right thing by avoiding Scottie's minion this way. I certainly didn't feel safer looking at those things.

"It's alright, Sis," I whispered to myself. "You can do this. Just find Maddox, get the tile, and be gone."

I was definitely through the looking glass, and I didn't even want to think yet about what I had to do to get back out. I needed to think about the next step. I could puzzle out the rest of it as I went.

I checked my phone. No signal, of course, but it told me the time. I set the timer on, reminding myself that the last check-in had shown me 23 hours remaining before the sorcerer torched my house and hunted me down. I reasoned that since it was still night, that time might run linear here and that my time in the portal had been mere seconds. Felt like a hell of a lot of minutes, but time did that sort of thing.

I hoped this once that would work in my favor.

I pulled down my shirt and set my sights on what was in front of me, waiting to be confronted and expecting to have to explain myself. If anyone noticed my entry, they didn't care.

Except for the door with the creatures half in and half out of a solid block of wood, the cobblestone courtyard could have been a marketplace in any place in the world. Ahead of me lay a world not unlike my own at first blush.

The bazaar seemed to be stretched out over several blocks with three main roads converging into the one courtyard. They reminded me of some of the older parts of Rome in some places and India in others. It smelled of burned things and sweet things and some fragrance that made my nose itch.

Things hung from above booths everywhere and were scattered along the ground on mats and carpets. A dozen or so doors lined the buildings behind the stalls and booths and it was my guess that only the wealthiest of proprietors were able to maintain old-fashioned shops. The rest were transitory and temporary.

Lights were strung over booths and stalls to better show the wares for sale. Dozens of them lined either side of the courtyard and several peddlers wandered about in the middle. On closer inspection, however, this was no ordinary market. It had the feel and flavor of a bazaar in India, but the goods and wares were nothing like I expected. Nothing like any human being could imagine.

I learned somewhere that we all suffer from confirmation bias. We've already decided what we're going to see or understand or believe long before we're confronted with the possibility of there being anything different about it. It's one of the reasons motorists don't see motorcyclists: they expect to see two headlights, a full car and four tires, so if that's not what's coming at them, they discount it out of hand. We lay down our own perceptions of reality onto something when we are confronted with something fresh to help us understand it.

I expected the marketplace to be filled with quilts and blankets and produce, and there certainly were all of those things if I looked hard enough. They were sprinkled here and there throughout the bazaar and attended to by patrons of all sorts. And so it did look like an ordinary marketplace at first, because I dearly wanted it to.

I decided to take it in stages. Get my feet wet, as it were. The stall closest to me held urns of spices and bowls of strange ingredients. I figured I'd ask the owner if she knew Maddox. She looked human. Her goods looked normal. I went to dip my hand into a stone basin filled with, I thought, rather large marbles. The wizened crone slapped my hand away before it touched down.

"Leave the eyes. You touch, you pay."

Eyes. I examined the contents again and my gorge rose as I realized what I had been about to run my hand through.

"Eyeballs," I said, breathless with sick. This old crone was selling eyeballs. Viscous and thready with the tissue that had held them in their sockets during life still clinging to them. "You have a bowl of eyeballs."

"Not just any eyes," she said, squaring her shoulders proudly. "Blind men's' eyes. The best. Not two days from the harvest."

"Harvest?" I echoed in a sick sounding repetition of her explanation.

She narrowed her gaze at me as she levelled her accusation. "You're not a witch are you?"

I shook my head, and she covered the bowl with the edge of her shawl. The way she edged in front of the bowl made me think she wanted to get rid of me. Fine by me.

"What are you?" she said. "If you be no witch, these are not for you."

She flicked at me with her shawl. "Go away."

I went happily, stepping backwards and heeled up against a solid frame.

When I turned around it was into the face of a rather large looking dog on a leash. It barred its teeth at me and I sidestepped quickly just in time to avoid getting my arm snapped between foot-long canines. The still sore wound on my calf ached in response.

The woman holding the other end of the leash glared at me and ran a loving hand down along the hackles of the beast – an incredibly large wolf, I realized now – and smoothed them back down again.

"You should know better than to look a werewolf in the eye," she snapped.

"I'm sorry," I said. "So sorry."

I held up my hand in surrender and stumbled away, my mind reeling. I butted up against an ancient looking fountain and sank down on the lip of the bowl. It was ludicrous to stumble around in alien looking bazaar without some sort of plan. It had been foolish of me to think I could just come in and find Maddox and get back out without thinking it all through.

I needed to take my time and let things come at me on my own terms if I was going to get through it. A leisurely scrutiny would be more appropriate, no matter how badly I wanted to hurry the hell up and get out of there. I panned my gaze back and forth, mapping out the lay of the land and trying to tell myself that the creatures, the people, and the things that I saw were nothing but figments of my imagination brought on by stress.

I knew better, but I badly wanted that confirmation bias back again. I wanted to believe that the pale and ghostly looking things that resembled wisps of smoke were not Will o the wisp but sewage steam coming up from the grates beneath our feet. That the half man, half deer looking thing that clumped its way over toward me with lust written over its features was not in fact a young Greek satyr with nubs for horns, but a small man sitting atop a pony.

When he was intercepted by a man of middling height but whose feet pointed the wrong way, I found I couldn't pretend any longer. Like it or not, this shit was real.

And I was already feeling as though I was having a panic attack. I was failing and I hadn't even started.

I looked around, seeking out those buildings and the multitude of doors. Maybe if I was going to find Maddox, the best place to start would be with the owners of those more permanent shops.

I'd make a grid in my mind to pan out from shop to shop, starting on the left and reaching all the way down the the street, then coming back up before trickling down to the next one. As I returned back to the apex of the courtyard, where all of the streets met in a triangle, I would check through each one of the stalls.

It wasn't a great plan, but I had no other. I pushed myself reluctantly to my feet and headed toward the farthest street to my left, aiming for the first shop so that I could work my way down and then back up again. I could be methodical if I couldn't be inspired.

The first door refused to open. I tried the next-door down. Same thing. The next one was also locked. There were no bells or buzzers or even windows to peer into. Frustrated, I spun around and tried the doors on the other side of the street. They were all closed as well.

I wasn't about to give up. Not yet.

I headed straight to the closest stall, intending to ask the proprietor how I could gain access to those shops. It had been built to withstand the weather, with a roof made of leather and stretching out for several yards in each direction. A thick iron bar framed it up on all sides and crossed the distance from one side to the other far in the back. Every length of it had feet buried deep into the cobblestones on either side.

At first I thought the stall was being visited by a dozen patrons all at once, but I realized that the patrons were far too small to be buyers. Children. The oldest looked to be about ten, and all of them were chained by the wrists to that bar. They looked dirty and disheveled, as though they had been running for a long stretch before being run down into the ground and collected up.

My stomach turned into a hard lump of glue. These were human children and the willowy woman inspecting them with a long thumb running along each chin looked more like a reptile wearing Prada shoes than the lithe looking human woman she presented.

The woman spun around when she saw me, letting a broad grin take over her face. I recognized the look of a con woman when I saw it. She would try to get me to buy something, and maybe I would. Maybe that was my in.

I sidled over to the stall.

"How old is your youngest?" I said, turning to the proprietor.

This close, she was even more terrifying. Her eyes looked reptilian, with the vertical pupils sat in the middle of yellow corneas. I didn't think I could stand it if forked tongue slipped out of her mouth as she spoke, but I held my ground anyway, reaching out to the closest child and laying my palm down on his shoulder.

The woman looked me up and down with narrowed gaze.

"How did you get in here?" she demanded. "What are you?"

What are you? The same question Maddox had asked me.

"If you can't tell," I said, "then maybe I should be the one who's asking."

She crossed her arms over her chest and tapped her foot twice as she inspected me.

"Who knows how old these things are," she finally said. "I don't track them, just sell them."

She rifled through the shoulders of the children as though she were flicking aside coat hangers on a dress rack. She yanked hard, and a small owl-eyed girl stumbled out from between two taller boys.

"This one is prepubescent," the reptilian woman said. "If you're a vampire, you'll know that these don't come cheap."

Vampire. I swallowed down a flood of sour water at the word and all that implied as I studied the poor soul.

"How old are you, honey?" I said as I knelt down to the girl. The proprietor beside me tapped her foot impatiently.

The owl-ish eyes welled up with water. I could see trauma behind that gaze, terror in the streaks of dirt on her face. And to think in all of this time, I thought missing children had met terrible fates at the hands of awful men. My heart went out to her.

"It's all right," I said in a whispered tone. "You don't have to be afraid of me."

"Her blood is better if she is," the woman said. "You must not be a vampire, then. So what is it you do with your human whelps?"

She stared directly at me without a hint of interest but still obviously expecting me to answer. It was the type of small talk any seller might make to seal the deal.

I peered up at the woman. "What makes you think I'm interested that way?"

She shrugged with what might look like a delicate shoulder if she had been human.

"You came straight here instead of the other shops," she said. "The shadow bazaar has all sorts of delicacies and precious wares, and buyers don't come here to acquire everyday items. They come here for something special."

Those reptilian eyes of hers narrowed again. "If you're not interested in children, then leave my stand. You're getting in the way of real customers."

She turned away from me, fully expecting, it seemed, for me to just walk away and leave these kids here with her. It was very possible these children might be sold as servants to cook and clean, but with the use of the word vampire, the woman had erased any doubt from my mind that they would see something far worse than slavery.

I took the little girl by the hand. She reminded me a lot of Kassie. Maybe it was the look of trauma in all of their faces that did it because it was in all of them, even the boys. I couldn't leave any of them here.

"You can't take that thing without paying," the woman said, catching sight of me. Her hand clamped down around my wrist.

"I'm taking her," I said. I didn't want to know how much time I had left because damn it, I wasn't about to let this child suffer whatever fate this woman had in mind.

"You take something," the woman said. "You leave something."

I faced her as though I were facing Scottie again. A bully, that's what she was. Didn't matter if she looked like a skinny stick with knobs and knots on her face, if her eyes were slitted with narrow pupils. All bullies were the same. They felt they owned your ass. The fact that this woman had these children chained to her iron bar in this foul-smelling booth proved she was the worst of bullies. One who thought she owned them and could profit from that sense of possession.

While I felt sick to my very soul at the thought of purchasing a human being, I couldn't just let this girl stay here left to God knew what sort of fate.

"What do you want?" I asked her.

The woman's smile turned ugly. "You."

CHAPTER 18

You. One word from the owner, but it made me step back-ward involuntarily. I looked at the girl and the way her face just sort of crumpled when the woman spoke. I got the feeling that she pitied me, and that couldn't be good.

My hand gripped the railing as I faced the woman.

"What do you mean?" I said.

She leaned in and I could swear she smelled my hair.

"As you can see, I have a market for exotic things." She waved a graceful arm over the heads of some of the smaller children. Her gaze ran the length of my throat. The way she said it, the way she eyed my pulse, I felt as though my entire body needed to be scrubbed clean. The hair rose on the back of my neck.

One look at the girl confirmed everything I thought about the woman's use of the word exotic.

"I don't know what you are," she said. "But you have a fine fra-grance. Like licorice and cherries. If you want the female runt, I'd be happy to swap for you and let her go free."

I heard a sharp intake of the girl's breath, the hope that she pulled in with it.

I looked from one child to the next, taking in the filthy faces, the look of trauma. All of various ages, and if I had to guess, not one of them over the age of sixteen. The oldest, a rather brawny looking teenage boy stared off into nothing. I couldn't imagine what was going through his mind to rob it of thought or expression. I just knew it had to be bad.

"Swap?" I said, testing the word.

The woman nodded. "Yes. You stay and I unlock her manacles."

I'd come to save my ass, not peddle it. The woman seemed to sense the offer would get her nowhere and she made a grab for the child's arm. Without thinking, I grabbed for the other one.

I tugged. Just because I didn't want to be martyr didn't mean I wanted to leave these children to her mercy.

We stared at each other over the mop of greasy hair. The girl started to cry.

"You can't do this," I said. Desperation clogged up my throat.

"They're mine," she said. "I can sell them to whomever I please. Now let go."

The girl cried even harder.

I felt as though someone had punched me in the stomach. I thought of all the missing children reports I'd heard over the years and imagined horrible things happening to those poor souls. Despite the fact that I could do nothing about it, I couldn't let the child's hand go. The little thing was clenched in mine so tightly, I could feel it shaking.

The woman had to use both of her hands to wrest the child's grip from mine and then she jerked her sideways, pushing her back into the line. I stood there helpless, looking from one child to the next and trying to work out some way to release them. There had to be some mechanism that could let them go. They all seemed to be shackled together on that rack. But my shocked brain just couldn't puzzle it out.

I inched closer to the girl again and was still trying to work through my rage and impotency along with the cuffs when a short fellow strode over and made a polite inquiry about the cost. He was wearing an old-fashioned cloak like the kind you saw in a Dracula movie. The proprietress smoothed down her glimmering dress and pasted on that same look every great salesman wore when confronted by a target.

"And what would you say the vintage is of that one," I heard the man say.

"That one is the youngest," the woman said, and I knew she was coming closer. I imagined she would trot out the girl again for inspection. If I was going to do anything, I had to hurry.

"I don't like them older than five," he said. "They get a funky taste after that."

My head snapped up. Taste?

It was only then that I noticed the extended canines in his upper bite. Vampire, my mind whispered. Of course. I shouldn't be surprised, not when the woman had already mistaken me for one.

The girl was already clinging to me and sobbing into my shirt. She smelled of urine and feces so strongly it was like someone had pressed a bedpan beneath my nose. It made my eyes water. I ran my hands over the bracelets of her cuffs, feeling for the shape of the lock and hoping it was big enough to take the tip of my penknife. I tried ever so hard not to lose my shit, but I was tearing up as I worked the lock.

I heard the woman telling the vampire to feel free to browse if he wasn't sure her offerings were as good as she said. I thought he was going to argue, but another man blustered over and declared that he wanted to take them all. I fiddled harder.

"My den is getting an influx of extra patrons tonight. Some sort of costume party in the East End, and I don't have time for my scouts to go hunting. These will do. Providing they're the right price."

The kids, even the blank-faced teenager started to cry. I stole a look at the owner.

The woman looked torn between a sure sale and the option of getting rid of all her wares at once, but something was holding her back. It didn't take long before the real reason came out.

"The last time you bought for your blood den," the woman said. "You didn't pay for months."

The first vampire shot her a look of complaint. "I was here first," he said.

They were so distracted with each other, arguing over which one of them should be allowed to purchase first. The second vampire wanted them all, and the first one didn't want to give up the little girl. I stood there in shocked disbelief for several moments before I realized it was an opportunity for me to liberate them. All of them. Perhaps with them all running, one or two of them would have a chance.

I ducked away from them as they argued and tried to work at the manacles of the young girl's wrist. I twisted the tip of the pen knife just so, hoping to hear the telltale click that would tell me I'd disengaged mechanism.

She was crying hard by then. They weren't cuffs of any special sort. Fairly archaic, actually, even if they were effective to the person shackled. Years of picking locks and jimmying my way into places enabled me to pop it in seconds. Her loud and piercing shriek of joy pierced a hole in my fear and for a moment I felt exuberant with her. I watched her dig her toes into the dirt for purchase and then she was off like a rabbit, weaving in and out of stalls.

In my mind, I ran with her. She was a smart girl, obviously. Traumatized, yes, but not so far gone that she didn't understand the need to run and run fast. I was working on the lock of the teenage boy when the proprietress and her potential customers noticed the girl streaking across the courtyard.

She shrieked in anger. "My goods," she yelled. "Someone catch them."

One of the vampires groaned.

"I already have my money out," he complained.

The proprietress caught sight of me working on a third cuff. She stabbed her finger in my direction.

"You," she said. "You stay. You freed it, you stay for it."

Everyone seemed to notice all at once, and everyone seemed to understand that it was beyond the normal. What I had thought earlier were people shopping became a seethe of creatures both humanoid and things distinctly otherwise giving chase to the product running across the courtyard in gleeful but terrified liberation. Those who didn't follow the children swarmed the owner's booth, to help her keep the rest of her goods intact.

The proprietress went a livid shade of white.

I'd done it now. Whatever consequences would come, I couldn't turn back. I unsnapped child after child while the chaos made it possible. I had about four more of them liberated before the proprietress got hold of me.

The seethe of creatures storming the booth marshaled the remaining shackled children into a sobbing cluster. Both vampires stood to the side, their nostrils flaring and bodies quivering as though they were working very hard to restrain themselves.

I felt like a field mole under the owner's gaze, terrified to move but knowing if I didn't I was vulnerable prey in an open field. I spun on my heel, fully prepared to sprint and dodge, but got no further than the middle of the courtyard before someone grabbed me by the hair.

The sickening feel of hair pulling free of my scalp dropped me to my knees.

The owner of the booth let go my hair and gripped me by the shoulders instead. She dragged me, kicking, to her booth. Muttered something that sounded like STAY.

And just like that, I stayed. She rained blows on me as I tried to deflect them.

"So many predators," the woman complained. "I'll be lucky to get any of them back, let alone alive."

She shook me and my teeth rattled. Where did she get that strength from anyway? She wasn't that much bigger than me.

I kicked and cursed at her and brought my heel down onto her instep. Elbowed her in the belly. She muttered another word. This time clearly.

"*Desisto.*"

Every small muscle in my face, hands, and thighs quivered to a halt. I was left staring at her and trying to struggle beneath her grip. My chest heaved with fear and rage.

"You freed it," she declared in a huff of rage. "You stay in its place."

"What about the others?" The second vampire complained. "I'm not paying full price for half the goods."

She glared at him and he snapped his mouth shut. I supposed some was better than none and he was willing to concede for the day.

The proprietress reached into her cloak and pulled out a new pair of handcuffs. These looked different than the others. Made of rusted iron and formed as one solid hourglass shape. She yanked my hands onto either side of the rail and then shoved them onto my wrists. She cut into the skin with the force, and I winced. She snapped them closed with a flourish of triumph.

"Got you," she said.

CHAPTER 19

I rattled the manacles against the bar with a rage that, in the end, did nothing but wear me out. They were too tight. Whatever metal they were made of burned like a brand if I moved too much. I eyed the bracelets speculatively. No lock on these like there had been on the girl's cuffs, which meant it couldn't be picked.

I might have settled for good old fashioned negotiation if I had any idea what to offer in exchange for my freedom. I couldn't very well argue my way out. Brash arrogance wouldn't work on this one. I eyed her as she argued with several would-be buyers. I might have had time to plan out my route of attack but one of the vampires sidled up next to me and inhaled as though he were testing an aroma above a bowl of hearty lentil soup. He was close enough I felt him shiver, and when he let his lips rest against my pulse, his lips quivered. Breath that I expected to be hot and moist rasped against my skin like the cold air from tundra.

"She smells delightful," he said against my skin and might have taken a nip except for the owner who throttled him with the back of her hand.

"You want a taste, you pay for it," she said. "This isn't a sampler buffet."

He recoiled under harsh words, as though he was insulted, but his eyes never left my pulse.

"What is she?" he asked bemusedly. "Not a human child, surely. Her eyes are too old."

I sucked in a frightened breath at his musing tone. He caught my eye at the sound. His were stunning. Mesmerizing, even. I thought I felt myself sinking into a warm bath and my legs sagged. What had made me think of cold dry land when those eyes were so intoxicating?

He smiled as though he enjoyed my reaction.

"No," he said in a voice like warm syrup. "Not a child at all."

Under normal circumstances, I might be delighted that someone recognized maturity in my gaze instead of the diminutive stature that made everyone mistake me for a teenager. But all I could think was how gorgeous those coal black eyes were and how incredibly tired I was.

He shifted his gaze to my throat again. My head cleared the way an airplane might if opened mid-flight. A secretive smile still played about his full mouth. This wasn't a vampire like Fayed, and in light of how this one had made me feel, I doubted Fayed was a vampire at all. Fayed was a looker, and I might have tossed him eventually, but he'd never done to me with his eyes what this one did.

This one lifted a lock of my hair and ran it beneath his nose. I knew my heart was beating like a rabbit in a snare, but I learned a long time ago not to quail beneath a threat. It gave the aggressor more power, and I reasoned that a vampire might be very much like a violent man in that way. And a vampire was no doubt dangerous enough without making him feel as though he owned me in some way.

I faced him with unblinking eyes, trying to keep my gaze between his eyebrows so he couldn't do that thing again with his gaze. I wondered if he could hear the steadily rising thrum of my heartbeat. I could certainly hear it and if I looked out of my periphery, I could see my chest moving with the awful beat of it.

He put a thoughtful thumb on the tip of my chin and ran it along my jawline, stopping to cup me behind my neck where his fingers could knot into my hair. He tugged playfully.

"Quite delightful," he said.

I felt sick and if I'd been able to, I'd have run like the girl had. I had to settle for yanking my head sideways despite the pain it brought to my scalp so long as my hair left his grasp and his hand left my skin. The owner of the booth must have recognized the opportunity to increase her profit because she bustled over as though she were somehow responsible for bringing me here in the first place.

"She's unique," she said to the vampire conspiratorially and, I thought, with a note of possessiveness. I hated that tone.

"The Shadow Bazaar has not seen her like before."

She was bluffing. I knew it. I was certain the vampire knew it. But it was part of the game and I understood that as well. Even so, knowing that didn't help my sense of blooming panic.

The first vampire, who had been hovering at the fringes, trying to look as though he wasn't interested at all, started digging into his pockets. Dear God. He was going to pay for me. Right here, right now and I couldn't do a damn thing about it. I bit my lip to keep the sob from escaping.

Even the lady holding the werewolf back with a thin leash drew closer. The children who hadn't escaped and who ended up tethered again to the bar cringed away from me. They didn't want to get caught in the crossfire. I couldn't blame them for that.

"You can't just sell me," I said with more bluster than bravery. Even I could hear the tremor in my voice. "I'm a human being."

The owner murmured something in Latin and clamped a sweaty palm down over my mouth. Just like that, my words died in my throat. Witch, my mind whispered. She whispered more in English that sounded like, "Shut up stupid human." There was no talking my way out of this and there was no fighting my way out.

It didn't stop me from thrashing about and screaming as hard as I could even if the only sound I could make was a deep, throttling groan.

It had all the result of turning a relatively peaceful transaction into something that resembled chaos.

I'd be damned if I just let someone pay money for me and lead me out of there on a chain. I kicked out at anything that came near, and there were a lot of things coming near. Too near. Things that looked like men and women but who I knew full well by now were not.

They all wanted to smell, taste, lick, look at this thing pinned to an iron bar that the witch assured them was special. Whatever they thought I was, they wanted a piece. I heard a riotous bidding begin. The owner's sharp retort that I was worth three times that. Another bid. The first vampire, I thought.

My vocal chords made some horrible shrieking sound in my throat that didn't make it through my lips. I rattled the chains. Something ran along the base of my neck toward my shoulder. A figure, I hoped, because if it was anything else, I'd lose my mind.

I whipped around as much as I could, panic making my vision muddy. I kicked and tried to buck my way out of the handcuffs. Brought down a tiny creature that had flitted close to my heel. I might have stomped on it.

The bids rushed out, gaining momentum.

I was done for. I could sense it. The first vampire whispered in my ear.

"You're mine."

A strangely ethereal man the width of a splinter came out of nowhere in the air in front of me and grabbed me by the throat. I went dead cold.

I might have lost the last shred of my sanity except for a sound that throttled through the courtyard. It could've been the trumpet of Gideon for all I knew, or the warbling of the horn that leveled Jericho. Everyone fell back as though they were the walls of that ancient city crumbling beneath the blast.

I looked up to see Maddox strolling down one of the side streets toward us through the narrow chasm left by the shop-keepers and their minions who had thrown themselves at me. Something hung from his shoulder on a leather strap. It looked for all the world like one of those old-fashioned gunpowder horns. Whatever it was, it was nothing to the way the crowd re-acted to his swaggering presence.

They might have been scorched by a stream of boiling water; they gasped as one unit, and fell back in a wave. Several of the booth owners cringed away or busied themselves with inspecting their merchandise. The woman with the wolf tugged on its leash and disappeared behind a wall of black, dripping candles.

"What's going on here?" Maddox said.

The proprietress pointed a shaking finger at me. "Her," she said. "She ruined my product. Set a good deal of them free. She's mine now."

The sound went up of assent throughout the courtyard as every booth owner supported her.

"That's no way to treat a guest," he said.

Even though he hadn't raised his voice, most of the shop-keepers looked as though they had been scolded by an angry parent. Those who didn't, just looked plain scared. The terrifyingly pale man who held me by the throat hissed in my face and then shrank away to disappear behind his stall. The rest of them followed suit and I could see them all cowering next to their booths as Maddox strolled toward me.

One quick flash went through my mind. They were scared of him. This was a man to reckon with, and I needed to remember he could make supernatural things cower.

The only one who didn't was the witch.

"Guest," she said. "You asked her here?"

He nodded but I was sure he refused to look at me because he was afraid she'd see the lie in his face.

"My product," she persisted. "She freed them."

"You should know I wouldn't let any of your more profitable items just escape."

He waved a hand over his head and the dozens of children who'd fled off in every direction now exited the mouth of a near-by door, led out in chains by a ghostly looking wisp of a man. He looked very much like the one who had gripped me by the throat.

I prayed there was just one of them and eyed the stall the wispy man had disappeared behind to be sure there was only one of them that had somehow re-located. No such luck. The first one still peered over his counter at me.

I shivered involuntarily as the wispy gentleman holding onto the children broke into dozens of clones and re-chained them to the witch's bar before re-assembling himself and staring at Maddox expectantly.

As sick as I felt to see a man split into several copies of himself, it was nothing to how I felt at the way each of the children—even the young girl—accepted their fate without protest. I stoppered down the disquieting sense of worry that Maddox could command a creature like that so easily because at least he might also be able to do the same to the witch.

Not so. I would have thought the witch would be pleased at the return of her goods. Instead she glared at Maddox.

"Humans do not come here of their own volition. They don't come here and live," she said.

"It's my bazaar," Maddox said. "My rules." He held her eye with an intensity that made several owners shuffle their feet and make themselves busy at their stalls. Not the witch, however. She met it brazenly.

"So she's either not human," she said. "Or she is here for your pleasure or profit. Which is it?"

He cocked a russet eyebrow. "Emissary, actually. Not that it's any of your business, Evelina."

He gave her a look of disappointment that finally made her wither backwards.

Whatever it implied, had unsettled her, it was obvious. She flicked her gaze at me, and it ran the length of my body from hair to heel. She didn't seem impressed by what she saw, but she reluctantly stepped close enough to run her hand over the locks. They fell free with a thunk to the ground.

I rubbed my wrists, avoiding the mark on my forearm where the sorcerer had placed his tracking tattoo. Not yet, I told myself. I needed to make sure Maddox still had the tile, then I'd call down that bastard and be done with all this.

She stepped aside as Maddox closed the distance between us. He leaned in sideways toward me without taking his eyes off the witch.

I should have been relieved to see him, but I wasn't. Fear gave way to anger at the whole thing. Never mind I had put myself in this predicament; I wouldn't be here if not for him.

"You," I said looking up at him and finding a carefully guarded expression that did nothing to impress me. In fact, it infuriated me. "You owe me."

I had to hold up a flap of my shirt that had been torn away from my shoulder. I noted that his gaze flicked to the curve of my breast and then back to my face but I could see there was a hunger there in his jawline.

"You stole something from me," I said with a bravado that thankfully carried in my tone if it didn't steel my spine. "The Odin Rune. I want it back."

His hand snaked out so fast, I didn't get a chance to react before it gripped me by the elbow hard enough that I bit my tongue. Water stung my eyes. But I wouldn't cower like the rest of them. I couldn't show fear.

"Are you trying to get killed?" he hissed, drawing me away beneath a pool of viscous and hateful glares.

"Funny you should say that," I said.

He was already shuffling me through the streets, nodding at his shopkeepers. "I took the damn thing to protect you. Now be quiet." he growled into my ear. "We'll go somewhere safe to talk."

I dared to yank my arm away as I halted like a mule in the street.

So he did have it. And he had the nerve to tell me he stole it for my benefit. My benefit, when I had just almost been sold to God knew what kind of creatures.

"What is it *you* sell?" I demanded. No doubt he had a booth somewhere in the back shadowy areas. I wouldn't doubt he had the rune displayed ever so nicely with a hefty price tag.

"I sell space. I sell safety. Protection."

"Sounds like the Mafia," I said, glaring at him.

He shrugged. "I give them space to peddle and protection to do so without interference. But I'm no mafia."

Scottie wasn't mafia either, but that didn't mean a damn thing.

"So you're trying to tell me you're a good guy."

He levelled an impatient but tolerant glance at me. "There are no good guys. Now come with me."

"I don't have time to visit or to talk," I said. "I need it back. And I need it now."

He dragged me rather than walked me three feet sideways into an alley where only half a dozen stalls hunkered against the walls of buildings. It smelled of urine and roasted pig. One shop looked like it was made out of human skin. I wavered on my feet.

"You're lucky I found you," he said.

I yanked my hand out of his grip. Stumbled a few steps sideways as he released me.

"I wouldn't call what I am lucky at the moment," I said.

He looked me over up and down, and there was something in that gaze that made me both uncomfortable and warm. My throat started to ache when he reached out to lift the flap of torn cloth and tucked it beneath my bra strap.

"You're the girl from Errol's shop," he said. "The one with the wig."

There was a thoughtful look behind his eyes. I imagined he was remembering how I looked then with the blonde wig and the thigh-high boots. I felt myself flush beneath that gaze.

"Revolting man," I raced through my memory to find Errol leaning over a counter, his thin lips wet with desire. The smell of the candy floss at the door, of all the ginger and cinnamon. The embrace of chocolate. I shuddered because I'd never be able to smell those things again without thinking of the man. "Disgusting. A man like him should be jailed."

"He's not a man. Just stupid. He's always been stupid. An incubus with his power stripped. He's always on the look out for that one person who can help him get them back than to rat on someone. That's why he's in the business."

I blinked as I tried to work through that. "He's not human?"

"Few of them are. It's a good business to be in. Sometimes mundanes find something they shouldn't and he gives us a chance to reclaim it."

"You say us," I said, narrowing my gaze.

He nodded at me as though he was surprised I hadn't figured it out. Maybe I would have if I wasn't still trying to make peace with the fact that the world could be something other than normal.

"We have a franchise of shops. That pawnshop I first saw you in? Leased to a shifter."

"A shifter?" I staggered backwards, trying to replay every transaction I'd made to see if there were hints of supernatural in them. I'd been oblivious, obviously. But then maybe there'd been nothing to notice. If supernatural things had been slithering around in the normal realm unseen all these years, maybe centuries, maybe longer, then they will no doubt good at camouflage. It was a disquieting thought.

"And those kids," I said throwing my hand in the direction of the courtyard. "Innocent children and you brought them right back to the insulting party. You don't even care they'll be sold?"

His russet eyebrow quirked. "Who said I didn't care?"

"You could've done something."

He turned toward where the crowd and the market that was still buzzing with activity, the vampires and proprietress trying to collect up one particularly quick child who had avoided recapture and was darting around and knocking things over. I smiled as I noticed it was the teen aged boy. He was fast. Not fast enough, though. A ridiculously huge looking man grabbed him from behind and carried him like a flour sack back to Evelina.

I felt something within me sag.

"Oh," I said. I wasn't sure why I thought he might get away. It was futile. All of it. The quicker I was done with this the better.

"So," I said. "Where's my tile?"

Maddox reached behind his back and ran his hand over one of those locked doors. It evaporated much like the Portal had when I'd come in.

I thought for a long moment. Then I shook my head. I didn't think I could go through that again.

A wicked grin slid over his face. "It won't be anything like the entryway to the Bazaar," he said. "We don't like those to come through who should not be here."

I cocked my head sideways, studying him. "You say we?"

He spread his hands wide. "I should have said me. This is my bazaar."

I balked as his hand found the small of my back and he tried to guide me through the doorway.

He slipped that hand over my flank and tugged me close, almost playfully.

"I promise you nothing will happen to you that you don't want to happen to you."

I pulled away, confused at my own reaction to his touch. I back-stepped two paces into the street. Distance made me feel less befuddled.

He sighed and looked over his shoulder at me.

"Suit yourself," he said then stepped through into the darkness.

If I wanted that tile back, I guess I had no choice. I looked down at my phone timer. Ten hours left? How had time moved that fast already?

I stepped over the threshold behind him to face whatever was inside.

CHAPTER 20

I expected the interior to be dark and gloomy but it shifted as quickly as I got across the threshold.

I stepped out of the coolness of the alleyway where the breeze bit into more than skin and into a room that was cozy and warm. Books lined shelves on every wall. Above me walls of spines lined an open concept second floor balcony. A third floor above that, same deal. Iron railings wound about the entire room, revealing that what waited above us weren't rooms and floors at all, but a spiraling staircase that circled one massive chamber with stages of balconies. What was up above the third level, I couldn't tell, but it was shadowy up there. I thought I heard whispers leaking down, and the hairs on my arms stood on end.

This was no place for a regular gal, no matter how welcoming it appeared.

He seemed to notice the direction of my gaze.

"Nothing up there that would interest you," he said and crossed the room to an open hearth fireplace book-ended by two great leather chairs.

He lifted a thick cushion from one of them and smacked it with his palm to fluff it into shape. Apparently satisfied with its state of comfort, he then placed it back onto the chair and spread his arm over it, indicating that I should sit.

I looked at him for a long moment before I decided to do just that. My legs were quivering with the release of so much adrenaline all at once and far too frequently. If I didn't sit, I'd fall.

The fire leapt to crackling life when I did. It was disconcerting but I appreciated it in light of the contrast of my frayed nerves. I thought whatever magic let him do it, I wouldn't complain. It was very much like a library of old, meant to make the person within feel comfortable and safe.

Then I wondered what the place might truly look like if he was trying to make me feel safe.

"Is this a trick?" I said touching the edge of the leather chair. It felt real enough.

"A trick?" he said. "You think I'm some sort of a witch or a warlock?"

I just stared at him. I didn't know what the difference was. Didn't think I needed to care. Actually, I decided I didn't want to know. I already knew too much. I didn't want to get comfortable with the notion of magic or supernatural entities slipping in and out of my life.

He seemed to take my silence for an accusation and sighed.

"Despite your folklore, not many creatures have the ability to glamour things. What you see here is real." He jerked his chin toward the hearth. "The fireplace has a timer."

"So you can't glamour things is what you're telling me." I squirmed in the chair as I thought of my demand from the sorcerer and realizing why he might have been so quick to agree to it. The sudden flush of heat from the fire made my face far too hot for comfort. I waved a hand in front of my face and eyed him warily.

"So what are you?"

His mouth twitched almost playfully. "I've asked the same of you."

I lifted my chin. "You already know what I am."

His gaze trailed to my throat and the pulse I knew was pounding out a choppy rhythm. The way his gaze remained on it did nothing to calm it down.

"Yes," he said. "I do. Nothing but a vulnerable human. A toffee we sometimes call you." His disappointment was palpable.

I didn't like the way he said vulnerable since I was sitting in a room of his own making while he stood there in front of me, a place where things whispered above me, and the door only unlocked at his touch. Nevertheless, in for a penny.

"My inconvenient humanity is the reason I'm here, actually."

I gripped the arms of the chair, letting the mark peek out from beneath my cuff. It was a good reminder for me to stay on track.

"I need that tile back. Now."

He tapped a finger against his thigh. "But it doesn't belong to you."

That old argument. No doubt it would be smarter to bargain with the chips he'd already given me.

"You said you stole that tile to save me," I said.

He nodded. "I did." His expression didn't shift. A better poker face I'd never seen.

I sank deeper into the chair. I simply couldn't hold my back straight anymore. Exhaustion and stress was robbing me of my will to even be there let alone keep my eyes open. The fire was doing its best to melt me into a puddle.

"You didn't even know me when you stole it. Why do you care what happens to me?"

He sighed heavily and pulled up a chair. Twisted it around backwards and straddled it. His arms hung over the back. They were broad and big hands, with blunt fingers that looked like they could stop your heart with a single jab.

"A vulnerable and mortal human doesn't stand a chance against Kelliope," he said. "A little kitten of a human like you...let's just say it would be messy."

There was an odd huskiness to his voice that, in contrast to the way his features remained placid, made me run my fingers along the column of my throat. His gaze followed the trail they made and rested on my mouth, making me nervous.

"Liar," I said and leaned forward close enough that I could smell whiskey on him. Good whiskey. He was used to finer things. His suit and his library were evidence of it.

"Just because you don't believe it, doesn't mean I'm lying," he said, nonplussed.

"What do you think it's worth?" I asked. "A hundred thousand? A million?"

He laughed, showing a crooked tooth toward the back. Strangely, it made him seem less threatening and encouraged me to press on.

"I make my living reading people," I said. "You don't have to pretend you didn't steal it so you could sell the thing for a tidy profit. Like a hundred percent profit since it cost you nothing." There was a note of bitterness in my voice but he didn't react to it.

"Enlighten me," he said. "You who are such a study in human nature."

He stressed the word human as though it should be evident that I couldn't read him because human he was not. But I could.

Supernatural or not, his actions in the courtyard proved it. He didn't want anyone out there to know he had the rune.

I squared my shoulders. "You saw a chance to take something and leave me to pay the consequences. And now that I'm here, I'm threatening your little farmer's market by letting them know you have it."

He guffawed at that, but I knew I'd hit a nerve with the taunt. He was too cool at the insult. Too calculated. Don't trust him, Fayed had said. Well, I didn't and wouldn't.

"Prove to me you had my welfare at heart," I said.

His eyebrow quirked. "I thought I'd already done that, kitten."

"Don't call me that." I said and he canted his head sideways as though confused.

"But you like it," he said. "It's all over your body language." He waved his hand over the air in front of me. "The way you squirm when I look at you, the way you flush when I use an endearment—"

"That's rage," I said.

"The way you lean toward me to get closer." He hitched his chair a few inches toward mine. I bit down on my lip as I steeled myself not to move. Any show of motion would only encourage the presumption that he was right and he wasn't dammit. I did not do dangerous men anymore.

He chuckled as though he'd expected my stubbornness.

"You modern women," he said. "You want to let go the stereotype but it's hardwired into your biology.

"Misogynist thinking," I said. "And archaic."

"Ah, The old feminist argument." He put up his hands in surrender. "It's sexist of me to say you enjoy it. I must not presume.

My apologies for being a...what do you humans call it? a sexist pig?"

"Maybe an old bitty from the sixties might," I said. "My generation would just call you a prick."

He sighed heavily. "Every generation, a new thing. It tires me out, honestly."

"You're changing the subject," I said. "I didn't come here to discuss your sexism, your misogyny, or your bigotry. My rune," I said. "I want it."

His only response was to cross one arm over the other on the back of the chair. The way he watched me made me uncomfortable. His gaze never wavered from mine, but he leaned forward, lifting the legs behind him into the air about half an inch. I expected him to topple forward, but his feet were well planted. One movement. That would be all it took for him to flash across the space to grab me by the throat.

It was such a visceral thought, accompanied so clearly with an image that my hand went to my throat protectively.

I couldn't keep his gaze. I had the horrible thought that he had planted that image in my mind and it took me a moment to recover. The man who would do that, use the suggestion of violence to get what he wanted, only understood violence. I remembered Fayed's warning. Don't trust him. He's dangerous.

His smile this time was long and lazy, and I knew he had done exactly that and now realized I knew it too. Whatever he was, it included telepathy of some sort.

"So," he said. "You wanted me to prove my chivalry to you but you didn't say how I could do that."

He laid his chin on his forearms and stared at me expectantly.

"It's simple. Your chivalry made things worse for me." I laced the word chivalry with icy disdain. "You can fix that by giving me the rune."

"And how did I do that?"

I summarized the night from the bar, the way I'd been threatened and then ended up trying to help the fallen man who disappeared, ending with the way he'd hung me by my jaw in plain sight on a busy street. "And no one noticed," I finished with. "It was as though we weren't even there."

"You probably weren't," he said in a musing tone. "At least not all the way there."

"He told me he was a sorcerer."

He eased his chair back.

"A sorcerer?" He thumbed his bottom lip. "There aren't many of those roiling about the dimensions, and the ones that still exist are tied together so tight into their guild, they rarely step out of it. I doubt you encountered one let alone stole something from him. They aren't so careless with precious things."

He sounded thoughtful. "You'll have to try again, little thief."

I twisted my wrist so that he could see the evidence hennaed into my skin.

"He put this on me, said he was some kind of tracker."

His sharp intake of breath was not the reaction I expected.

"Lovely isn't it?" I said, testing.

He pushed up from the chair and twirled it around before settling it against the fireplace.

"You certainly do have a special talent," he said curtly.

All pretense of trying to charm me was gone.

He pulled down the cuffs of his shirt. "Very special. But not for the things you think."

He strode several steps before stopping mid tread and swinging back around. I thought he wanted to say something and waited for him to speak. But he turned heel again and headed to a small tabletop box beside a row of leather bound books. A decanter appeared when he lifted the lid. He poured a shot and upended it. Poured another.

"Want one?" he said, holding it up toward me.

I stole a look at my timer. Five hours left? Sweet Jesus, was the time accelerating?

"I don't have time for a drink. I need that rune."

"Before you decide that's what you need, maybe you should know more about who you're dealing with."

In my experience, knowing led to compassion or empathy or fear and other nasty things that got in the way of a successful transaction. Best to treat everything as objects to be traded. Even people. Easier that way.

"I don't need to know," I told him.

"No?" he said. "Maybe I just want to tell you." He flashed a grin and tilted the glass toward me in salute before he downed it.

"There's only one sorcerer who has flesh magic," he said and began meandering throughout the space, now and then touching an object, laying his hand along a spine of a book.

"Each has their own specialty in addition to some pretty nasty energy wielding. If you've got in the way of Finn as well as Kelly...Well, let's just say it takes a special kind of stupid."

He looked directly at me when he said this, the insulting bastard. But if he thought to bully me into letting him keep that rune he had no idea what this little kitten had already been through. A few words weren't likely to change my mind.

"I don't do things in half measures," I said with a thin smile. "Even stupid."

By this time, he'd found his way back to the fireplace and was leaning against the face, one shoulder pressed into the bricks, one foot crossed over the other. He might have been at a cocktail party setting himself up to tell a humdinger of a tale, and I guess he was.

"There are plenty of factions in this world," he said. "I won't lie to you. Not all of them are pleasant."

"I don't care about the factions," I said. "I don't care about the things that are in this world. I just want to get out of here safely and get back to my own world where I know the demons I face. If that means I need to deliver some ridiculous supernatural artifact to someone I've never met before, never care to meet again, then so be it. What happens in your world is nothing to me."

I gave a long thought to the children outside. No doubt they wanted the same. No doubt they were blissfully unaware of this realm the same as I was until they found themselves in it, and would have done anything to avoid it if they could.

I let that pass. I had no bargaining chips for that. Only for the issue at hand.

"Do you still have it," I asked. "The rune. Or did you sell it so you could buy a couple more books?"

He might say he stole it from me to save me, but we both knew better. I met his eyes. The fire crackled impatiently. I watched as he reached over to throw a log on top. Strangely enough, I didn't feel its warmth any more.

"I have it," he said.

I very nearly gave myself away with a sigh. I chewed the inside of my cheek as I regarded him. If I pressed the tracking mark right now, would Finn the sorcerer be able to get past whatever lock Maddox had applied to the door? It might be the fastest way to expedite this entire bit of nastiness.

"I want it back," I said. "If I don't give Finn that tile, he's going to kill everyone I know."

"Let me guess," he said. "Then he'll kill you."

He didn't sound impressed by the threat.

"I take death threats very seriously," I said.

"As well you should."

He crossed the room to the bookcase. Ran his fingers down along a few of the spines. I waited, breath held. My fingers trailed down toward the tracking mark.

I hesitated though. I needed to see it. Make sure he really did have it. Time was running down faster than I could sense. I couldn't risk making a mistake. One glimpse and I'd yank in that bastard Finn and I'd turn my back on this whole world and try to forget any of this ever happened.

When Maddox turned back around he held what looked like a velvet jewelry box like the one rings came in. Both of his index fingers tapped the side of it thoughtfully. My eyes were glued to the hinges. I tried to will him to open it.

"I own this place, like I said," he said. "This whole bazaar. It's mine. I conceived it. I built it. They came."

I waited, wondering what any of that had to do with the tile or with me.

"Humans come here sometimes, but it's rarely of their own volition. Evelina was right about that. The ones that do come are here for rather dastardly reasons."

Was he accusing me of something?

I thought of Scottie's henchmen. And Finn. And Kelly. Caught between a rock, and a hard place, and a sharp pointy stick. I looked up at him because it finally dawned on me what it was he wanted.

"I don't plan to come back."

He nodded. "Good decision."

He held out his hand between us, the box lying in his palm. In my own it wouldn't look quite so small, but in his, it seemed tiny. In another lifetime I might have wanted to feel those hands on my skin.

The way he laughed at me when I tried to grab for it ruined that.

"You think I'm just going to pass it over?" he said. "When you have no idea what it is? What Kelly is? Finn is nothing to Kelliope. You saw her. You saw him and what she'd done to him."

"You're scared," I said.

"Me? I'm afraid of very little, but a healthy respect for the most notorious fae the rogue lords have is a smart thing. Kelly is an anomaly among even her own kind. She has an affinity for several elements instead of just one. Light for example. She can harness it like a laser to either harm or heal."

"Let me guess," I said. "She chooses to harm."

"Not a choice," he said with a sigh. "She is bound to her over-lords. They send her to do their bidding. And she obeys."

He closed his fist around the box.

"You can have it, but it won't be safe."

"And yet it would be safe for you?" I sucked the back of my teeth. "You are an old misogynist, aren't you?"

He didn't take the bait.

"We walk among you without being noticed," he said. "The ones who can wear human faces either by magic or glamour or physiology. But there are others. So many others."

I balked at the thought. I'd seen enough unpleasant things outside in the bazaar to keep me peering under my bed at night for the next twenty years. That didn't preclude my need to have the tile now.

"If you're trying to scare me, you're not as effective as Finn," I said, pulling my T-shirt collar back up over my shoulder.

He watched the movement keenly and I had such a vivid image of him peeling away that shreds of shirt and touching my shoulder that I flushed hot and I put my hand out again as a distraction. For who, I wasn't sure.

His gaze flicked to my face and I thought I saw humour in its depths. Had he done that on purpose? Made me imagine his touch? I scowled up at him.

"Again," I said, mostly to goad him. "Not as effective as Finn."

"Maybe you prefer Kelliope," he said with a grin.

I worried my bottom lip with my teeth. This was most frustrating.

"Just give me the damn tile."

He smirked. "What do you think would happen if every supernatural creature from every world could cross the threshold between them at any time they wanted?"

Worlds? Had he said worlds, plural? I lifted my chin. Focus, Sis, I told myself. Focus.

I was used to playing odds. Dealing with Scottie had made me appreciate the law of averages in a keen way. The chances of finding someone's super secret password when they have to change it frequently. The chance of stumbling upon the one thing they love enough to do anything for you. The odds of someone spilling every dirty little secret he ever knew if you exacted just the right amount of pain in just the right spot.

"Not my problem," I told him.

He put the hand holding the box into his pocket and I followed the path with my eye.

"Most folk don't believe the runes exist," he said. "But those who do, think they are part of a mosaic crafted by Odin."

"Odin," I echoed, anxious for him to pass over the box. He held it tight in his trouser pocket. I could see the ball of fist it made.

"Odin was a god—"

"I know who he's supposed to be," I snapped.

"Was," he said, correcting my verb tense. "Odin was one of the only gods who could travel all nine worlds at a whim, sometimes all of them at once. Legend has it when he died, his bones shattered into a thousand pieces and reassembled into a map of the nine worlds that hung itself on the wall of the Enochi Hall of records. No one could read it. The codex was in a language unknown to even the angels. Runic types of markings. It got destroyed somehow. Some say Odin's greater spirit saw the terrible power of the mosaic and destroyed it, scattering the runes throughout the worlds. Some think the runes themselves were so powerful, they couldn't hold together without shattering.

"Even in the underworld, we have our fables and legends.

I shrugged. "Then it's only a problem if everything you say is accurate. So far you only have legends and conjecture. Nothing solid. I can't base my decisions on theory. And I can't base my life on your guesses."

I held my hand out and waited until he deposited the box onto my palm.

His fingers brushed against mine as he withdrew his hand and his eyes never left my face.

"Tell me, Kitten," he said with a sad smile. "What if this is the last piece? What if it's the only thing keeping evil at bay?"

Unbidden, my thoughts went to those terrified children chained to the witch's booth, knowing they would end up in some blood den or worse. I thought of the vampires, both of them, their lust for my blood evident on faces and in their actions. I thought of the woman barely holding back the werewolf on a leash. The eyeballs I'd seen in the bowl.

And all of that was just at the front of the bazaar. The surface things. The more palatable items. Everyone knew the seedier things were at the back of the shop; that the vanilla items were in the windows for the common, conservative customer.

There were dozens of alleyways in the deeper pockets of the bazaar. Places I hadn't inspected or strolled through. What things did those shadows hold that I hadn't seen?

If this man, who could make those creatures fall to heel, was afraid of what might happen should the tile be delivered then what things were yet to see or suffer?

"You're trying to trick me," I said. "You've been caught and you want to keep it and you're trying to scare me."

I wanted to see the truth of it in his face. I peered up at him, inspecting his features the way he had mine in the pawn shop. I wanted to see just how accurately I'd hit the mark.

He stood still, very still under my scrutiny then he murmured, so quietly it might have been my imagination, "I don't need to resort to tricks and lies to get what I want, Kitten. I just take it."

He just took it. I felt naked suddenly. I met that steady gaze as bravely as I could, but I could barely hear anything but the hammering of my heartbeat in my ears as the horrible realization of it all struck me.

"I can't give this tile up, can I?" I said and fell backwards, reaching behind me for the chair. "I won't be safe anywhere. No one will."

I collapsed against the arm of the chair because I couldn't hold to my feet any longer. I would have tumbled over it backwards except Maddox caught me before I could. He held me firmly, let me hover between the chair and his chest, looking down at me with something like bemusement in his features.

His hands lingered on my forearm for an instant longer than I expected but then they were shoved into his pockets and he was unreadable again.

I was dead whether I collected the rune for Finn or not. Maybe we all were.

CHAPTER 21

There was a sort of release in the realization that my free will was gone. Much like the look of relief I'd seen in a hundred men's eyes when they knew that no matter what they did or said next, death would release them from the agony of not telling, and the guilt of saying too much.

I laughed but somehow it sounded more like a sob.

"You don't have to be the thin red line between chaos and calm," he said, and the smoothness of his tone was like warm chocolate and tiny marshmallows. I know he felt me yielding. He inched closer.

"I can help you."

I looked at the velvet box that held the strange looking tile and its odd little scorched-in markings. So much ado about something so small.

I lifted my gaze to his. There was an earnestness behind his eyes that didn't make sense. Fayed had told me not to trust him. Kassie had told me not to trust him. And now here I was, in the belly of his territory, off my game, not thinking clearly.

He had to be working me. The entreating look in his eyes could be faked. He might be very practiced at all this. The manager of a very large market, dealing with all manner of retail, he had to be good at negotiating. A con woman should know a con when she saw it, but for all I knew, his supernatural skill might well be to compel people the way vampires did.

Hadn't he said earlier that there were no good guys? That meant him as well. No good guys anywhere. That's exactly what my experience had been over my lifetime. Scottie. My foster fathers. Even the mothers sometimes. A dozen people or more who had used me and abused me. I was used to it, but it didn't mean I had to accept it.

I needed distance. I couldn't think with him looking at me that way. I closed my hand over the box and stumbled away from him. I headed for the door only to realize that there was no handle. I swung around, feeling an unwanted wetness on my face.

"Let me out," I said. I swiped a hand across my cheek to rid it of water.

He didn't move.

"Let me out," I said, stronger now.

"Ms. Foster," he started to say and I interrupted him.

"It's Isabella," I said. "You might as well know my real name if you're going to screw me."

His shoulders slumped but he nodded toward the doorway. The movement seemed to be enough to make it yawn open. Beyond the threshold lay brightly lit streets. I'd come mid night, and it still seemed so, but like it had when I'd arrived the streetlights and oil lamps burned hot enough to make the alleyway and courtyard beyond seem mid-day. The market in full swing bustled with noise. I thought I could hear children crying.

And I knew right then why I'd felt uneasy about his convenient submission.

I took a deep bracing breath and lifted the box to eye level. I fingered the clasp.

I was my own woman. I'd almost given in to him. Almost believed him.

"Don't do that," I heard him murmur from behind me. I swung around, not sure how he'd got so close again without me hearing him move.

"Why?" I demanded, but I knew the answer. The rune was not in there. I was as sure of that as I was of my own heartbeat.

I snapped the top open as a way to shove my knowledge of human nature in his face, ready to demand my property all over again.

My shock at seeing the rune lying cushioned against the velvet must have been comical because he let go a short burst of dry laughter. I met his eyes, confused.

"It was warded," he said shortly.

"Was?"

He nodded and pulled his hair up into a bun before crossing his arms over his chest. He looked like he was daring me.

"I'll live with it," I said and started to leave.

I halted when I noticed him unhooking a large and heavy looking mace from the side of the door.

"You planning to bash my brains in?" I clenched the little box behind my back.

He hefted it into both hands, obviously testing its weight.

"I wouldn't need such a brutal weapon for that," he said. "This is insurance."

I wasn't sure whether or not that was supposed to make me feel safer or not. Better not to think about it. I backed my way out of the door and into the alleyway where I'd turned on my heel and headed doggedly toward the mouth of the alley.

I was certain I could hear him behind me, but I refused to turn around. I wanted to get as close to the exit as I could when I pressed the tracking mark. Let the sorcerer Finn have the damn thing. What did it matter to me? What did it matter to all of humanity? One small piece of tile with scribblings on it that might be a key to a bunch of worlds or someone's bathroom tile for all we really knew.

Even if it could bring down the entire universe as I knew it, I personally was not going to die here in this miserable bazaar over it. No. I would die in my own home.

Presuming all of those legends were true in the first place. Which I doubted they were. More like the thing had some more tangible magics that offered up its owner something profitable. Men were greedy. No doubt they were in the supernatural realm too.

As I got closer to the main bazaar, I was aware of a strange scuffle ahead of me in the courtyard. The tension was almost electric. Something was wrong. I could feel it.

I panned my gaze left to right. Everyone was frozen to their spots. Evelina, the witch, was hovering next to her cash register with both hands holding onto its sides like she was going to pick it up and hurl it. The children were gone, no doubt sold to the highest bidder, and I felt a nagging guilt at the back of my neck. The wispy man from before had gathered back to himself and was gripping two rather large rocks. The vampires, the lady with the wolf, patrons of different types, all of them seemed to be in a state of alertness.

It was only when I followed their gaze that I realized someone new was in the courtyard. Someone who had come through the entrance. Someone who could make them all afraid enough to arm themselves with whatever they had to hand.

I heard Maddox behind me shouting my name even as I realized that the person who had come through the entrance wasn't just an everyday somebody. She was petite in stature like me, wearing combat boots and a sly, confident smile.

I knew that smile. I knew that demeanour. My legs still ached from the memory of running from it.

Kelly.

While I expected the discomfort of realizing my assailant from the back alley behind Fayed's bar was here, I was not expecting the shock I felt at seeing who was with her.

Kassie. Being held tightly against Kelly's side by a death grip the woman had in her hair. The girl's eyes were wide and darting about as she no doubt sought to find an escape. I knew the girl wouldn't cry out. I doubted she'd even whimper. There was a resolute toughness to the teen that was as impressive as it was sad.

Kelly gave her a shake as though she wasn't getting enough attention and needed to draw all eyes to her. Kassie winced visibly.

That's when the dam broke. Someone threw a rock. I assumed it was aimed at Kelly, but it struck the girl in the temple. She went limp in Kelly's grasp.

"Kassie," I said, breathing the name out like a gasp.

I expected things to change in that moment, and they did. Whatever Kelly had been hoping for in bringing Kassie here, she seemed to have lost that edge when Kassie fell unconscious. And it didn't make her happy.

She dropped the girl, who crumpled to the cobblestones in a ball of filthy clothes and tangled hair. She looked like a small child lying there and something in my chest ached to see her looking so vulnerable.

The wolf lunged, tearing the leash free from its handler's grip. The blast Kelly sent toward him as he ate up several yards in one leap left him transforming with shrieks of agony back into a man. He lay quivering on the cobblestones as each bit of hair and claw retracted into his flesh.

Kelly took the opportunity to throw both hands out in front of her, her shoulders back, light gathering in her palms as it ebbed out of the lamps and lights. She heaved soccer ball sized balls of light in every direction. Where they landed, things disintegrated, caught fire, or blew into dozens of pieces that sent shrapnel in every direction. Bolts of long, zagged light sizzled creatures into smoldering husks. The air stank of burnt fat.

Dozens of creatures surged forward, uncaring, it seemed, of their own welfare. But it wasn't enough to quail her. Maddox grabbed my elbow and pulled me back, just out of sight of the assassin's view.

I tried to shake him off. That was Kassie out there. A young run away that got tied up in this mess for a hundred bucks. I sobbed without meaning to. It was my fault she was here.

"I can't just leave her," I said.

"She doesn't need you," he said.

He tugged me backwards, into the alley way and out of sight. Back where we'd come from. We got maybe three feet when I lost Maddox's hand. The onrushing crowd became a conveyor, moving me helplessly about.

I lunged forward instinctively, my thoughts on the girl. I found myself in the courtyard amid the heart of the chaos. People ran, rocks sailed through the air, light exploded like bombs all around me. A rush of customers and patrons, some of them small things that barely looked human jostled past me in a bid for escape.

I felt my legs shoot out from beneath me as I was shoved sideways. Maddox. I recognized the smell of fireplace and smoke.

We skidded sideways together into a booth made of leather, pulling down swaths of it on top of us. The bowl of eyeballs upended with a clang to the cobblestones and the viscous eyes dropped on me before rolling off in every direction. I fought the urge to gag.

Maddox was on top of me. The pressure from his weight was squeezing my lungs and making it hard to breathe.

Another crack split the air. I peered out from over his torso. The bazaar and its occupants had turned into a seething roil. The ghostlike man split into two dozen clones this time, each of them carrying a rock that had somehow got larger than the one he'd held originally. Each clone heaved the stone at her. She deflected each thrust with a wave of light that warbled through the air like a fast forward ebbing tide.

"You need to get out of here," he said.

Yeah, I thought. No shit. Therein lay the trouble. I rolled over onto my side as he pushed himself to his feet. He grabbed the mace he'd dropped, then hefted it over his shoulder.

He gave me one last lingering look, one that was full of expectation and something else. Sadness?

I stared at him and he reached down to yank me to my feet.

"Run," he rasped. "I won't tell you again."

Obviously believing I'd do just that, he stepped out from behind our cover and stepped into the throng, the mace resting against his shoulder. I thought I heard him whistling. *Lounge Fly* by STP, I thought, but it couldn't be. Because why in the hell would he ever pick that song?

I was torn between wanting to run away and wanting to go scoop Kassie up. I wasn't sure what to do. I had the rune. I was good at getting through tight spaces. Kelly was busy. They were all busy. I could easily find my way around the market and out the entrance.

I could. I should.

I found myself stumbling out from behind the booth and running toward Maddox. Kelly had yet to see either one of us, and was busy catching the rather large stones that came her way and either heaving them back or splitting them into tiny pieces with a laser -like focused stream of light.

Kassie still lay unconscious at her feet.

Maddox halted at the mouth of the alley where it met the courtyard. I was still at least two paces behind him but was close enough that I could tell Evelina had seen him. The relief on her face was obvious.

Then she pointed at me, and everything changed.

Kelly followed her gaze and her face brightened enough to war with the bolts of light she gathered on her palms.

Maddox swung around, his features a bruise of fury.

"You're not a very good listener," he growled.

A blast of light skittered past my head and I felt my hair move with it.

"I heard every word," I said shortly.

He swore and his hand snaked out to take mine. He yanked me along the perimeter of booths searching for one with good cover, dodging shopkeepers who had taken by then to running. Only a few remained on the offensive. We were hurtling deeper into the bazaar, toward those shadows. Coward, I thought. What happened to the guy strolling through the market with a mace?

"You're just going to leave her out there?" I wasn't sure if I meant Kelly or Kassie, and I supposed it didn't matter.

"No choice now," he grumbled. "You ruined that."

He dove behind the fountain, dragging me with him. The still-healing dog bite reminded me why moving was painful. A splash sounding, drawing my attention and I peered up to see balls of steaming water sailing from the basin toward the fae assassin. Something inside was heating water and hurling it.

A lilting yodeling sort of yell came from Kelly's direction. A type of victory cry, I thought. I wondered who she had taken out. I peered around the side to see the two vampires had shifted into large, hairy bats the size of vultures and were railing about her head. She swatted at them almost absently and when one of them dug claws into her scalp, her hand whipped out to shoot a trail of light like a lasso to wrap around its neck. She whipped that light viciously behind her then thrust it forward, flinging the vampire to the ground, where it transformed.

It railed again at her, blood draining from its ears and eyes, this time in human form. Battered, it forged forward only to be thrust again to the ground. This time it stayed there.

Her gaze landed dead on to the fountain.

"How does she know I'm here?" I said.

"Not you," he said. "The rune."

The rune. Right. It had been warded until I opened the box. I still clung to it, my fingers spasmed around it in terror.

A blast of light skipped across the ground and blasted a hole in Evelina's booth. The witch let loose a cry that that made my blood crystallize. It spoke of anguish and fury. She launched herself at the assassin and for a moment, I thought her sheer rage might change the tide.

Kelly staggered backward as the witch struck her with a blast of wavering air. No light. No sound. Just a heat wave of shock. What the vampires couldn't do, the witch seemed to manage. Emboldened, she stepped closer, threw another blast.

Then I realized Kelly was toying with the witch. When she landed within reach, the fae assassin gripped Evelina by the face, those diminutive fingers of hers crawling over the features like a spider legs. I watched horrified as Evelina went rigid and then seemed to glow from within.

It might have been beautiful as the glow grew brighter and brighter except at the zenith of it, the witch's very skin caught fire. For several seconds she looked like a lit match being consumed and yet not one lick of flame touched the assassin's skin.

She died shrieking beneath Kelly's grasp. Her cry echoed over the courtyard for a long moment after she had crumpled into ashes in a pile at Kelly's feet.

It wasn't just Kassie at risk now. I would never get out. I could see that. And if I did, this fae would follow.

"We have to do something," I said.

He gripped me by the elbow and yanked me to my feet. "We are doing something. Running."

"But all those people—" I gagged on the last words as the taste of roasted meat struck my palate and I knew exactly what that meat was. I heaved over, clutching my stomach. That could have been me. So easily have been me a dozen times over.

What if it ended up being Kassie? Could I live with that? Knowing that I had involved her in this mess and now she was out there in danger because of me. She had managed to survive city streets on her own, maybe by luck or skill, who knew, but she had carved out some sort of existence.

Maybe she could survive this.

"Isabella," Maddox yelled. "Move."

He pulled me behind one of the booths but it did nothing to blind my vision from the way Kassie lay unmoving amid the chaos.

I flashed back to the night I had run from Scottie. The hours I spent in that ditch because I had managed to get only so far on my own steam. I remembered praying for a car to come by to save me and when one did, how I cringed, terrified, deeper into the ditch because the driver might be one of Scottie's men. I'd been paralyzed by fear. No good to myself.

I peered out around the booth to see a long trail of light, very much like a lasso, sizzle through the air but stop short of the booth. Just inches short. I gasped at the way it left a dark and smoking stain on the cobblestones where it landed. Maddox hauled me out of sight again against his chest.

His heart hammered against my back.

"My God," I said.

"Yours and everyone else's," he muttered against my shoulder. I felt him trying to fold me out of sight and climb to his feet. He hunched behind the booth with his legs alongside my shoulders. I tried to get up but he held me down with one hand.

"What is she doing?" I said.

"Which she?" he said, pushing me backwards as I tried to look again.

"Kassie."

He wouldn't answer.

"Well?"

I winced as a cracking sound rent the air. Then everything went silent. It felt wrong somehow. Like those moments in that wet ditch when all sound got soaked up by the dark. My feet stung, remembering the pain of the cold.

I saw Maddox wince at the sound.

"That's not good," he said. He swung his gaze to mine and I noted the corners were tight with anxiety. If the silence was bad, those eyes said it was worse than I could imagine.

And Kassie was out there with it. In her own ditch, probably just as terrified.

"We need to get you the hell out of here. Now," he said.

"But Kassie—"

"She's fine."

Fine. A young girl out there next to Kelly's boot, lobs of deadly light all around her. Creatures of every sort engaging in ways that left them dead all around her. What might that do to a tender psyche? And what was Kelly's reasoning for bringing her here in the first place? Leverage, obviously. Kelly knew I had that tile. She knew I cared about that girl.

It was my fault she was here. I couldn't just leave her there.

I tried to crawl over him, not sure what I could do, but knowing I couldn't let that girl suffer because of me.

"Stop it," he said. He gripped me by both shoulders with those broad hands of his and I could swear his fingers met across the span of my back. He forced me to meet his eye.

"Listen to me. She doesn't need you," he said. "It's the rune we need to worry about."

I met his gaze but I didn't like the steeliness of it. He was as heartless as I'd thought. Cold. I wasn't sure why I expected better.

"She's just a kid," I said. "What kind of man are you, anyway?"

"I'm not a man, remember?"

No. he wasn't. Whatever he was, whatever all of these creatures were, they might fight the fae, but they'd not win. I knew that because they were dying all around me. Maddox said he'd give a healthy respect to the most notorious fae assassin the rogue lords had. He wanted to run with me, get the rune safe.

None of these creatures could do anything. I knew that. There was only one thing that could help. And I had it.

I shook Maddox off and managed to stagger forward. My legs hurt. My head hurt.

I shouted Kelly's name and her head swiveled in my direction. She smiled.

"What are you doing?" he hissed.

"Stopping this," I said.

I could hear Maddox's whisper from behind me.

"You can't," he said.

"The hell I can't," I said.

CHAPTER 22

The velvet box felt like a thousand pound weight in my hand. Kelly canted her head to the side, took several steps toward me. Kassie stumbled along beside her and could barely keep her feet from dragging as the assassin strolled closer. I heard the first vampire from earlier suck in a breath and mutter that I was insane.

Maybe. But I'd let one girl down today. Since I was as good as dead anyway, I could at least save someone else.

I held the box high above my head. Strange how it seemed to feel lighter the higher it went. Just doing so seem to flip a switch. Everything in the market stopped as though I had frozen play on a DVD.

Heads swiveled in my direction. I fancied I saw Kassie moving. Her foot scraped against the ground.

"I have it," I said, bolstered. "The Odin rune. It's what you want, right?"

A shocked gasp went up from the courtyard. I gathered it had nothing to do with the fact that I was offering it to her, but rather the fact that they didn't know it existed in the first place.

And that made me question what it was they were fighting for. Not the safety of the bazaar, not their booths or the fact that they'd been attacked. Certainly not even for the rune. They were fighting for something else.

It was on the fringes of my mind. A puzzle worthy of solving and I might have had it except Kelly's gaze swiveled to mine. She dropped her hands to her sides and although she didn't take her eyes attention from me, she nudged Kassie with the side of her boot. The girl shifted, scrambling away from her several inches before butting up against a dead body. The wolf man, I thought.

Without taking her eyes from mine, Kelly leaned sideways, and grabbed hold of Kassie's hair.

"I knew it was here," she said and her voice was lilting. Musical. A stark contrast to the tough look of her. "But I didn't think a human was stupid enough to hold it."

I ignored the insult. "Release her," I said. "And you can have this thing."

Kelly laughed. "Have it?" she said. "The way I see it, all I have to do is take it from your dead hand."

Despite the threat, I inched forward. Held my hands out, supplicating.

"You just have to let her go," I said.

I knew the risks. I'd be giving over the rune, and even if I lived, I wouldn't see many sunrises afterward. Once my time ran out, Finn would kill me as surely as Kelly would. The least I could do was save Kassie in the process.

"It doesn't belong to you, does it? I said. "You're stealing it."

"Not stealing," she said. "Liberating."

I chuckled. "I've used that term myself many times."

I stepped closer. I had already gained several yards and the assassin so far seemed content to wait me out.

Just a few more. I watched as Kassie climbed up to her hands and knees. She lifted her face to mine and I smiled encouragingly. I wanted to tell her with my eyes that everything would be okay. Instead of the relief I hoped to see, there was panic. She shook her head back and forth.

One of the creatures ran in from the sidelines, aiming his track toward Kassie. Without so much as turning sideways, Kelly lifted her hand out and blasted him with a jagged bolt of lightning. He crumpled a hand span away from the girl.

I canted my head sideways, confused. I expected everything to stop now that I had produced the rune. And yet they were still trying to get to Kassie.

Maybe there was hope for this world after all.

From the corner of my eye, I thought I saw Maddox creeping forward, the mace in his hand.

"You want this thing?" I said, and snapped open the lid. I tilted it so she could see it clearly.

She took an involuntary step forward. Progress, I thought.

"All you have to do is relinquish the girl," I said. I winced at the memory of Maddox using the same phrase of me back in the bar with Fayed.

"Deal," Kelly clipped. She stepped forward again. Put out her hand.

She was close enough now I could see her face. The irises were purple. Several scratch marks ran down her cheeks to her neck. I chuckled to myself, recognizing the look of those scratches. I knew them well.

If she had the type of affinity for light that Maddox said she did, she hadn't missed me back in the alleyway at all; she had been aiming for the bag. Obviously thought the Odin rune was inside of it.

I could just imagine her fury when she opened the bag and my cat jumped out at her.

"My cat," I said hastily. "I want my cat too. And don't tell me she's dead because I won't believe you."

Her brow furrowed. "Cat? That mangy thing I found in your suitcase?"

"Bug out bag," I corrected her. "My way out. You stole that too and I need it."

"And you know this because?"

"Because it disappeared. It didn't burn or fizzle like everything else you've attacked. So you weren't trying to destroy it. Just acquire it. It's still whole and unharmed somewhere. At least it better be."

She laughed at that. "You can have that hellish thing."

I was almost close enough. Almost.

"Then give it to me now," I said inching forward more. "All of them. The bag. The cat. Kassie." I jerked my chin in the girl's direction.

My timer sounded in my pocket. One minute left? Couldn't be. Was everything accelerating? From the side of my eye I could see Kelly take a step sideways. She was giving me a wide berth. I inched the other direction toward Kassie. I wasn't sure what I would do once I got there. I only had a few seconds left before Finn found me. Didn't matter. I planned to press the mark long before that. I just had to get Kassie in my arms, and get that bag.

I crouched down next to the girl and gathered her in my arms.

"Can you walk?" I asked her.

She nodded. I looked up at Kelly. "The bag."

"Not without the exchange," she said. "And be aware, I can strike both of you in a second if you don't."

"Just put the bag somewhere I can reach it," I said. I eyed the distance between myself and the door. I didn't know how I was going to get through those creatures. Their stinging tails and barbed tails made me shudder. But I had to do it.

"The bag." I said again.

A sizzle like the sound of meat landing on a hot griddle sounded and the bag popped into view a foot away from me. The belly of it was moving. I told myself it was the cat inside.

Kelly's boot came into view and I glanced up. She towered over me. Her hand extended.

"Your part of the bargain, human," she said. Her head was cocked to the side, as though she were studying me.

I reached up and passed the velvet box over. It was time. There was only one thing I had left to do.

I looked down at Kassie and squeezed her tight.

"It's going to be okay," I said not knowing whether or not it was true.

I let my hand play over my wrist, the thumb pressing into the tracking mark. I held it for a long second. It burned terribly. Kelly's face went from cocky and confident to bewildered.

My back arched with pain as the mark stripped away from my skin. It danced in the air between the assassin and me and slithered within itself as though both fire and serpent were being borne from it. It began to take solid shape, fleshing out to a black cloak.

Kelly gasped. Then she outright laughed as she realized what had happened.

She might have the rune but she was going to have to fight to keep it.

In the next instant, the calm around me turned into chaos.

I had to believe that the sorcerer had made it through although I couldn't see anything but the smoke as thunder crackled. The sounds of several battle cries rose to the air. I imagined every creature within the bizarre was either running or fighting and I had no doubt that they were enjoying it.

I told myself that the resulting chaos had nothing to do with the rune. It didn't just allow Kelly to do what Maddox had said it would, but that the sorcerer had made it through and was fighting for possession of it.

The smell of fire and smoke pushed us forward toward the entryway.

"Almost there," I heard Kassie whisper. "Hold on."

She sounded incredibly calm for someone who had just gone through what she had while I, who had done nothing but give away a precious artifact could barely speak for the terror that clumped up my throat.

I froze at the entryway. The tails were lashing about everywhere, striking at whatever came close.

I balked, terrified that I'd get stung or stuck or worse. I couldn't go through that thing again.

Into the pause, a grim face loomed in front of me. Blood. There was blood on his face everywhere. I caught sight of the mace in his hand as it raised above his head.

He was going to strike me. Vengeance. Anger. Fear. Whatever it was, he was going to make me pay for creating it.

I gripped Kassie tight and ducked to avoid the blow. A soul-crunching sound met my ears like the thunk of a cleaver striking meat. Hot fluid sprayed my neck. A grotesque creature fell at my feet, clutching at his face where the mace had landed.

I gaped at Maddox. The next thing I knew, he was pushing me through the portal.

I fell through on the other side without a single sting or stick. My bug out bag lay beside me, dropped in my arrival.

My knees skinned against the tread of the first stone steps as my cheek struck the edge of it. There'd be a nasty bruise around my eye within hours.

I was disoriented and nauseous, but otherwise, safely through. The distance between the entryway and the steps where I lay indicated I hadn't just been pushed, but rather thrown like a sack of potatoes.

But Kassie was gone.

I scrabbled onto my side, searching for her. My bug out bag lay at the bottom of the steps close to the entryway, but the girl was no where to be found.

I stumbled to my feet and considered going backwards into the portal. I lay my cheek against the door. Nothing. No sounds. No heat. It was as though it was a regular old wooden door, ages old. Nothing special except its age. I lifted the knocker and dropped it. Nothing. I wrapped several times. Still nothing.

When I'd gone through the first time Kassie had told me it wasn't the regular way. She had spoken words that sounded like Latin. Cut me on the wrist. Obviously, it was harder to find that realm than simply knocking on the door.

But what had I done for Kassie after all that? Nothing, it seemed. She was gone like a summer breeze and I had no idea if she even survived the journey through the Shadow Bazaar's peculiar entrance or if she simply stayed behind.

But at least there was no sorcerer. No Fae assassin. That had to count for something, right?

My cat meowed from inside the bag. I bent to retrieve her and unzippered the top.

When she poked her head through, I started to cry.

I looked above me to see that the sky was turning pink. I could make out the tops of the skyscrapers poking through orange tinged clouds. Dawn. Just seeing it exhausted me.

How many hours had I been on my feet? How many hours with nothing to show for it. I considered going back to Fayed's bar, but I knew he wouldn't be there. If he was a vampire as I thought, he was no doubt already snug in his little coffin, waiting for nightfall again.

Perhaps the best thing would be to go home. At least I knew now that the person who had been in my apartment hadn't been Scottie or his henchmen at all. It had been Finn, searching for the things I had taken from him. Of course he hadn't found it, because it went with me when I sought out Errol.

An old incubus without powers, according to Maddox. How many other people in my world were supernatural creatures and entities?

I didn't feel victorious at escaping. In fact, I felt rather cruddy. I wanted nothing better than to soak into a warm tub and crawl into bed. I needed to sleep for days.

I caught the subway and sat in silence. My cat began purring as though she missed me. We both knew that couldn't be true. She was a finicky thing. Given to bouts of hissy fits rather than purring.

I exited the subway tunnels half a block from my apartment.

By the time I unlocked the door and crossed the threshold into my apartment, I was far too exhausted to even get in the shower. I dropped the bag onto the floor of my kitchen and the cat leapt out, tearing across the apartment into my bedroom. I could see her jump up onto the bed from the doorway.

"Good idea," I said and followed her.

Last thing I remember, she was curled up at the top of my head on my pillow, and I was thinking about the events of the past few hours, trying to sort through the complexity of it all, feeling like it was a puzzle I couldn't crack. Through it all Maddox's words about Kassie haunted my thoughts.

She doesn't need you.

Maybe she didn't. The entire market seemed ready to die for her; she probably didn't need me. I'd never know because I left the market burning behind me and the answers with it.

I was asleep long before I figured it out and when I woke, it was the last thing on my mind because staring down at me was the business end of a pistol.

CHAPTER 23

I leaned back into the seat of a familiar limousine. It smelled very much the same as the last time I'd been in it: like caramel and scotch and just a bit of blood. Scottie's henchman sat opposite me, holding his gun leveled at my chest. He wouldn't dare pull the trigger; we both knew that, but if it made him feel more in control, so be it. I'd wait him out. He was a burly man, and so I knew his muscles would fatigue easily. He might have sinew somewhere under all that bulk, but I was willing to guess his huskiness was mostly fat.

"How was your night in jail?" I said, imagining that the sour look on his face was more about sleeping on a narrow cot than any a stern effort to keep me nicely controlled.

"A night at the fuckin' Ritz," he said. "The strip search especially."

Under normal circumstances, I might laugh, but I was still too exhausted to feel anything.

I looked out the window through the tint and watched as the buildings blurred by. Everything looked so sedately normal. As though the world hadn't just almost toppled in on itself. Maybe it hadn't. Maybe I had dreamed the entire thing.

"So how far?" I said.

"You'll see," he said.

I flicked my gaze at the pistol. "I don't think you need to hold that on me," I said. "It's not like I can run away."

He smirked. "You bet your ass you can't."

I sighed. "My ass isn't worth betting on anymore."

It was my own fault I was in this deep with a man no one should have to owe anything to. I'd chased him as a stupid teen. I'd ran from him as an adult. I was returning to him feeling very much like a chastised child. Running was stop gap measure at best.

"So what does he have in store for me?" I said to the minion.

"You know the boss," he said. "Thinks of all the best punishments."

"Indeed I do," I said. "No doubt a hot bath and a few rounds of tequila."

I fidgeted in the seat. The tequila was a certainty, laced with sedative, of course, to make me compliant. He'd wine me, perhaps, over a splendid meal complete with foie gras and hand-spitted game. He'd pretend he wasn't furious that I'd run off and I'd smile beneath a tight mouth as I tried to find a way to keep him at bay.

If I got a bath it would be filled with bubbles and be the perfect temperature. He'd wash my back. Soap my hair. Hold me down beneath the water just long enough for my lungs to ache.

I blinked at the minion holding the pistol.

"What did you say?" I asked him because he was glowering at me over the barrel and I had the feeling he'd said something to me.

"You ain't got a hot bath waiting, you stupid woman," he said. "You got a tracking chip. Gonna put it in your ear like any good bitch."

A tracking chip. I'd never known Scottie to use one. He was more of an old fashioned kind of thug. But times changed.

I hadn't truly known Scottie for three years. Maybe he'd gone techie.

"Apparently, it's all the rage," I said, thinking of Finn and heard my bald humorless chuckle. I looked down at my arm to be sure the mark was gone.

It wasn't. My heart ached to see it. It should be gone. I'd seen him arrive, felt the mark's burn as it pulled from my flesh. Was I destined now to be monitored like some stupid iPhone?

I groaned inwardly. It was always coming to this anyway. Never mind the Fae. Never mind Finn or Kelly. Maddox or Kassie.

It was all coming down to this moment I would face Scottie. All of my years since I left him were just borrowed time. Much like the clock ticking down faster than it should as Finn made me reclaim that Odin rune. Except this time there'd be no magic to save me. It would be just me and Scottie.

I thought back to the night I'd run from him in the first place. While most people tried to escape him because they had betrayed him, I wanted out because he wanted to hold me closer.

He'd slipped an engagement ring on my finger over a spaghetti dinner at the fanciest restaurant who owed him. Lots of employees over hundreds of shops and restaurants owed him. Lots of people. He made sure to work them at first by coy and dulcet means: paying for childcare so a young mother could work, leaving packages of food on doorsteps, even sending a kid or two off to college. The larger organizations owned the owners. Scottie owned the workers. He was smart. The front line was where the info was. The key to knowledge and opportunity.

I'd fallen prey to his charm too at first. I couldn't blame any of them. But the exterior and the interior of a man are often dichotomous. None more so than Scott Lebans. By the time I stared down at that H color diamond ring, I'd already been walking the razor edge of his personality for five long years.

I started to hyperventilate. My spaghetti sauce tasted sour, as though the meat had gone off. I couldn't swallow down enough Cabernet to wet the palette that went dry the moment the ring went on.

I blustered to my feet, begging a few minutes to compose my weeping, blissfully happy self.

Scottie was no fool. He let me go and when I returned he smiled that heart stopping grin of his and bustled me into the back of the very limousine I sat in now.

Even as I was running over the knowledge that I'd be tied to him forever, he'd pressed the button that motorized the partition separating the back from the driver.

He kissed me. Long. Hard. Possessive. I tried to respond but couldn't, even knowing it would infuriate him.

While I was doing my best to make my lips act as though everything was an ecstatic, celebratory occasion, he snapped a set of cuffs on my wrist.

"You're mine," he said. "Always."

He repeated the words over and over as he lifted my dress and invaded me so callously I couldn't see any familiarity in his touch. I fought him. He enjoyed it. Later at home, he did the same. I'd lain like a doll while he invaded me, telling myself the moment he was through, I'd pull out the bat he kept beneath the bed.

When he finished, he peeled himself off me and went to the kitchen sink to pour a glass of water. Rape was thirsty work, it seemed. He was still muttering that I was his dammit and needed to understand that and admit it when I snuck up on him from the back. I still remember the horrible sound of aluminum cracking bone as the bat struck him in his right shin.

I winced at the memory now.

It had been so long ago. I'd given him most of my youth and most of my skills. He got richer because of me. Every heist in my early days I had done because I'd been dying to please him. Having pleased him, there was no way out. He wanted to keep me. Like a doll that sat on a shelf, or like a key to a safety deposit box that he pulled out when he needed to dip in.

I looked at the henchman who sat across from me in the same limousine where my new life had struck its new course. I'd sat exactly where he was in that moment of genesis. He couldn't know it, but his life would change too. He was new. He wouldn't last long. He had no idea what Scottie was capable of. I did. And although I knew what he wanted of me would mean my survival, it would come at a cost. My freedom.

It was why I had run in the first place.

Now he wanted to put a tracking chip somewhere in my skin? Just like Finn had? I'd never be the same. I'd never be my own woman again.

I went meekly to my doom like a lamb to the slaughter, but inside I was seething with anger and determination. My doom turned out to be a posh hotel room in the upscale neighborhood close to my apartment. I could've walked it, but Scottie was never one to waste an opportunity to impress. Although I'd been in the limousine plenty of times, he would see this journey as an opportunity to remind me that no matter how far I went, he could always simply pluck me up and transport me to wherever he wanted.

I smiled to myself as his minion tugged me from the limousine and into the lobby of the hotel. There were plenty of times when I could have ducked out and ran. He was sloppy. But I was done running. Whatever faced me with Scottie, this was the moment when I stared it down.

I'd been to the Shadow Bazaar, for heaven sake. I'd faced the most notorious assassin the Fae owned. Survived Finn.

I'd almost been sold as vamp feed for shit's sake.

I could take on a man. A regular man for all his bluster.

So why did I feel so anxious?

The henchman bypassed the doorman altogether and sailed right past the front desk. So Scottie had been here long enough to check in and register. No doubt had been holed up in this hotel for weeks. I knew him. He wouldn't have taken me rashly. He'd have planned it out. Wanted to make sure I would be where he thought I was.

Except I'd not done as he'd expected and he couldn't possibly have accounted for the supernatural community that had thrown half a dozen flies into the ointment.

I smiled to myself. At least that was one thing that whole mess was good for.

The concierge nodded politely at the henchman as we walked past. I thought he muttered a name along with good morning. Alvin? Was that the name he used? It certainly fit. I started humming an Alvin and the Chipmunks song to let him know what I thought of him. He gave me a sidelong glance but kept his mouth pursed into a tight line.

"Hoola Hoop," I said brightly as we headed to the elevator. "Me; I want a hoola hoop."

He responded by jerking me along when we got to the elevator, probably expecting me to fight him off. No dice. I wasn't that chick anymore.

I looked at him with all the ennui of a beleaguered hooker.

"Which floor?" I said even though I didn't plan to wait for his answer.

Because it would be the penthouse. Of course it would be.

I stabbed the button with my finger and smiled at him, knowing that every single tooth was showing.

He looked bemused.

"What's wrong. Alvin?" I asked him. "Too fat for a hoola hoop?"

"Stupid bitch," he muttered and then turned to face the door. We waited in long silence as the lights blinked on and off one by one.

It took forever to reach the top. When the doors opened, it was into a lush corridor that led down a few feet to a set of broad golden doors.

Mottled glass on either side made them look even wider. The shadows flickering within told me Scottie wasn't alone.

I squared my shoulders and puffed out my chest. Thinking at the same time that it wouldn't make me any larger, broader, or scarier, but if it worked for the animal world, it couldn't hurt.

Alvin pushed me toward the door.

"Move it," he said.

I twisted the knob and yanked.

CHAPTER 24

Scottie was nowhere in sight and I let go a relieved breath. Instead, a trio of well-dressed, well-groomed men I'd never met before reclined in chairs, holding onto champagne flutes with one hand, and onto lithe, impeccably dressed women in the other. I looked down at my now ratty jeans and stained T-shirt. The same clothes I'd been wearing since meeting with Errol. My God, had I even showered? I crossed my arms over my stomach and hung back.

Alvin gave me a hard shove, making me stumble into the room. Some entrance.

The gazes that landed on me were assessing and judgmental. I straightened myself up and pulled my T-shirt down. Smoothed the jeans over my backside. My fingers met a tattered hole mid thigh.

"Lovely to meet you all," I said.

Someone tittered and I swung my glance their way. A young woman, maybe nineteen or so. She was dressed like a movie star. Scottie's date, no doubt.

"Careful, love," I said. "You might get used to this."

Alvin bumped into me with his stomach and pushed me further into the room. He jerked his head toward the left.

"Your room is over there," he said. "I'll tell the boss you're here."

I faced him. "I'm not going anywhere," I said. "You can tell him I'm here. Right here." I stabbed the air in a downward motion.

"He told me to put you in the room."

I shook my head. "Whatever he has to say to me, he can say in front of all of our friends."

I extended my arms spread them wide to encompass everyone in the room. He muttered something again about me being stupid and then gave me the same line again, like a robot stuck on one line of code.

"The boss told me to put you in the room until he's done with his business."

His business. I knew what that meant. He was schmoozing somebody. Conning them. He was multitasking. Some bosses might think that a bedraggled stranger being dropped into the midst of an upscale cocktail party might ruin the ambiance. Not Scottie. It was his way of showing exactly how far his reach extended. It was meant to both impress the victim and to impress the people at the party. They would feel as though they were in good hands with someone who understood how to deal with the riffraff.

Or maybe he just hadn't timed it at all. It was entirely possible I was giving him far too much credit.

I crossed my arms over my chest. "I'm not going."

Alvin grunted and made a rather unceremonious grab for me. He hefted me over his shoulder and lumbered toward the bedroom suite's door. When he threw me down on the bed I bounced twice before he made it back to the door. He pulled it closed with a loud click.

I jumped off the bed and tried the door knob. Locked. Of course. What would I have expected?

I pressed my ear against the door. One thing hotels were notorious for was cheesy and cheap building construction. This one was not.

I sighed, thwarted, and scanned the room.

It was obvious by the way the room looked that Scottie had been here longer than I thought. Not a couple of weeks at all. More like months. His dresser was filled with clothes. A second tallboy was also filled with clothing. Mine.

I recognized the pajamas, lingerie, the yoga pants, and the slinky black dress he'd made me wear the night he'd asked me to marry him. No, correct that. Told me I was going to marry him.

What revealed his true length of stay, however, was the pure Scottie touches on the room. He'd obviously hired workers to alter the stately, everyman decor into a home away from home for a thug.

There was a gun locker hidden beneath the bed. I could see the latches on the half sized locker peeking out beneath the skirt. The chest in the corner would have ammo. The sedate looking sofa would be stuffed with money.

I wondered how long he had been watching me and biding his time.

On the wall next to the window, he'd installed some sort of safe. The painting that was meant to disguise the fact that it was even there was pushed to the side, revealing not just the handle, but the pin pad.

I crept closer, laying my hand on the wall next to it. At first blush, it might seem that he'd simply forgotten that it was there. Maybe he wasn't expecting me to arrive so quickly and didn't have a chance to disguise it again. Maybe he'd even been interrupted while looking through it and only had time to close the safe door and not cover it again with the painting.

I knew better. He wanted me to see it. He knew my skills. He knew I could crack it, be into it, and out of there given enough time. He probably even had a camera built into the mirror to video tape me breaking in and stealing enough money to hop out the window and down the fire escape.

It was too convenient. All of it.

That made me wonder exactly why he'd set up the entire party. Why he was purposefully busy when I arrived.

This was no mistake or accident. He'd planned this. All of this.

I looked again at the pin pad. Fractions. Several of them.

A cold shiver ran down my back.

The house at the McMansion had a fractions pin pad. I scanned my memory, trying to decide whether or not this one had the same ones.

I ran my eye over the figures. Yes. They all reduced to prime numbers. My fingers pressed the buttons instinctively, calling to mind the pattern that I'd used at the McMansion.

The door slid up to reveal two drawers.

I felt as though someone had thrown a bucket of ice cold water on me. I stepped back involuntarily. I wasn't going to open those drawers because I knew exactly what was in them. Or at least one of them. The top would be empty.

I'd underestimated him. Here I thought all these years I had been out of his sight. Out of his reach. Not so. It was he who had set me up to go to that McMansion. The evidence was right here in front of me. He'd thought it all through. Knowing how I worked. Knowing I wouldn't be able to resist the opportunity to make enough money to flee the city. He put in my way at the coffee shop on purpose. Setting all of these things up like a domino toppling event.

And I'd fallen for it. I should have seen it but I didn't.

I swung around in the room. Started pacing. I didn't need to open those drawers. I wouldn't.

I had my hand on the handle of the bottom one when the door opened behind me. I swung around, expecting to see Alvin again, and my heart jumped into my throat.

Scottie. Finally.

He hadn't aged much in the years since I'd seen him last. A dashing 35 had turned into an even more dashing 38. He wasn't a tall man, more mid sized, but his shoulders were broad and muscled. To some he might remind them of a bulldog, all torso and muscle, but on a man that knew how to use it.

All of that was a holdover from the years when he'd done all of his own hard work. He still enjoyed what he called discipline now and then, but usually left the worst of the jobs to his minions. Now that build looked like it was going a bit soft. Maybe without regular beatings of his woman, he couldn't keep up the muscle. He was still handsome. Sandy blond with grey eyes. A mouth you could kiss forever.

How had I ever found him attractive?

He looked me over as though I weren't standing there in filthy jeans and a dirty T-shirt. I knew I smelled of sweat and fear. He seemed not to notice. Instead, he circled me as I stood in the middle of the room. He smelled of my favorite aftershave. That too, was a concerted move.

He waited until he had circled me at least three times before he stopped in front of me. His gaze went to my throat, watching my pulse hammer.

I clenched my fists at my side.

It seemed an eternity before his hand reached out for mine. He tangled his fingers in them and raised them to his lips. Kissed the fingernail of each. Once that had made me melt. Now he did it without moving his gaze from my pulse. I hoped it was steady.

"What do you want?" I said to him finally.

"Just to give you your bridal gift," he said.

I refused to look over in the direction of the safe. I didn't need to see it again to know what was in there.

"You still want to marry me?" I said.

He ran his hand down along my arm. "Of course," he said. "That's never changed."

The way his hand roamed my skin, I believed him. His touch was greedy for me. I had to hold my breath to keep from screaming. He hesitated over my left wrist, lifting the hand and inspecting my skin.

I don't like the tattoo," he said. His thumb ran over my wrist and twisted my arm up so that I could see what he was talking about.

"Why would you get it done?" He peered a little closer, almost as though he was trying to make out the mark. "And what kind of ink is that?"

I rubbed my hand along his, brushing it away. "Henna. It's only temporary."

I looked him in the eye and lied, hoping that it really was temporary, and that he wouldn't see the processing going on behind my gaze. There was no reason it should still be there. Surely

Finn should be dead at Kelly's hand. Surely if he was gone, the mark should be as well. If he wasn't dead, he would've come for me by now.

I twisted my wrist to see it better. It was faded, but not gone. I tried to think back to the time when I'd first met Finn, when he told me that he needed to recover after Kelly's first attack. He'd been too weak to accost me physically. He had to bide his time until he had enough energy to rejuvenate so that he could finally corner me in the street. I wondered if it was the same now. If he'd somehow survived Kelly's attack in the shadow bazaar.

Maybe things weren't as I'd thought. Maybe the bazaar was running along smoothly. But how much time had that been? A day? Two? Twelve hours?

"Why?" I said to Scottie and yanked my hand away. "Marry me, I mean. Why?"

"Because you're mine," he said. All emotion left his voice then. No coyness. No charm. Just flat possession.

"No," I said.

I was not a possession. I was not a minion to be commanded or a handy tool to be pulled out of a chest at whim. I stuck my chin out, defiant, even if I was afraid of the reaction.

"I'm not yours," I said. "I'm not anybody's. I'm just here to say goodbye."

His response was fast and brutal. I didn't have time to back away or escape before his hand closed down around my wrist and his free one crawled up to my neck.

"You most assuredly are mine," he ground out through clenched lips. The webbing of his thumb butted up into my jaw-line as he clutched my throat. He kneed my legs out from beneath me so that I fell against him, pinned to him and trapped on the other side by the wall. "Don't ever forget that. You are here because I wanted you here."

He eased up the pressure some, enough for me to cough and find my voice.

"And what about all the people in the room out there?" I jerked my thumb toward the door. "Why are they here?"

"Buyers," he said. "Most of them."

"Most?"

He nodded. "The women are hookers. Real classy stuff. University degrees all of them."

Right. University degrees. All those girls he'd put through school. The true cost of that fancy education coming to roost like filthy little homing pigeons.

"So you own them too," I said.

He smiled. Ran his thumb across my bottom lip. "Ownership is such a strong word. I prefer benefactor."

I sucked the back of my teeth. "You don't do things for nothing."

"You know me so well." He slipped his arm around the small of my back and pulled me close, hip to hip. I strained away from him, and the harder I leaned backward, the more he pulled me close.

"You've got too skinny," he said.

"Starvation will do that to you."

He laughed. "I doubt you're starving, Sis. You're too good at stealing to go that hungry. Besides, my men left a few crumbs for you. Enough to keep you going."

It was then that I realized that all of these last months when information and opportunity had gone lean, that he had found a way to bottleneck it. Cutting off all of my opportunities so that when the chance to rob the McMansion came up, I wouldn't be able to resist it.

"You're a bastard," I said.

"How can you say that when you've met my mother?"

I managed to struggle free and stumbled backwards.

"What do you want?"

"I need you," he said.

"Need me?" I was hesitant. It could mean so many things.

Thankfully, he lost all pretense of the charming lover and started to pace the bedroom.

"I found something, Sis. A puzzle of sorts."

"And you need me to figure it out." I relaxed somewhat. It was clear by his frenzy that he was preoccupied with whatever it was. Enough to postpone meting out my punishment.

He swung around on his heel. "I do need you," he said. "And I missed you. Did you miss me?"

There was no good answer to that.

"I thought you'd enjoy a heist like this. You did go for the Incan gold after all."

"So it was you."

He crept closer and toyed with my hair. "I would've expected you to figure it out far earlier than this," he said. "But I must say it was fun watching you."

Fun. I imagined he watched me for weeks and the knowledge made my blood run cold. He ran a palm over my arm, raising the hairs. I shivered but it had nothing to do with the air conditioning.

I clenched my fists at my sides as he yanked my pants and panties down in one rough motion. There was nothing sexual in the act. Only command. He wouldn't take me now, but he would later, and it would be rough and painful and humiliating. I tried not to cry. I snuffed up the snot that started leaking unwanted from my nose.

"Go wash up," he said and dug his fingers into my ass cheeks. "You need to show our investors they've backed the best pony and I don't want you out there smelling of rotten eggs and cat piss."

He followed me to the bathroom and watched me as I pulled my T-shirt over my head and unsnapped my bra. Like some chivalrous knight, he pulled open the glass shower door for me and bade me stand toward the back of the stall. He ran the water from the tap, sticking his fingers beneath to test the temperature. When it seemed to suit him, he waggled his fingers at me until I came forward.

I stood there with my arms crossed over my breasts as he ran the frothy soap over my skin, lingering between my legs in a promise that made me catch my breath in my throat. If tears ran down from my eyelids, neither one of us would know.

With the care of a mother, he tilted my head back and cradled it in his palm as he worked shampoo and then conditioner into my hair. I kept my eyes closed, not wanting to see the look of satisfaction on his face.

I felt like a kid as he helped me back out of the shower and scrubbed my skin with a coarse towel. He spun me around in front of him, checking out every inch of my body.

"Too skinny," he muttered. "But the ass is still good."

He swatted it then spun me back around to place his finger beneath my chin. He tilted his face to mine.

"Mine," he said. "To have and to hold till death do you part."

I could barely swallow through the tightness in my throat. All I could do was nod at him like a supplicant as he lifted the terrycloth robe on the hook on the door. He swathed it around me like a blanket.

"Now let's see what we can do about keeping you safe."

CHAPTER 25

There was a knock on the door outside of the bathroom and his face brightened.

"Your doctor is here," he said and stretched his arm out toward the door to indicate that I should go through it. Such chivalry. Such manners. His mother would be so proud.

"What are you waiting for, Sis?" he said. "Your new future awaits."

"Hell to freeze over I guess," I said, but I took a bracing breath anyway and left the bathroom ahead of him, knowing that he was smirking behind my back, and probably planning exactly how to test that safety later.

He called out to Alvin to allow the doctor to enter, and the door opened just enough to let the man through. I could hear a quick clinking of glasses and the gaggle of girls laughing before the sound shut off again.

I was more surprised to see my drunk enter the room than anything else. This was my doctor? The man who guzzled down a bottle of vodka? The man who had patched me up in the street after the dogs had bit through my pants? It seemed so long ago now.

I supposed it made sense. Once I'd realized Scottie had been trailing me all along, it would only be logical to think that he'd put the drunk in my path to give me an opportunity to make think I was keeping my anonymity. I could accept that, and I could accept that Scottie would use an innocent man down on his luck. But it was a bit of a stretch for me to think he'd planted a viable doctor there for days to live on the streets just to lull me into a false sense of security.

Although, come to think of it, that sounded exactly Like Scottie.

I was more surprised to realize that my old drunk was actually capable of looking professional. I'd already presumed he had medical skill of some sort, so doctor wasn't out of the playing field. The clinical way he inspected my dog bite after the heist and the way he patched it up gave him away.

I barely recognized the man now. Clean-shaven and dressed in a suit with a lab coat slung over his arm. He could barely meet my eyes as he walked over to the credenza and laid a black bag on it. He turned around and faced Scottie instead.

"Is everything ready?" he said.

Scottie reached his arm out to me, slipped his hand around the small of my back. "She's ready."

The doctor nodded mutely. He dug through his bag and lifted out a very long needle, a scalpel, and a small satchel of what looked like Band-Aids and bandages. I hoped the top of the bottle that I saw him peeking out was antiseptic.

I tried to get out of Scottie's grasp.

"You're not performing surgery on me in a hotel room," I said. "I'll do a lot of things for you Scottie," I said. "I'll marry you. I'll solve your puzzles. But I won't let you cut me open."

His voice was soothing, almost infuriatingly so, when he spoke.

"It's not surgery, Love," he crooned. "Just a little nick in the skin."

I pinwheeled backwards and out of his grip. The damn over-sized robe caught in my legs and I fell backwards onto the bed. "No," I said. I tried to scrabble over the bed to freedom and butted up against the headboard.

The doctor took a step forward, hesitating. The needle winked in the light and my mouth went dry. It had to be at least an inch. No way he was sticking that in me.

"Go to hell," I said, pulled my legs up and scrabbling backwards to the headboard.

The doctor looked from me to Scottie. "You said she'd be willing."

Scottie gave me a hard look that made me clutch the robe tightly together.

"She is willing," he said.

The doctor strode closer with the practised deportment of a man who had to do terrible things to unwilling people all the time.

"Stay away from me," I said.

Scottie sat down on the bed next to me and smoothed down my hair. "Shhh, Sis," he said. It's just a little nick. I've never seen you balk at a little needle before. And you need this. It's a very small tracking device. And the doctor is very practised. I wouldn't put you in the hands of anyone less than exceptional."

I shoved him away with the flat of my hand, but I kept my eye on the doctor who was drawing fluid from a vial into the syringe.

"I'm sure he is," I said. "I'm sure you have had him implanting all your little minions."

Scottie put his arm around my shoulders and squeezed. "Not so many," he crooned. "Just the ones I care about."

The doctor seemed satisfied that he had enough fluid in the syringe. He eyed me with a clear gaze. Last I'd seen him, those eyes had been cloudy with drink. Had that all been an act too?

He sidled closer, bag in one hand filled with alcohol pads and paraphernalia and needle in the other. Scottie held me tight, pinning me against his own torso so that I couldn't fight the doctor. Couldn't run. The panic bloomed in my chest.

The doctor leaned in close as he put two fingers over my pulse in my neck. "Don't worry," he said. "I'm very good at giving needles."

I glared at him.

He turned to Scottie.

"I might need to take her into the bathroom for this," he said. "You know, sink. Water. A more clinical atmosphere."

Scottie helped me ever so chivalrously to my feet and the doctor put up a hand to stop him.

"I think we'll be fine," he said. "I've cared for Ms. Hush before. I think she trusts me."

While the words were innocent enough, and his face showed very little change of expression, there was some subtle movement of his eyebrow. Just enough to encourage me to take the hand he held out. With a gentle ease, he guided me into the bathroom just off the suite and closed the door behind us. He bade me sit on the toilet lid.

"I'm sorry," he whispered as he knelt in front of me. "I have to do this you understand."

I was speechless with fury. So much for trust.

"But it isn't what you think," he whispered.

He rifled with the plastic bag, pulling out an alcohol swab.

"I have to do it, but I don't have to implant what he asks me to."

He laid the swab on the sink and pulled out another smaller baggie from inside the first plastic bag. Then he extracted an even smaller one from his lab coat pocket. He was so adroit at it, with such a practised sleight-of-hand, that I imagined he had spent years substituting medicine for lollipops.

I didn't dare pull my eyes from his to look around the room, but I knew there was a camera somewhere. Scottie didn't believe in privacy. I couldn't expect even this room to be free of his invasive eagle eye.

The doc held both baggies up against the front of his coat in between us. The one on the left looked identical to the one on the right, except the one on the left was a little bit bigger. Both had little oily beads of black plastic.

He jerked his chin down ever so subtly toward the smaller one.

"It's just a harmless bit of silicone."

He stared into my eyes meaningfully. "As far as Scottie is concerned, you'll be implanted with the tracker and I'll put the bug in a nice little rat who's been romancing the neighbourhood."

Yeah, right. And my knight in shining armor would gallop in to save me at any moment.

"What kind of trick is this?" I said.

"No trick," he said. "You have to make a decision to trust me or not."

"A rat, huh?" I said.

He nodded.

Fitting, I thought. I really shouldn't blame a man who was under Scottie's thumb. After all, I'd been an involuntary recruit myself all those years.

"Do it, then," I said through gritted teeth.

The implantation was painful, but not terrible. He numbed my skin enough to make it easy. We faced Scottie together on the other side of the door and I noted the careful, almost covert way Scottie slipped a wad of cash into the doctor's bag.

He was gone moments later and Scottie stood in front of me, slipping his palm beneath my robe and running his thumb over the bandage on my collarbone.

"Perfect," he said. "Now you don't have to worry about getting lost again."

His hand slipped further down as he trailed the backs of his fingertips against my rib cage. For a moment I thought he might decide to take the time to prove his true possession of me. It would be a very Scottie thing to do, and I waited, breath held, muscles tense for that second when I would hear his zipper rattle against its teeth.

But the night was full of surprises. Instead, he patted my backside beneath the robe and then nodded toward the dresser.

"The black dress," he said. "Your heels are in the closet."

"And what is it you expect of me?" I said.

"I told you I found something."

He strode across the room and hooked my shoes from the floor and tossed them on the bed.

"I think it could be good for us."

Good for us. I thought about those words as he went back to his guests.

This party wasn't for me, to celebrate my return or our "engagement" because he knew I'd be here. He couldn't have known of my involvement with Finn or Kelly or even the shadow bazaar. I'd no doubt been lost to him completely while I was on the other side. Alvin had seen me enter a door that he couldn't go through. Had he questioned it at all? Or had he simply reported the strangeness to Scottie without giving it a moment's thought.

I was willing to bet he reported it and he waited till I fell back through. Then he followed me all the way home. Gave Scottie the Intel. Waited to be told to extract me.

So why the party? Why try to impress anyone at all. This party had something to do with his puzzle and my arrival was a happy happenstance, occurring just when he needed it the most. He wouldn't question it. He expected everything to go his way. That didn't bother me. What bothered me was what nasty bit of business he wanted from me.

The dress bagged on me, of course. I had lost weight over the last six months. Pickings had been lean. I sighed as I inspected the fit in the mirror. I had planned to come here and face my demons. Cut ties between us for good. All I had managed was to make him think he could find me anywhere anytime he wanted.

I opened the door to the bedroom suite to find him waiting on the other side. He smiled broadly, as though the last three years had been nothing but a discomforting dream.

When he reached his arm out for me, I hooked my hand around his elbow. I could play the game. For now. If only to find out what was really going on.

"This, gentlemen," he crowed to the room. "This is my fiance. The one I told you about."

The assessing glances ran the length of my dress and stopped at the cleavage. I tugged the edges together self-consciously.

Scottie guided me toward a high-backed stool near the bar in front of a bank of windows. He didn't need to tell me to sit. I perched on the edge, with my feet dangling because they couldn't reach the first rung. I crossed my legs sedately.

Scottie panned the room with his gaze.

"I told you I had a very special artist at my disposal," he said and nodded toward me. He smiled as though his lips were greased.

"This is Isabella."

There was a murmur that ran through the men as though they had heard everything they needed to hear about me already. I felt at a distinct disadvantage.

"And what have you told them?" I said, looking up at Scottie. Even on the highboy stool, he was still taller than me.

"About your skill set," he said. He picked up a glass of champagne and meandered around the room, jerking his chin at each man in turn.

"Professor of History," he said of one. "Cryptology specialist," he said of another. His eyes landed and stopped the longest at the man who I'd seen upon first entering the room.

"Archaeologist."

"How lovely to meet all of you," I said and thought I did pretty good at keeping the level of sarcasm out of my voice. Scottie seemed to think so too because he smiled thinly. He'd obviously thought I would be difficult.

"And what do all of these have to do with me?" I said.

"These men are in my employ, Isabella," he said. "They report to me when they find anything interesting, anything they think might be useful or valuable."

I nodded mutely. So what was so different or special about that? Scottie had a lot of people in his employ. A lot of people who fed him that kind of information.

He crossed the room to a tattered box that sat by itself on the bar. It looked like it had seen better days. There was dirt scuffed into the creases and I thought it was made of leather.

"Sarah here is the mistress to one of the most influential antiquities dealers in the area. In all of North America, actually," he said with a gloating grin. He nodded at the young woman I had mistaken for Scottie's date.

"He told her about a new discovery. Completely unexpected and unprecedented. He'd come into possession of it but had nothing but bad luck ever since. He locked it away in a special safe in his home. Mostly because after all of the things that happened at his research centre, he was too afraid to leave it out in the open. Sarah here couldn't get the safe open no matter how hard she tried. And you did try didn't you?"

The girl nodded amiably.

"He did tell her what was in it, though," Scottie said. "She can be very persuasive." He smiled at the girl who blushed.

"And then of course she told you," I guessed.

He beamed like a proud patron should. I was beginning to understand.

"This safe that she couldn't open," I said. "Did it happen to be locked away in a beautiful library behind a rather lowly hung painting?" I tried to keep my voice light, but my disdain leached through. I looked at her with a calculated eye.

"I would've thought a girl with a university degree could figure out a few prime numbers."

She gave me a cold look. She hadn't been able to figure it out. But then, it wasn't just a matter of finding fractions and prime numbers. It was figuring out that the code was giving the order of the fractions as well.

I uncrossed my legs. "That box was in the bottom drawer," I said. "Along with the Incan gold."

Scottie smiled.

"Indeed," he said. "And yet all of these men haven't been able to figure out what the contents mean."

I didn't need him to spell it out for me. He wanted me to crack the code because he knew I could do it. It was why he held onto me, after all. Why he felt he owned me.

"You used me to crack that safe," I said. "You sent the Lolly to brag about the gold, knowing I would break in."

Scottie nodded. "Except you didn't extract everything, did you?"

I shook my head. "I couldn't. I was attacked." I twisted my leg so that he could see the still healing scar.

He winced. "We'll have to fix that. Maybe the same time as we fix that tattoo. Is it darker?" he asked and lifted his lip in revulsion. "Ugly, Sis. Not your best choice."

He spun on his heel as though none of those things were important as I stole a look at the tattoo. It was darker. Enough to notice. But I didn't have time to puzzle it out. Scotty lifted the box from its place and carried it over to the table and laid it in front of me. Each one of the men craned forward. Whatever was in the box, they had no idea what it meant. They were hoping I would.

"They all agree," Scottie said nodding in each man's direction. "We all agree that these things are valuable," he said. "Ancient, even. But what we can't agree on is what they mean."

He lifted the cover of the box. Inside, clustered together as though they were coins in a leather pouch sat four small tiles. I swallowed down hard. I recognized them all right. The sight of them froze the words in my throat.

He stuck a finger in, separating them from each other. "There is some strange writing on them," he said. "A puzzle of sorts," he looked up at me expectantly. "We need to know what it means before we can negotiate."

That's why the men were here. They'd each seen these runes and none of them knew what it meant. But they suspected they were valuable, same as I had. Thieves had a way of seeing opportunity. They were all here to bid on the merchandise, based on whatever message I might find hidden within.

Scottie had no idea what he had. None of these men did. At a glance, I could see that two of them were fake. After having seen and held the real one, I knew the frauds when I saw them.

I put my hand in the box, lifted all four out into my palm. Yes. There was heat in the two that I knew were real. I shook them about in my palm.

"Strange," I said, faking a sense of awe. "I've never seen anything like it. But it's definitely a message."

I looked up at Scottie. I could feel the tracking mark on my wrist beginning to ache.

I flicked one of them out onto the table with a clattering sound. It spun and warbled for several seconds before coming to rest.

"Interesting," I said in a musing voice. I flicked the other one down next to it. Then the third. I moved them about with my index finger, clutching the heat of a real one in my hand.

"They definitely fit together," I said.

I could feel the tension in Scottie's shoulders as he stood next to me. I could almost smell his eagerness.

My own thoughts were a confusing muddle as I tried to feign interest in but not knowledge of the origin of the small tiles in front of me. Two supernatural factions had gone to war over another tile. The question was: were both of their soldiers dead or alive? Which one would come for their loot first?

The aching mark on my wrist told me it was Finn. He had to be the victor and he hadn't yet come to punish me for failing to bring back his rune.

That had to mean he was in possession of it and thought me dutiful.

So the real question was could I make use of that? I surreptitiously peered down at my wrist as I fingered the tiles on the table. I tried to muse things out loud, to make Scottie and the others think I was working out the problem. I wasn't aware of the things that I was saying. They might've been ridiculous, confusing ramblings. All I could think about was what might happen if I pressed that mark.

The authentic rune in my palm grew warmer.

"Well," Scottie said demanding. His tone was tense and harsher than he might've wanted. It was a good indicator of how much money he had riding on this.

I looked him in the eyes, trying to disguise the butterflies he would no doubt see in my gaze. The tension in the cords of my throat.

"You want to know what it says?" I said. I tried to give it a teasing tone. One that would make him feel off guard.

He nodded. His eagerness was slick across his face.

I took a breath, ran my thumb along my wrist. But where I knew the tattoo was by now without looking. I pressed the pad of my thumb into it. Held it for several achingly long seconds. All while Scottie pinned me with that grey gaze of his.

"Isabella?" he said. "What does it say?"

I thought I heard a buzzing behind my ears. I had one rune in my hand. The other lay on the counter. Bait, that's what it was, although no one but me would know it.

My skin burned like a bitch but I held tight. The shadows in the corner of the room shifted. I doubted anyone saw it. All eyes were on me, and no one would see the cloak edge being clearly delineated at the perimeter of the shadows. They wouldn't see the wavering shape of a man take form. I smiled to myself. This was it. This was my moment of true emancipation.

I held Scottie's gaze with my own. Toed off my high-heeled shoes. They were no good for running. Bare feet would be much better.

"Isabella," he snapped. "Tell me."

"They're authentic," I said. "And their message is pretty damn clear if you know how to read it.

I tightened my grip on the one in my palm.

"Well?" he said.

It was in that moment that Finn came all the way through. One of the girls—the nineteen year old mistress, I thought—screamed.

"It says fuck you, Scottie," I said. "Fuck you and your tracking chip."

Then I spun on my bare heel and I ran.

I was to the door when I heard the clamor behind me. It sounded like someone was choking. Scottie, I hoped. I imagined him hanging from Finn's grip with his feet dangling as Finn demanded his property. The women screamed.

I didn't look back. This time I wouldn't be Lot's wife. This time I would be Lot. And I would run from the city of Gomorrah as though there were angels on the heels of my feet. Maybe there were. I didn't doubt any of that anymore.

I slammed the door behind me and ran for the elevator.

CHAPTER 26

Iplunked the tile down on Errol's glass counter within the hour. He wouldn't recognize me, not without my blond wig and dominatrix outfit, and I doubted with his laser focus on my breast that he'd question the voice. He'd recognize the tile, though. Of that I had no doubt.

"How much will you give me for it?" I said.

He eyed me speculatively. I knew he was trying to piece together the sound of my voice with the petite brunette he saw in front of him. I tried to pretend that the last time I'd been here he hadn't tried to force me into the back room.

"Doesn't look very valuable to me," he hedged. "A little piece of rock with Sharpie marker all over it."

I laid both palms on the counter in front of him.

"Cut the crap. I've been to the Shadow Bazaar. I know this is valuable."

His eyebrows rose about an inch.

"That's right," I said, nodding. "I know all about it. I know what you are. And I know what this is."

I tapped the edge of the tile with my fingernail.

"You do?" he said, but his tone gave away nothing. Very noncommittal and practiced. I expected that.

"I know quite a fair bit about you, Errol," I said. "For example, I know that you've been supplying children to Evelina."

Instead of rising, those eyebrows scuttled down. He was pissed. Mark hit. It had been a long shot, one that I hadn't truly pieced together until I'd come back into the shop. It was gratifying to know that my brain was still working somewhere in there despite all of the post traumatic stress it had suffered.

"Oh, yes," I said. "I know about Evelina and her booth made of human skin and rather—what shall we call it?—tender product."

I pushed the tile sideways across the counter with my fingernail. Now that it wasn't physically on me, I felt less tense. But there was no way I was going to pick it up again. I'd been nothing short of lucky to have got this far without some shadowy creature like Kelly announcing herself with a bolt of lightning and sizzling my insides. I didn't want to carry that risk any longer than I needed to.

If I was going to unload it, I needed to unload it fast. I couldn't risk keeping it, and I couldn't risk it falling into the hands of another human being because who knew what kind of creatures would fall onto their doorstep, or what they'd do to retrieve it. I might not be one of the good guys, but I certainly wasn't an unfeeling bitch.

That didn't mean I was going to let the tile go without a hell of a lot of cash coming my way. Whatever happened to it after that was the supernatural realm's problem.

I jerked my head toward the back room. I certainly wasn't going to tell him that Evelina was dead. Doing so would only queer the transaction and he'd find out sooner or later anyway. I wasn't exactly negotiating in bad faith.

"I couldn't piece together your reason for that candy counter at first," I said. "It seemed a strange mix of business. But after what I've seen, it makes the most sense. Occam's razor, Errol." I tapped my temple with my finger.

"Do you see any children in here?" He spread his arms wide, but I had him. And we both knew I did.

I thrummed my finger on the glass, unmoved by his flimsy defense.

"I wonder what the police would say should they get a tip, anonymously of course, that you're a human trafficker" I said.

"You're reaching."

I shrugged. "Whether or not it's accurate, doesn't matter. All it takes is a little bit of doubt cast in your direction. You'd be under investigation. I'm quite sure you wouldn't want that."

He glowered at me. "If you were in the Shadow Bazaar, you would know how dangerous it is to level that accusation at me."

"I'm not trying to see you arrested, Errol," I said. "I'm just trying to impress upon you the things that I know. I'm trying to gain your trust. Show you that I'm not just some regular weak human walking in off the street."

"All humans are regular and weak." His eyes lit up with the words. I knew he'd lost his power, Maddox hadn't said why. Just that it had left him bitter. I saw a tinge of that anger now. He was powerless, but he still thought he was superior.

Of all the things I learned from Scottie, both good and bad, I discovered that you might not be able to change the way someone thinks, but you can use it to your advantage.

"I'm not just here for money, Errol." I flicked the tile in his direction. "I'm here to make you an offer."

He didn't try to hide his disdain.

I ignored it.

"I'm willing to give you the tile, but I want something in return."

"How much?"

I chuckled. "Not money," I said. "A service."

I wasn't worried about him trafficking children to Evelina anymore. She was dead and he was nothing but a powerless incubus, but he did have something. A network I didn't.

"I'm small," I said. "And I'm human, and I'm vulnerable. I need someone who can create some sort of spell, some sort of glamour that can act as a supernatural security system."

He crossed his arms over his chest. "That's a tall order."

"I'm sure you know someone."

He was very good at not giving away his thoughts through his expression, but there was a glint in his eye that he wasn't able to master.

I let my gaze linger on the small candy counter at the front of the shop. "I do have one other place I need to go today," I said and looked down at my watch. "One other place that can serve and protect."

He gripped my wrist across the counter.

"Don't be hasty," he said.

I let my gaze trail to where his thumb rested, and was pleasantly surprised to see that the tracking mark had disappeared finally. Good. Things were looking up.

"So?" I said. "Can you help me?"

He nodded slowly, but a sly grin spread over his face. "I do. But you'll need to go back into the market."

I wasn't sure the market existed anymore the way I left it, but I wasn't about to take that chance.

I shook my head and pulled my hand out from beneath his grip. "No. I'm not going back through the portal."

"Rough ride?" he asked with humor in his voice.

Answering the question would only show weakness, and I wasn't about to do that. Not when I was almost ready to close the deal.

He obviously saw through it, but wanted the tile enough to ignore it.

"You must've gone through the blood gate," he said. "There are several gates in if you know the way." He inclined his head ever so slightly toward the back room. Interesting. I hadn't factored in his delivery method to Evelina when I'd taken that shot in the dark. Even so, I wasn't interested. I didn't want to ever go back there.

I watched his fingers trail toward the rune. I laid my palm down around it.

"If you want this," I said. "You need to make it happen now. I'm not leaving until you make the arrangements."

"And what's to stop me from killing you in your sleep?"

"Who's to say I haven't already met with that police officer?" I said.

He blinked at me. We were at an impasse and we both knew it. We would have to trust each other if only for the short term.

"I know someone," he finally said. "Wait here."

While I waited, I picked my way through his shop. Usually, I came to the counter to unload merchandise and went straight back out again. The thigh-high dominatrix boots were a bitch to walk in, and so I spent as little time as possible in them. Now wearing the heels I'd clutched as I'd run from Scottie, I was a little more inclined to scan the shop.

Besides the candy counter at the front, he had other, more age-appropriate merchandise that would account for the teen aged boy I'd seen at Evelina's. Video games and comic books and even a nudie magazine placed covertly inside a Marvel comic. I swallowed down my gall as I thought of those kids in the bazaar. I'd seen only the tamest parts of the place, I knew that. I couldn't imagine what other things might have been peddled in that place. What other services offered behind those doors that were locked.

But I couldn't change that. And I couldn't do anything about the kids already lost. I gave a thought to Kassie and hoped she was safe somewhere. She was a resilient little thing or she wouldn't have been able to survive this long the streets. I had to believe that.

I sighed audibly and crossed my arms over my stomach. The survey of the shop showed mostly books and the odd fake piece of merchandise meant to look like ancient artifacts. Some of the more authentic pieces were history based: World War II helmets and blades, the odd hand grenade. Clothing and hats lined shelves. For all intents and purposes, Errol's shop looked like it offered real service to those who were interested in that sort of thing. He no doubt had a robust business just from his regular fare.

Of course, he was just one outlet. One doorway into the supernatural, according to Maddox. If Errol was peddling something, it probably had nothing to do with money. And if he supplied just the right thing to just the right person, perhaps he might achieve it.

Maybe the old incubus was smarter than I'd given him credit for. No doubt he'd just conned the con. I just hadn't figured out yet what he wanted badly enough to make a deal. I had made a mistake. I was sure of it.

I was on my way back out of the shop when I heard him behind me.

"It's done," he said over my shoulder.

I spun around, not expecting him to be so close. He was right on my back, for heaven's sake.

"I changed my mind," I stammered out.

He ran his tongue along the bottom of his mouth, letting it linger in the corner as he looked me up and down. Did he look just a little brighter?

"This isn't a deal we can negotiate," he said.

I inched backward, nodding, but not quite sure how I felt about it. "All right," I said.

"All you have to do is go home," he said. "Everything will be in place."

"And I can trust you?"

He shrugged. "I guess you'll have to see."

There was something off about him that I couldn't put my finger on.

By habit, I got off the subway four blocks from home. I zigzagged up and down several streets before taking the one that would lead to my apartment. My feet hurt from all of the walking, but a girl couldn't be too careful. Never knew who was watching.

When I did stand in front of the place where my brownstone should be, I saw only an empty lot. I knew that even with the landlord's fight with the zoning committee that an entire construction crew couldn't have demolished and cleaned up a building in the few short hours I'd gone.

So Errol had come through after all. I heaved a sigh of relief and strode straight toward where I thought the steps should be. I hesitated, not sure what would happen if someone were to see me stepping up onto a tread that wasn't there.

The moment the tip of my toe nudged against the stair, everything went washed in green. It wavered for a second and then steadied. I climbed stairs until I reached the top, and then I turned around to face the street.

Everything was tinted. Somehow, whoever Errol had struck a deal with, had managed to place the entry into some sort of between worlds reality. I swung back around to face the door and clutched the handle. Solid. It opened the way it always did.

It all felt very regular.

But I knew that nothing would be regular ever again.

I plucked my cat from the floor next to her bowl and fell down onto my sofa, smoothing down her fur till she purred. It was a good sound. A sound that made me feel like anything was possible.

I felt safe for the first time in years. I felt hope.

Maybe a good guy would've pretended those runes meant nothing and spared those people in the room. Maybe a good guy would have saved them from themselves and told them they were fake. Two of them were fake anyway. Two authentic: one to bait Finn and let him believe I had somehow kept my bargain. One for my fist. With enough value to buy me a whole new life.

Maybe a good guy would have found a way to spirit the real ones away to safety where they couldn't do any real harm.

But like Maddox had said: there are no good guys.

Not even me.

And I could live with that.

-Finitio-

THANKS for READING

37305759R00158

Made in the USA
Middletown, DE
25 February 2019